HARD WIRED

Bennett Security Book 3

HANNAH SHIELD

Cover design by Damonza

Editing services by The Wicked Pen

Published by Diana Road Books

Edgewater, Colorado

HARD WIRED

Chapter One

Sylvie Trousseau took the moniker of "hacker" seriously. It was an identity, not a job. Hacking was all about the intellectual challenge, the thrill, the beauty of finding novel solutions. Sylvie knew how to use her creativity and cleverness to achieve things that should've been impossible.

So her boss's latest request had her more than a little irritated.

"Let me get this straight. You want me to install a security system? Isn't that something our techs can handle?"

"Usually, yes. A tech would do it. But this isn't the average install."

They were in Max Bennett's office, perched above the workroom. Through the glass walls, Sylvie could see her coworkers bustling around below. To her left, through a massive bank of windows, lay a panorama of blue sky and white waves crashing into the rocky shore. Just another perfect sunny day in West Oaks, California.

Max twisted back and forth on his swivel chair, squeezing a stress ball in one hand. "I need my top person."

"Aren't my talents slightly wasted on this, though?"

Hell, these days most security setups came straight out of a box, no need for technical knowledge at all. Of course, a Bennett Security system wasn't the typical off-the-shelf product. Sylvie herself had written the code, and she was damned proud of it.

Sylvie was in charge of the Bennett Security software, research, and analytics department. It was a big umbrella because she had a wide variety of skills, including a photographic memory. She had ten people working for her now, including a brand-new assistant she was still training. She didn't have time to make house calls. Schmoozing with customers was Max's deal, not hers.

Sylvie liked to have fun while she worked, but she had no interest in flattering the egos of their wealthy clients.

She wasn't conceited, of course. And she didn't expect every single day at her job to fulfill her intellectual curiosity. "Hacker" was nowhere in her written job description, for good reason. It was far too loaded a term. But she wasn't going to sell herself short, either.

Max's face remained impassive. "You're absolutely right. You could do this install in your sleep. But I promised I'd send my best, and that's you. I owe this man a favor."

This man?

There was a hint of something in Max's voice that Sylvie didn't like. He was holding back important information, probably because he knew she wasn't going to be happy.

"And who exactly is this client?"

Not him, she thought. *Please not him.*

"Dominic Crane."

Sylvie closed her eyes, cursing under her breath. Yep, it was him. "Crane is a criminal. And you're sending me to his house like some sacrificial lamb?"

Max chuckled, though his fist kept tightening around that stress ball. "I'll send a bodyguard with you. But it's not like

Crane will lay a hand on you. Not when he knows you work for me."

"Wow, how reassuring."

"He provided some extremely important information to me at risk to himself. You know that."

"Yeah," she said through gritted teeth. They all knew what Crane had done to help Max.

"And think about it, Sylvie. Isn't it better that I square up with him on something like this, that costs me basically nothing? Who knows what he might want later on? Or how questionable it might be? Instead, Crane asked for a security system with all the bells and whistles. I'm getting off easy."

Until recently, Dominic Crane had been the head of the Silverlake Syndicate, a criminal organization from Los Angeles. The group had made inroads into West Oaks, and they'd been involved in several nefarious dealings around the otherwise-sleepy town.

But none of that fully explained her concern. Sylvie did *not* want to tell Max why she was so reticent to meet Dominic Crane.

"*Please*, boss. Send someone else."

Max's handsome face slid into a smirk. "Don't tell me you're scared of the man?"

Sylvie's boss was a master manipulator. But she was immune to his tricks. "I'm not scared of Crane. But he *is* awaiting trial for murder. Remember? That's not exactly nothing."

"The murder charge is puffed up and probably won't even make it to a jury, from what I hear. Plus, he's wearing an ankle monitor. He's declawed, stuck in a cage. Honestly, I don't think he's all that dangerous."

"But would you let Lana near him?" Lana was Max's girlfriend.

He huffed. "I wouldn't go that far."

Sylvie knew the real reason Max wanted to keep his girlfriend away from Dominic Crane. It was the exact same reason that Sylvie preferred not to get near the former head of the Silverlake Syndicate.

Crane was gorgeous. Like, model gorgeous. The man had the face of an angel and a wicked smile that promised he was anything but. He was the type of flirtatious that made women weak in the knees, even as they knew they should stay far away. Sylvie had never even met Crane in person, yet she could tell he was irresistible.

As a human being, the man should've been repulsive. But she had a schoolgirl crush on him. She *liked* the idea of Crane laying a hand on her.

Of course, she would never actually mess around with him. But if she got tongue-tied in front of the most attractive criminal defendant in West Oaks, her co-workers would never let her live it down.

"I thought his former friends were trying to kill him." Sylvie had heard about the civil war within the Syndicate from her law enforcement contacts. "It can't be safe to be hanging around his place."

"Why else do you think he needs this security system so badly? Like I said, you'll have one of our bodyguards with you. Take your pick. It'll just be for a few hours. It's *possible* the man isn't as bad as he seems."

Max put down the stress ball and folded his hands together. Sylvie noticed the new addition on his ring finger. She lurched forward, pressing her hands onto the surface of his desk.

"Wait, what is that? Did you and Lana get *married?*"

He looked down at his hand, splaying his fingers. "No, not married. I would've told you about something like that. It's…" He trailed off, then gripped the back of his neck, as if he wanted to hide the ring from view.

Max Bennett was looking downright sheepish.

"I've started wearing it whenever Lana and I are apart. Just to make sure everyone knows I'm taken."

Sylvie burst out laughing. "That's possibly the most adorable thing I've ever heard."

He wasn't just her boss. Sylvie considered Max a friend, and she knew him well enough to have noticed his tendencies.

Before Lana, he'd been a bit of a man-whore. He'd left a wake of satisfied ladies in his path, always making clear it would be no-strings attached. Sometimes those women still called the office, hoping for more, and the receptionists knew how to deflect when needed. It had been a very big deal for Lana to take the title of "Max's girlfriend" in the first place.

"Usually, men remove their rings when their significant others *aren't* around," Sylvie pointed out.

"I'm aware of that. I can't help if I happen to be an enticing guy. Women can't stay away from me. The ring helps explain why I can no longer return their affections."

Sylvie snorted. "Good to know your ego remains firmly in check. I was afraid you'd gone and changed on me."

But Max *had* changed, that was obvious. While Sylvie was thrilled for him and Lana—and relieved that Max occasionally took days off now instead of working himself into the ground—she didn't trust the idea of change in a person. Sylvie refused to change herself for anyone, and she would never expect anyone to change for her.

So many people in this world had fought for the right to be their true selves. Sylvie had personally given up a lot, even friends and family, to be able to live her life as she wished. Those sacrifices hurt. She still bore the scars.

But it had always been easier to assume that she had no choice. That there was no going back. And here was Max Bennett, making change look so effortless.

But this isn't about me, she reminded herself. Max could do whatever he wanted.

"Some women are even more enticed by a guy wearing a

wedding ring," she warned him. "If you really don't want women after you, just be uglier."

"Well, that's not going to happen." Max held out his hands, as if asking, *What can I do?*

The topic of attractive men brought her right back to Dominic Crane. The long ski slope of his nose, his plump cupid's-bow mouth...

Sylvie was surrounded by muscular former-military men daily. Guys like Max. Most women found them panty-dropping hot. But guys like Max weren't Sylvie's type.

Dominic Crane and his aura of wickedness? Oh, so exactly her type. And so wrong.

She had one final ploy. "Look, I'll make sure everything about Crane's system is perfect. Custom coding, whatever he wants. But I can do that much more effectively from my desk once he's connected to our network." That was how Sylvie usually handled their most demanding clients. From behind her wall of computer screens.

In fact, she liked to handle most things from behind a screen.

Max stood up from his desk, staring down at her from his full height. "You're going to install Crane's system, and that's final. But I'll make it up to you. You decide what that will take. A bonus, extra time off? Some new gadget you've been wanting? Done. But I'm finished with this conversation. I don't want to hear from you on the subject of Crane until the assignment is finished."

Sylvie left Max's office, shaking her head. Why had she bothered arguing in the first place? Max Bennett always got what he wanted.

～

SYLVIE WENT DOWN to her corner of the workroom. She had three massive screens on her desk, positioned so they created a cozy alcove. She checked her email, then sent off instructions to several people on her team so they would stay busy while she was gone.

Sylvie had worked at Bennett Security for the last three years. Most of the time, she loved her job. She'd gotten testy upstairs about the more basic aspects of installing their systems, but she always felt gratified to provide safety and security to their clients.

Sylvie was Max's unofficial right hand in their company. He trusted her with their most sensitive and difficult assignments, whether it was poring over crucial video surveillance, working her contacts in the state and federal law enforcement agencies, or using her hacker skills to find answers no one else could provide.

For the most part, their clients were West Oaks elites. But Max donated his time to help the larger community as well, like consulting with the police on cases, or funding non-profit services. Usually, his pro-bono projects served more sympathetic characters than a crime boss like Dominic Crane.

Ugh. Why did her kryptonite have to be sexy bad boys? Why couldn't well-adjusted accountants turn her on?

Well, fine. She had a theory. Sylvie had never liked being told *no*. In fact, the word *no* had always felt like a challenge. That was why she loved hacking so much.

Sometimes, knowing something was forbidden made it that much more enticing.

Priyanka, Sylvie's brand-new assistant, appeared at her desk. "I got your email. We're going out in the field?"

"Don't get your hopes up. It's just an install."

Priyanka puffed out her lips. "Boo. I was hoping one of the bodyguards would be coming with us."

"Oh, one will. We're going to Dominic Crane's house. Max owes the guy a favor."

Priyanka's eyes widened. "This is so exciting. Do I have time to run home to change?"

Sylvie narrowed her eyes at the girl. Priyanka was twenty-two, a recent grad from college. She knew how to code, and her grades suggested she had an eye for detail and the patience for research. But so far, she seemed a lot more interested in her male coworkers than in learning everything Sylvie had to teach her.

"Definitely not. You look fine." She decided to do Priyanka a favor and not insist they wear the Bennett Security polos most techs sported on house calls. Even Max had known better than to suggest it to Sylvie. "Just pack up. We'll be leaving within the hour."

Sylvie checked their log of current assignments. A few of the bodyguards were out of the office today, but Tanner wasn't busy. Excellent. He was her top choice.

She found him downstairs in the gym, where a lot of the bodyguards liked to hang out while awaiting their next project. Tanner was currently grunting underneath a barbell loaded with huge iron plates. She saw his eyes land on her in the mirror. Sylvie waited until he finished his squat and the bar landed with a crash on the rack.

"Hey, Sylv. What's up?"

"I've got something for you today. Want to come with me to Dominic Crane's house?"

"That asshole? Please tell me we're escorting him to a federal holding facility."

"No such luck. Max wants me to install a system at his place. So Crane's Syndicate buddies can't off him like they want."

Tanner shrugged one shoulder. He was one of the biggest guys on the team, a former Navy SEAL around six-five, with shoulders that spanned twice the breadth of Sylvie's. He had a bushy beard to match, as well as an unruly mop of curls on his head. Tattoos covered his arms and shoulders, one of the things he and Sylvie had in common. They went to the same artist in L.A.

Tanner was also one of the most laidback guys Sylvie knew. He didn't even look askance at Max's orders.

"Whatever. If Max says so, then I'm there. When do we start?"

"As soon as you shower and get dressed. I just want to get this over with."

Maybe the gods would smile upon her, and she wouldn't have to see Crane at all.

Chapter Two

*D*ominic Crane had one leg draped over the back of the couch, his eyes fixed on the ornate plaster moldings on the ceiling. Chopin played on his stereo.

His body was still, but his mind was working. Plotting, just as his enemies were plotting against him.

But it really sucked not being able to move. Not beyond the walls of this house, anyway. Seriously limited his options—both for business, *and* for fun.

His phone rang. It was his lawyer, Aaron Sandford. Dominic reached over to grab the device from the coffee table and answered.

"Yeah?"

"Dominic, how are you?"

Sandford pretended to kiss Dominic's ass. But he knew the lawyer hated him. The feeling was mutual.

"You have news?" Dominic asked. "From Warren?"

"Not your brother, no. I've been assured he's safe. But not so talkative lately, it seems."

"Why is that?"

"I really couldn't say."

Originally, Sandford had worked for Dominic's older

brother. But Warren was in prison now, serving a sentence for tax evasion like a modern day Al Capone. Warren, at least, hadn't written off Dominic altogether. If he had, then those attempts on his life probably would've been more successful.

But Dominic's last message to his brother had gone unanswered. It was concerning. The two brothers had been trying to fortify their support to retake the family business. It didn't seem to be going well.

In just the last week, Dominic's few allies had stopped taking his calls. Which meant *something* new had changed. But what?

Sandford cleared his throat. "I just got a new offer from the district attorney's office. They've sweetened their plea deal considerably. I'm obligated to let you know, even though I'm sure you won't be interested. But this is a positive sign. It means they're willing to negotiate. We can come up with a counter that would be more palatable."

Dominic looked down at the ankle monitor strapped to his left leg. The band of black plastic itched. His skin was getting pale and shriveled underneath it. He'd been wearing the thing for the last several months, ever since he'd been granted bail.

"What's the offer?"

Sandford coughed again. Either he had a buildup of phlegm in his throat, or he really didn't want to pass this on. "They're asking you to turn state's evidence. Inform on those you used to work with in the Syndicate. Although, as usual, we deny there is any such organization as the 'Silverlake Syndicate.'"

"Yeah, sure." The "Syndicate" was a term for outsiders. To the Cranes, it was just the family business. A burden Dominic had never wanted, as if he'd had a choice in the matter.

But now, Dominic was technically an outsider, too.

"What's the rest?" he asked.

"Well, in exchange for your testimony bringing down the

so-called Syndicate, they'll grant you full immunity and witness protection. As I said, it's not something you would ever consider. But I'll keep working on them. At the very least, I should be able to loosen some of the conditions they put on your bail. Like the electronic monitoring and movement restrictions."

"You do that." Dominic wasn't allowed to go more than thirty feet from the perimeter of his house in West Oaks. Hard to take back control of his life without the freedom to navigate. To meet with the remaining captains who were loyal to him, demand to know why they'd gone silent. And persuade—or threaten—the others into submission.

"I'll get back to you as soon as I can," his lawyer said.

Dominic didn't bother to say goodbye. He tossed his phone onto the table and put a hand over his eyes.

Rat out the Syndicate? Rat out his family?

The DA called him a criminal, and he'd definitely done bad things. Cruel things. *Violent* things. But only to people who'd deserved it. He drew the line at destroying the lives of innocents. For that reason, certain of his former allies had betrayed him. Called him *weak*. As if he didn't have enough blood staining his hands that he sometimes thought he could still smell it.

In the power vacuum that had followed his ouster, half a dozen different factions within their group had begun warring for control. His uncles headed some of those factions. Not *real* Cranes—they'd married in—but still technically family, and feuding just as bitterly as the Medicis or Borgias ever did.

He didn't even know who was in charge of the business at this point, if anyone was. It was a fucking disaster.

Dominic's own mind was at war with itself, too. A secret part of him wanted to just wash his hands of the Syndicate, like he'd tried to wash away the blood.

But like it or not, the business had become his responsibility. His duty. Warren had told him growing up—*there's always someone worse.*

That meant he was trapped with few options, just as surely as he was stuck within the confines of their West Oaks house.

Dominic's fickle friends and lovers had deserted him. Most of his former business associates had betrayed him. Some were even trying to kill him.

But at least nobody could call him a traitor.

He forced himself to get up and leave the room. As he went down the hall, he could hear Maureen bustling in the kitchen.

She smiled as he padded across the tile. "Well, look who it is, up and at 'em. I was just about to bring lunch in to you." Her soft southern accent brightened his day, as it always did. "I made you a smoked salmon and cucumber salad. I hope that's up to your taste this fine afternoon?"

"Whatever you make is always my favorite. I really don't deserve you."

She mimed smacking the side of his head. "You're in a mood today, I see."

He gave her a sardonic smile.

Maureen had been working for him the last two years. He liked to think Maureen didn't mind him so much. Perhaps even had affection for him. She certainly wasn't intimidated by him.

He followed her out onto the balcony, which overlooked the ocean. Dominic's house was situated in the West Oaks hills, the toniest neighborhood in town. This place had once been a second home for Dominic's family. They hailed from Los Angeles, and he'd spent many childhood weekends and summer days playing on the grounds here.

Maureen set down his lunch on the patio table, then went back to the kitchen to fetch her own. She gave him company at mealtimes, which he gratefully accepted.

She settled into the chair across from his. "So what's on your agenda today, Mr. Crane?"

"Try to call Raymond. I'm getting worried about him."

"Oh. Any specific reason?"

"Just haven't spoken to him lately." Dominic's younger brother was a college student. Not part of the Syndicate, thank god. He was busy with school, and he'd been active online. But he hadn't been answering his phone.

Combined with the resounding silence of his captains, and the fact that Dominic hadn't heard from his eldest brother, Warren? *Very* concerning.

"I'm sure Raymond's well. Must have a test coming up." She took a bite of salmon. "Interested in a game of rummy later?"

Though Dominic had several video gaming consoles, Maureen preferred cards, and she'd taught him to play. Those old games were elegant, deceptively simple.

"Not today. But thanks."

"Too busy contemplating the inevitable demise of everything in the universe?"

"You've got me."

She giggled. "Then nothing too out of the ordinary, I suppose."

Even before his arrest, when he used to host wild parties here that lasted for days—or when he came home with blood all over his suit—Maureen had never seemed shocked. Instead, she quietly scheduled their cleaning service and looked at him with sad disapproval, like she might've expected better from him. Even though *no one* had ever expected much better from him. Certainly not his parents or the Syndicate captains.

"I would've thought you'd be dressed for our guests, though," she said.

Dominic sat up straighter. "Guests?"

"That nice Max Bennett fellow called. He said they'd be

here sometime today to install your new security system. That'll be quite a relief, don't you think?"

He slumped into his seat again. "Oh. That."

The new security system had been Aaron Sandford's idea. The lawyer had argued that the old alarm was installed on behalf of the Syndicate, which meant his current enemies could've had access to it in the past. It was a fair point.

Maureen had mentioned seeing cars with tinted windows driving past the house. No one had actively tried to kill him since he'd gotten out of jail, but Dominic preferred to be on the safe side, especially since Maureen could be at risk, too.

Through the open patio doors, they heard the doorbell ring.

Maureen set her silverware aside. "That must be them. It's about time. I was starting to wonder. I can handle them, and you can take your lunch upstairs. I'll let you know if they need anything."

She always bossed him around like an overbearing grand-mother. Usually, he liked it. Made him feel a little closer to human.

But he was too eager to see a different face, even if that face belonged to Max Bennett.

From the first moment they'd ever spoken, Dominic and Max had not gotten along. Max was one of those people who considered him a bloodthirsty murderer, worse than dirt. Yet recently, Max had begrudgingly expressed his gratitude for Dominic's help with a sensitive matter. Dominic even thought that he and Max were developing an understanding.

He followed Maureen to the front door, standing behind her as she opened it.

"Welcome," the housekeeper said. "You folks must be from Bennett Security?"

Three people stood on the doorstep: a gigantic guy with an overgrown beard. A girl with large eyes who seemed to be around twelve.

And in the middle—like she was in charge—a petite woman in black jeans, a long black sweater, and combat boots.

"You're not Max," Dominic said, his gaze fixed on the woman in black.

She wore her strawberry-blond hair in a blunt bob. Chunky pink glasses dominated her face. She had her sleeves pushed up to her elbows, and black tattoos peeked out along her arms. She was like a little rock 'n' roll pixie.

"Astute observation." The pixie's eyes were down, as if she couldn't be bothered to raise them. "Max told you he'd send his best. That would be me." She really didn't sound happy about it.

"Thanks for making the trip," Dominic said, voice dripping in sarcasm.

She hummed noncommittally.

The huge guy tilted his chin in a lazy greeting. "You're Crane, right? I'm Tanner. Here to keep an eye on things."

"And I'm Priyanka," the twelve-year-old squeaked. "I'm Sylvie's assistant."

So that was the pixie's name? Sylvie?

Dominic stepped back to let them all inside. He was trying not to be offended that the women had brought a bodyguard along. Did Max honestly think they wouldn't be safe around him?

Sylvie dumped her bag onto the ground. Tanner leaned against a wall, taking a peek at his phone. At least the bodyguard didn't seem to expect Dominic to attack at any moment. A minor vote of confidence.

Dominic crossed his arms over his chest. "Will the install take long?"

"Shouldn't." Sylvie unzipped her bag, then stood. "Where did you…" Her blue eyes finally lifted to his.

And it was like an electric shock passed through her.

She'd frozen in place. Her full lips opened slightly. A pink flush spread in her cheeks.

Her eyes flicked downward, and Dominic didn't miss the way her gaze lingered on his chest. His arms. Then lifted back to his face, her focus softening.

He knew that look. He'd seen it in plenty of other people before.

Sylvie was checking him out. Like, a lot.

Huh. She'd seemed annoyed to be here, but she was cute. And after months without any sex to speak of?

It wasn't like he *minded* some female attention.

He put his hands in his pockets and shifted his weight, angling his head. Dominic let his eyes rove over her right back. She had a boyish figure, not many curves, at least none that were visible beneath her baggy sweater. He wondered what other tattoos she had. She was intriguing, not the typical person he'd have expected to work for straight-laced Max Bennett. He wanted to know her story.

"Anything I can do to help, Sylvie?" Yeah, he was turning up the flirt. And he was rewarded when she sighed, gaze settling once again on his snug T-shirt.

This was turning into a straight-up eye fuck.

"Sylvie?" her assistant prompted. "What's first?"

"Uh, right. Let's see." Sylvie's voice had gone all high and funny. She gestured vaguely at the wall. "Should we do it right here by the door?"

Priyanka giggled.

Dominic tilted his head the other way, fighting a smile.

"I mean the panel." Sylvie coughed. "The security panel."

"Wherever you want it is fine by me," Dominic said, leaning into the innuendo. He couldn't resist teasing her.

Priyanka giggled again, and even Tanner snorted.

Come on, Sylvie. Don't you want to laugh? A little?

But her expression shut down. "Do you want the panel by the door," she snapped, "like the old one you've got here?"

He shrugged. "That works. You're the expert."

"Great," she ground out, narrowing her eyes. "If only all

my degenerate-murderer clients were so accommodating and helpful."

Sylvie wasn't eye-fucking him anymore. Her glare was more of a *fuck you*. Like she wanted him as far away from her as possible.

He couldn't understand these mixed signals. Did this woman actively dislike him, even though she'd just been giving him a serious once over?

His mind repeated what she'd said.

Degenerate murderer?

He forced out a laugh, like he couldn't care less what she thought. But he was quickly feeling that the joke was all on him.

Chapter Three

From the minute she'd stepped inside, Sylvie had been trying not to look at him.

Instead, she'd been examining the architecture like she was a real estate agent. Dominic Crane's house looked like a casino hotel in Vegas. There were garish marble floors, gold trim on the light fixtures, even paintings on the walls of European cities like Venice and Paris. How much tackier could the man get?

But then, she'd made the mistake of briefly glancing up. And had found Dominic looking back.

With his regal features and dark curls, he was part rockstar, part anime character, with a sprinkling of emo boy thrown in. He was nearly as tall as Tanner, but with the elegant, lean musculature of a runner.

That tight T-shirt and loose pants that he'd obviously just thrown on without a single thought, the scruff on his face, tousled black hair... No human person had a right to be that effortlessly beautiful.

And now she was thinking about all the bad things those large hands had done. Such bad, bad things... *Stop staring. He's probably already noticed.*

Sylvie suspected she'd been saying something nonsensical, because Crane and Priyanka were both snickering at her.

Gah, this was so embarrassing. Crane's presence had put her off balance, just as she'd feared. She had to get her brain going again.

"Do you want the panel by the door, like the old one you've got here?"

"That works. You're the expert."

Okay, now he was mocking her. She'd claimed to be Max's best, but she was making herself look like an ass. "Great. If only all my degenerate-murderer clients were so accommodating and helpful."

He barked out a laugh.

She braced herself and looked at him again. But his smirk had faded. Now Crane just looked bored. Good. Maybe he'd leave her alone and let her get this finished as quickly as possible.

"Could I get some room to work, please?" Now she sounded petulant, but it was better than shooting heart eyes at him like he was in a Korean boy band.

"Dominic, perhaps you and I should go finish our lunch." The housekeeper waved him toward the living room, where Sylvie spied a set of open patio doors. "My name is Maureen, by the way. You just let me know if you folks need anything at all."

Sylvie held out her hand. "Thank you, Maureen. I'm Sylvie Trousseau. Pleased to meet you."

Sylvie hoped she hadn't offended the housekeeper by calling her boss a murderer. But then again, she couldn't imagine anyone would work here by choice. Not unless Crane was paying Maureen bucketloads of money. And in that case, she probably didn't care what anyone called her boss.

The woman took her hand and patted it politely. Sylvie felt a twinge of homesickness. Maureen had a Louisiana accent, like her dad. It had been years since Sylvie had left, but the old melancholy still crept up on her occasionally.

Crane and Maureen went out onto the patio, and Sylvie got to work. First, they needed to install the new panel. Luckily, the old one was already hard-wired, so Sylvie just had to switch them out instead of setting up any new connections. She told Priyanka which tools she needed from the bag, happy to focus on her task instead of on her distracting client.

Quickly, Tanner got tired of watching them and went to sit on the porch. He was the type of person who always craved sunlight, while Sylvie was usually worried about getting burned.

She took the opportunity to walk Priyanka through the steps of connecting the wiring for the panel. Priyanka seemed to pick it up quickly, as she did everything when she was paying attention. But then, her focus started to wander.

"Isn't he hot?" the assistant whispered.

Sylvie sent a worried glance over her shoulder, but Crane was still sitting out on the patio with his housekeeper. A breeze ruffled his hair, and his profile was every bit as striking as any model in a perfume ad.

"I guess so. But we shouldn't be talking about this."

"I can't help it. All that man... Damn. I just want him to break me in half."

Sylvie bugged her eyes at her assistant. "Priyanka, that is not a way to talk about a client."

The girls nose wrinkled. "Crane? Oh, he's okay. I'm talking about Tanner. Is he single? Do you think he might be into me?"

Good Lord. "I'm not answering any of those questions. Can we please stay focused on work?" Sylvie was going to have to show the girl that sexual-harassment video—again. Otherwise, Priyanka would end up in some sort of compromising position, and Max would blame Sylvie for a lack of proper training.

"Come on, Sylvie, you know I was kidding. Sort of. You're not usually this serious."

"She isn't?" a deep voice asked.

Her shoulders tightened. Crane had snuck up right behind her.

"Why are you so serious today, Sylvie?" He said her name like he enjoyed rolling it around his tongue. The same way a cat might enjoy toying with a mouse.

"Because I have a lot to do when I get back to the office. I don't usually waste my time doing installs."

And she didn't usually get so mouthy with their customers, either. She knew she was probably getting close to the line here. But would Max be that mad at her? He didn't like Crane either. Not really.

"I'm wasting your time? Then why are you here?" He didn't sound mockingly flirty anymore. He had the same tone of annoyance she'd been using on him.

"Because Max told me to."

"You always do what he says?" Each time he spoke, Crane moved closer. He'd shifted to leaning against the wall beside the panel, where she had no choice but to look at him.

"I tried to talk him out of it."

"Because I'm a degenerate murderer?"

"You guessed it."

He took a step forward. His nostrils flared. Was he angry? Or was he *smelling* her?

Now that she thought of it, the man smelled pretty enticing himself. Not like soap or aftershave or detergent. Not the things Sylvie's co-workers, or her exes, ever smelled like.

She couldn't describe Dominic's scent in any terms other than *sex*. The guy smelled like sweat and salt and arousal.

"You're in my space," she said.

He didn't move. Just stared down her. Priyanka was eying the two of them with her teeth digging into her lower lip.

Sylvie couldn't tell if her assistant was nervous or really enjoying this.

"Are you afraid of me, Sylvie?" His voice was a smooth, dangerous murmur. "Do you need to call your bodyguard back inside to protect you from me?"

"I can handle you just fine myself." She poked a finger into his chest, finding firm muscle underneath.

But he didn't move. And she didn't lower her hand.

The corner of his mouth quirked. "How exactly do you intend to handle me?"

His exhales tickled her skin. His eyes bored into hers, utterly hypnotizing. One of those snakes that mesmerizes its prey. Sylvie's foot lifted, and somehow she ended up another inch closer. Like he had some magnetic pull on her. The smell of him, his heartbeat...

Words vanished from her brain. A small noise snuck out of her, almost a whimper.

Then just as suddenly, Crane retreated. His smirk was back. "That's what I thought," he whispered. "Not an expert at everything, are you?" He pivoted, hands dipping into his pockets as he strolled away.

Sylvie could only stare after him. He'd been toying with her. The *asshole*.

Priyanka was right beside her. "What the heck was *that*?"

Crane was making a fool of me. And I just stood there and let him do it. "Nothing. Let's get the Wi-Fi password from the housekeeper."

"But I was totally getting angry-sex vibes from you two. I thought you guys were going to strip down right in front of the security panel. At least, I was hoping for that."

Jeez, Sylvie's assistant needed to get laid. The girl was over-the-top horny. "I don't know what you're talking about. Wi-Fi password, Priyanka. *Focus.*"

She didn't see Crane again for the rest of the afternoon. Yet Sylvie couldn't get him out of her head, either.

It was like he'd known exactly how to push her buttons, all for the purpose of walking away and leaving her cold. He'd definitely known what he was doing.

Her dislike for the man had been purely abstract before. Now, it was personal.

Rationally, she knew that a man like Crane wouldn't lead her anywhere good. He knew exactly how attractive he was, and he was a fucking jerk about it.

But unlike Sylvie's boss Max, who also had a decent-sized ego, Crane didn't care whom he hurt. In fact, proving his effect on her had been the entire point. Well, the guy could take his beautiful face and his athletic body and shove it into a wood chipper for all she cared. She was never going to see him again if she could help it.

She didn't care what Max said. She didn't even care if every gang in Los Angeles came after Crane. No way was she doing him any favors again, on Max's behalf or otherwise.

Chapter Four

*I*t was three in the morning, and Dominic was haunting the upstairs hallways. Maureen had her own space on the first level, so this floor was his for wandering and brooding at all hours of the night.

He couldn't stop thinking about the pixie with the pink glasses and the oversized attitude. Sylvie.

I don't usually waste my time on installs.

She might as well have said, *I don't usually waste my time on trash like* you. Even though she'd looked at him like she wanted to lick him head to toe. As if he was good enough for an eye fuck, but not common courtesy.

So yes, he'd toyed with her a little. Just to prove he could. It had felt so damn satisfying to hear that sexy little moan, after she'd claimed to want nothing to do with him.

But sexual desire wasn't the same as respect. Or even basic civility. He might've proved that Sylvie wanted his body, but she'd never feel anything more than disgust for him as a human being.

Why did that bother him so much? He didn't even know the woman, and she didn't know him. Why did he care what she thought?

Degenerate murderer.

Fine, some people thought he was a degenerate. Sure. But Dominic was innocent of that ridiculous murder charge. Max Bennett knew it, and the district attorney's office knew it.

They'd accused him of ordering a hit on the victim—which he hadn't done—and then the police had uncovered a separate conspiracy related to the killing altogether. But the DA and his minions wouldn't drop the charge unless Dominic agreed to rat on the Syndicate. It was bullshit.

Sylvie's tattoos and fierce attitude had hinted that she might not view the world in black and white. That she *might* give him the benefit of the doubt. But he'd thought wrong. Sylvie was as judgmental as most anyone born with the privilege of moral superiority.

Dominic had never had the luxury of being so pure.

He noticed a light blinking. It was the new security panel Sylvie had installed for this floor. A touch of his finger lit up the screen. It had various controls for the cameras, a silent alarm, an audible panic button. Sylvie hadn't asked him for any further opinions during the set-up, so he wasn't exactly sure where she'd placed the cameras. Nor did he really care. He was glad to see that Maureen had armed the system before going to bed, since he'd forgotten.

As he watched, the screen pixilated, then switched to "not armed." Then back to "armed" again. Weird. It was probably some technical glitch. Not like he understood any of that stuff.

But this fresh reminder of the pixie in pink glasses and combat boots annoyed him. He stalked down the hall, looking for something else to take his attention.

A few minutes later he found himself in an unused guest room. Dominic stretched out on the bed, took out his phone, and video called his younger brother again.

Raymond answered. His dorm room was dark, and the screen lit up his face. "Nic?"

Thank goodness. Dominic sat up against the pillows. "Did I wake you?"

"It's okay. I fell asleep working on a paper, so it's good you did. I need to finish."

"It's been a while. How've you been?"

Raymond had an unpredictable sleep schedule, just like Dominic. The brothers usually ended up talking at odd hours, usually sometime after midnight and before breakfast. But they'd been speaking even less since Dominic's arrest and ouster from the Syndicate. He didn't know the exact reason, and that made him nervous.

Raymond was Dominic's half brother. They shared the same father, but Raymond had been born to their dad's mistress when Dominic was around twelve years old. His own mom lasted a bit longer in their marriage, but the affair helped explain why his mom took off eventually, unable to stand her husband's philandering. It was a bit cliché, a mobster with a mistress and a long-suffering wife. But the whole drama had given him a younger brother, so while Dominic didn't approve of his dad's cheating, he also couldn't really complain.

Raymond had moved in with them when he was just a baby. He'd had a special nanny and lived in a secluded part of their L.A. house. The rest of the family had laughed at Dominic for playing with Raymond in the nursery. But he'd known, even then, that his brother's innocence was something precious. Worth protecting.

When Dominic took over the Syndicate, Raymond had just graduated high school. Dominic had ensured that his younger brother went off to college instead of joining the business. It was the single accomplishment he was most proud of. Now Raymond was working on a history degree and planned to become a teacher.

Sometimes, Dominic wondered what he might've done if he hadn't joined the business at eighteen. His father hadn't given him a choice, really. It was either join or get the fuck out of town, never see his brothers again, and hope nobody was pissed enough to track him down.

But Dominic also couldn't imagine having some generic day job with a boss and paperwork. Even as a junior member of the Syndicate, he hadn't been very good at staying focused.

Raymond scratched at his scalp on the screen. "I've been busy with school. The usual. How about you? Any news on the trial?"

"They keep delaying it. Which is fine with me for now. I don't like being stuck at home, but at least nobody's gunning me down on the courthouse steps."

As long as he remained alive, a few captains would remain loyal to him as a Crane. His enemies would stand a better chance of taking over if they got Dominic permanently out of the way.

Raymond flinched.

"Sorry," Dominic said. "Bad joke."

"It's going to blow over, right? All this stuff with the business. You and Warren are going to get it back."

"That's the plan. It's all going to work out." An unsettling thought came to Dominic's mind. "Have any of the captains been contacting you? Any of our uncles?"

The most dangerous was their uncle Charles Traynor, who claimed he had both a right to run the Syndicate as the husband of a Crane, and the clearest vision for the business's future success. To Charles, that meant being more merciless than anybody else out there.

"I don't hear from hardly anyone except you." Raymond cut his eyes to the side.

Dominic sat forward. "Is someone else there?"

"No. But I better finish that paper. I'll talk to you later, Nic. Miss you."

"Miss you, too. Love you."

Raymond nodded, though he didn't return the sentiment aloud.

Dominic hadn't mentioned the DA's latest offer. He didn't want Raymond to worry. And it wasn't important anyway because Dominic wasn't going to accept the deal.

But if… If.

If he was even going to consider accepting the district attorney's offer, then he'd have to ensure Raymond's safety first.

He'd have to get his little brother away from their uncles, who might try to use Raymond for their own ends.

From the time he was a little kid, Dominic's whole family had talked about "the business." Yet it wasn't a store or an office or a medical clinic like any of the businesses his friends' parents ran. Dominic had no idea that his family's "business" wasn't legal until he was in the seventh grade.

That was when he'd overheard some kids call his house the "mob house." He'd asked his older brother what that meant. Warren had been seventeen, but he'd looked and acted far older. He'd finished high school early and joined the "business" with their dad.

"Some people would call Dad a mobster," Warren had said. "But who the fuck cares?"

Dominic had cringed at the curse word. He'd never liked to hear his brother or father swear. It made them sound angry. "But what does 'mob' really mean?"

Warren had just looked at Dominic with pity and laid it all out.

"Look, Dad helps people with problems. He might take something that somebody else wants. Which might be called stealing, except insurance just pays the first guy right back. Or he helps other people hide their money from the government."

"Okay…"

"Plus, there are certain neighborhoods that his men

protect from really violent guys, gangs, and Dad charges a fee for that service. Stuff like that. Get it?"

These activities sounded vaguely problematic. "But I thought the mob was a bunch of really bad guys."

"Well, sometimes Dad helps people who want to buy drugs, too. Or people who want to buy sex with an attractive, willing woman."

"But why? Dad's a good person. He loves us. Why would he do those things?"

"Because if he didn't, somebody else would. There's always somebody else who's more cutthroat, more violent, like those gangs that he protects his territory from. You can't see the world in black and white, right and wrong, kid. There's only *better* and *worse*. The sooner you accept that, the sooner you'll be able to take your place as a real member of this family. A real man. If you don't? Then you'll probably never sleep at night again. But it won't make a single ounce of difference because Dad will keep on doing what he does, and the worst people will keep on doing their thing, too. The only person you'll be punishing is yourself."

A year ago, when Warren had been convicted and sent off to federal prison, there'd been nobody else with the Crane name to take his place. By then, their father had premature dementia. Raymond had only been nineteen.

Warren even tried running their organization from within prison for a while, but it just wasn't practical. So Dominic reluctantly became the new head of the Syndicate, over the vigorous objections of many of Warren's captains—like Uncle Charles.

Dominic had told himself he could still run the family business and not be an evil person. There was always somebody worse, just as Warren had said. Somebody who would offer the same services but use more extreme violence or demand more outrageous terms.

Dominic had seen the corruption within governments and

corporations, which only made him more convinced that his family's Syndicate was just as legitimate as the companies that traded on the New York Stock Exchange. If anything, the Syndicate was more honest about its true nature. Dominic had to lie, sure, but somehow the lie felt cleaner because it was so bald-faced.

As the Syndicate's leader, Dominic had ordered deaths only a few times. Like punishing a ring of betrayers who'd engaged in underage prostitution on the sly. Or another guy who'd assaulted and murdered a girl. Dominic absolutely couldn't tolerate hurting women.

He'd tried to walk a fine line between being ruthless enough to control the Syndicate and holding onto his humanity.

But he saw more clearly now. To the Syndicate, Dominic had always been a joke. A sensitive aesthete who'd never be able to cut it as a real gangster. They'd only been willing to tolerate him for so long.

And to people like Max Bennett and Sylvie? Dominic was a monster in a cage, where he belonged. They stood back, so superior, acting like he didn't deserve to spit shine their shoes.

So fuck all of them. He didn't need the Syndicate or Bennett Security. He could solve his problems just fine on his own.

No matter how impossible a task that seemed.

Chapter Five

Tanner stopped by Sylvie's desk. "Fish tacos after work today?"

She glanced around for her assistant. "Yeah, but don't let Priyanka hear that. She'll invite herself."

"You don't like her?"

"I do like her. But she *really* likes you. I don't want to give her any new excuses to be hanging around you."

Tanner chuckled. "You sure about that? Don't you think I'm a little old for her?

Tanner had well over a decade on Priyanka. "I completely agree. But she clearly doesn't see it that way."

Tanner just shrugged, shaking his head.

Sylvie felt nothing for him but friendship, but even she could attest that Tanner had sex appeal. He was one of the few men in their office who didn't have an inflated ego to go with his massive body.

"I'm just warning you," Sylvie said, "because I'm afraid she's going to try to feel you up in the hallway one of these days."

"Then you'd better protect me. Good thing you've been working out. You've got some serious guns going on."

Sylvie flexed her biceps. She was wearing a tight black T-shirt today, which showed off both her muscles and her newest ink—a heron with its wings outstretched.

She'd been working out in their gym lately, as well as practicing her shooting at the range. Sylvie made her living behind a desk, but her visit to Crane's house had reminded her that she still worked for a security company. Her job had inherent dangers, and she wanted to be ready for them.

It had been three weeks since she'd seen Crane. She hadn't heard anything further from the man. Nor had Max mentioned him. She figured that Crane hadn't complained about her bad attitude, probably because he'd put her sufficiently in her place. And Priyanka hadn't spread any rumors about their confrontation in the entryway, which had definitely increased Sylvie's affection for her new assistant.

All in all, the whole incident was behind her.

So why couldn't she stop thinking about him? Replaying that scene inside his house, only with a different ending than him smirking at her and walking away?

The workouts had helped distract her, but clearly, it wasn't enough. She needed a new guy to take her mind off things. But every time she swiped through a dating app, her mind wandered off to Dominic Crane again.

She *had* been pretty rude to him. Would he have behaved differently if she'd been kinder? Even mobsters had feelings, presumably.

Not like it matters, she reminded herself. *Because you aren't going to see him again.*

An hour later, she and Tanner were walking along the beachside path to their favorite fish taco stand.

"What's new with you, besides your fitness regimen and your fresh ink?" the bodyguard asked. "Seeing anyone these days?"

"Um, what?"

He laughed. "That wasn't a proposition. I'm asking as your friend. You seem…different."

"Why would me seeing someone make me different?" She'd never change herself for a man.

"Not different in a bad way. You just seem a little dreamy. Sometimes you're looking off into space and smiling, and I'm just curious what you're thinking about."

Tanner might not be able to tell when a girl was crushing on him, but otherwise he was pretty damn observant. "I guess I've been thinking of someone. I'm surprised I'm smiling about him though. Because there's definitely no potential."

"Do I know this guy?"

She was so not going there. "Not really. It doesn't even matter. He's not remotely interested in me."

"Our Sylvie? You kidding? What's this guy's problem?"

"It's okay, Tanner. You don't have to make me feel better. I'm a big girl. He wouldn't be good for me anyway."

Tanner stuck his hands in his shorts pockets. Max had a pretty easy-going philosophy when it came to their dress code, but Tanner was always pushing it. His flip-flops slapped against his feet.

"Then it's better he stays away. You shouldn't waste your time. There must be plenty of guys knocking on your door. Whether you'll answer them is another question."

That was fair. She was picky. Sylvie hadn't had a boyfriend for at least a year. The last one had been a professor at a state school in Los Angeles. Theology, of all things. They'd had engaging conversations, even though their chemistry had only been so-so.

But Sylvie rarely had experienced intense passion in real life, as opposed to just in her fantasies.

She'd been on countless dates and had plenty of boyfriends in the years since she'd moved to Southern California. She didn't do one-night stands, but she'd slept with all kinds of men. Nice guys, some not-so-nice ones. But no matter how attracted she felt to them, or how much desire she experienced beforehand, the actual sex always turned out disappointing. She'd accepted the fact that it was her issue and not theirs. She just wasn't cut out for experiencing that kind of pleasure.

Specifically? She'd never had an orgasm. Not once. With anyone.

She only knew she was missing out because of the experiences other women described. Sylvie was an intellectual creature, not a physical one. That was nothing to be ashamed of. Or so a multitude of doctors and therapists had told her.

Of course, in Dominic Crane's entryway, she'd wondered if maybe he could get her to places she'd never been before... But it was probably better she hadn't tested that theory. Crane could stay in her fantasy world, which was better for all of them in more ways than one.

"What about you?" Sylvie asked. "Why haven't any ladies managed to tie you down yet?" She poked his side with her elbow.

"Because I'm wild and untamable." He shook out his mane of curly hair to emphasize the point. "But if you and I both stay single forever, you could be my wingwoman in the nursing home. You could handle my schedule of horny widows who want to come take a ride."

She cracked up at that horrifying yet hilarious image. "And what would I get out of this?"

"Job satisfaction? I could offer prescription discounts and a pension plan. Gotta keep that juice flowing, even in retirement."

"Now you're speaking my language. Investment portfolios get me all riled up. Talk dirty about 401(k)s, please."

This was all she needed—good friends, a challenging job, a boss she respected. Her cousin Ethan was her roommate and best friend, another refugee from their former life.

Sylvie didn't lack for many things. She was determined to

be grateful for all she had, instead of dwelling on what might
be missing.

SHE WAS BANGING around in the kitchen when Ethan came
downstairs. "What's for dinner, honey?"

"Why, baked ham and boiled peas, sweetheart," she said
in a falsetto.

Sylvie and her cousin had bought this house together a
year ago. He lived in the upstairs, while she took the lower
part. Ethan had his own kitchen up there, but he loved
mooching off her when it came around to dinnertime. And of
course, she didn't mind.

Actually, she was making lentil soup and homemade sour-
dough. Ethan bent over the pot on the stovetop and inhaled.
"That smells amazing. I'll set the table."

Ethan had been Sylvie's inspiration for moving to Southern
California in the first place. Sylvie's dad was from Louisiana
originally, but he'd put down roots in a small town in the Texas
Hill Country where cows outnumbered people. There were so
many things that Sylvie loved about growing up there. The wide-
open skies, the beige color of the local stone used to construct
their grandparents' home, line dancing on Friday nights.

But Sylvie had always felt like an outsider there. Like a
foreign plant someone had stuck into the soil but didn't know
how to care for.

It was her nature to question things, and her parents never
appreciated her attitude, nor had her Sunday school teachers.
She used to doodle tattoo ideas on her textbooks and got in
trouble for drawing on everything—her arms, her hymnals,
even her clothes—with sharpie marker.

In high school, Sylvie decided what books to read based
on whatever the local parent community wanted to ban. As

soon as she had access to an internet connection, she got into coding and joined every message thread on hacking she could find. She'd instantly felt drawn to the hacker ideology and culture. In her mind, information should be widely accessible to all, and anybody who abhorred free and open communication didn't deserve their power.

She'd daydreamed of going so far as Austin to attend the University of Texas and was thrilled to receive a scholarship.

But then, her cousin Ethan came out of the closet. Their entire family disowned him. He'd known it was likely to happen, but still, the loss devastated him. For Sylvie, it was the last straw.

When Ethan called her up and told her he'd moved to L.A., she'd decided to drop out of her freshman year at UT and follow.

They'd lived near one another ever since. Ethan was a freelance graphic designer, so his work was flexible. After Sylvie got the job at Bennett Security, Ethan moved with her to West Oaks.

Neither of them had any family now but each other. None worth mentioning, anyhow.

"Where's Luis tonight?" Sylvie asked. Often, Ethan's boyfriend joined them for dinner. They'd been together for five years, but Luis still had his own apartment closer to Los Angeles, where he worked as a photographer.

"Out of town for a few days on a shoot in San Diego. You want to go dancing? We could meet up with that friend I was telling you about, the one from the coffee shop with the soulful eyes who's recently divorced…"

"Why are people so concerned about my love life all of a sudden?"

"It might be that cranky look you've had on your face since your birthday? The big three-o?"

Tanner had implied that she seemed spacey, and Ethan

was calling her cranky. Maybe she *did* need some new friends. "I'm fine with being thirty."

"Yet you still haven't opened that birthday card. It's been sitting there a month now." Ethan pointed at the console table by the door, where the envelope waited.

"Not because of birthday anxiety. I saw the postmark."

It had come from Texas. Every once in a while, Sylvie received a postcard or birthday wishes from one of her siblings. But neither of them had ever asked after Ethan. So, she'd chosen not to write back.

She wasn't angry anymore at her family back home. Just sad for them that they were so closed-minded and afraid.

"But did you turn it over? Did you see the name on the return address?"

"No. Why?"

Ethan shrugged. "Not like it's my card. But if I were you, I'd be curious."

She pushed back from the table and went to get the envelope. The back flap had a name she hadn't seen in a very long time.

Faith Townsend. Sylvie's closest girlfriend from high school. Back then, she and Faith had schemed together about how they'd escape. How they'd both go to college at UT and assert their freedom. Faith, Sylvie, and Ethan had been inseparable.

But when the Trousseau family shunned Ethan, and Sylvie decided to leave, Faith had ghosted them. All their years of friendship, all their shared dreams, and Faith had chosen to give it up. The last Sylvie heard, Faith had married an ex-football player from high school, a guy they'd both decried as a bully.

Sylvie ran her fingers over the envelope. It had little hand-drawn balloons on the outside. She should've known it wasn't one of her siblings. Faith had always enjoyed sketching, just like Sylvie.

"Going to open it now?"

"Nope. I don't see the point. People are who they are."

And they don't really change. Faith had shown her true nature by her choices all those years ago.

"But don't they deserve a chance to make up for their mistakes?" Ethan regarded her sadly, as if *she* were the closed-minded person who'd earned his pity and not Faith. "You're thirty now. Older is supposed to mean wiser."

"Apparently not. It just means crankier."

Sylvie opened the lid on the trashcan and tossed the envelope inside.

But later that night, after Ethan had retreated to his own space upstairs, she went back to the trashcan, opened it, and stared down at the blue envelope. It had a stain of grease at the corner.

Faith. Who'd once drawn a line of hearts down Sylvie's arm on Valentine's Day, because neither of them had a boyfriend.

She plucked the card out and wiped it with a paper towel. It went into a drawer, still unopened.

Chapter Six

*M*aureen knocked on the door and poked her head in. "Dominic? Your security system was acting strange again last night."

Groaning, he sat up from the couch, bumping his ankle monitor against the coffee table. "What's it been doing?"

"Turning on and off, like it was before. I pushed that button and spoke to someone at Bennett Security again. But they still insist they don't see any problem."

"Was it Sylvie?" He felt a twinge of something, though he couldn't say if it was anticipation or annoyance.

"Not her. Some technician. Should I try again and ask for her?"

He pushed off the couch. "I'll handle it later." He'd have to go straight to the top and call Max Bennett. The man owed him, after all, and this glitchy security system of Bennett's wasn't nearly enough to make them square.

But Dominic didn't feel like doing that right now. He was already busy avoiding his lawyer, who'd called three times that morning.

Then his phone rang yet again. Damn it, didn't Sandford have anything better to do?

"Just answer it already," Maureen said. "I'm sick of hearing that thing ring." She left the room, shaking her head.

Fine, he thought. *I should get it over with.*

"This is Crane."

"Dominic, Aaron Sandford."

As if he didn't know. But did he detect a new hint of backbone in his lawyer's voice? "What do you need?"

"What I need is to talk. Are you available? Can I come by?"

"What do you think? Of course, I'm fucking available. I can't leave my house."

"There's no need to take that tone with me."

"I'll take whatever tone I feel like. Just tell me what the hell this is about."

"Hold on. I'll call you back."

Sandford hung up. Dominic stared down at his phone, wondering what was going on. The lawyer called right back, but this time using a secure app with video conferencing.

"Since you insist on discussing this now, instead of in person, then I'll accommodate you."

Sandford was in his office in downtown Los Angeles. Dominic could see the next skyscraper through the man's window.

He sat back down on his couch. "Then out with it. Obviously, something's changed?"

"That's right. The Syndicate has a new leader."

Dominic worked hard to keep his face expressionless, though inside his guts were roiling. "And who is that?"

"Your uncle. Charles Traynor."

Fuck. "Have you spoken to Warren?"

"I have not. But I don't work for Warren, I work for the organization."

Unbelievable. The lawyer was jumping ship on them? So much for loyalty. "What about the other captains? Have they recognized Charles?"

"They have. Otherwise, you and I wouldn't be having this conversation. The factions have almost fully united behind your uncle. I'm calling to extend his offer of friendship and forgiveness. I'd suggest you fall in line."

He paused a moment, processing what Sandford had said. "Is that a threat?"

"Of course not. You know how much family means to your uncle. He wants to bring the Crane *and* Traynor family back together again."

Dominic snorted a laugh. "I'm sure he does. What is he offering in exchange for my stepping aside and not challenging his authority?"

"Like you have any chance of that in your position?"

"Humor me."

"All right, then. He's offering your life."

Cold sweat broke out under his arms. "How generous."

"And the lives of your brothers."

Dominic shot up to standing, his fist tight around the phone. "He'd better not lay a fucking hand on Raymond."

"Or you'll what? Accept the district attorney's deal? Rat out your family?"

An icy shiver threaded through him. So this was Sandford's real play. But how much came from the lawyer and how much from Charles?

"I have no intention of turning on my family," Dominic said carefully.

"Glad to hear it. I'll pass on the good news to your uncle. So, he has your allegiance?"

"I'm no betrayer. But even you must admit, this is pretty sudden. Let me think about what I'd like my role to be in the business going forward. Can you at least give me a few days?"

"I'm sure your uncle won't have a problem with that. Take a little time. But just know, your bank accounts are being emptied as we speak. It's the Syndicate's money after all, not yours."

So this *was* coming from Charles. Sandford wasn't smart enough or brave enough. A small carrot, and several large sticks. Dominic wouldn't have expected anything less from his uncle.

"I'll be in touch," Sandford said.

"I'm sure you will."

Dominic had a choice. Fold quietly back into the family business, with no authority whatsoever, or burn every connection between himself and the only life he'd ever known.

If Dominic even thought about turning on the Syndicate, then his uncle would go after Raymond and Warren. He assumed Sandford was passing on a similar threat to Warren in prison. His older brother was already segregated from the general population because of past assassination attempts. But would that truly protect him?

There was next to nothing any of them could do.

The minute Sandford was gone, Dominic called Max Bennett.

"Crane. Haven't heard from you in a while. I thought maybe your old Syndicate buddies had finally gotten to you."

Max's idea of a joke. Obviously, the entire town would've heard if that happened. But every day, the possibility was getting more likely, especially after the news about Uncle Charles.

"I'm still here. But your fancy custom security system is useless. Keeps switching itself on and off."

On the line, Dominic heard the squeak of Max's chair. "That's weird. Nobody's complained about anything like that before."

"Well, it's happening now. How am I supposed to know my house is secure if I don't even know the alarm is working?"

"You called our techs?"

"Yeah. Can't you send someone competent to look at it?"

"Jeez, and people call *me* demanding. You're not even paying me."

The subject of money irked Dominic even more. "Do I have to remind you what—"

"Yeah, yeah, what I owe you. I was only kidding. I'll send Sylvie out again to look at the system."

Dominic felt his jaw tighten. "Not Sylvie. Someone else."

"You're not a fan of my Sylvie? But she's my—"

"Your best. Yeah, I've got it. But she's the one who screwed up the install."

"I highly doubt that. Whatever the problem is, Sylvie will sort it out."

He thought of Sylvie's soft mouth. Then her sharp voice repeated the accusation in his head: *murderer.*

"Maybe I just want to save her some embarrassment. She's into me, and I turned her down."

Max didn't hide his laughter, though he didn't specify which part he found so funny. "Right. I'll tell her to swing by." He seemed like he was about to end the call.

"Wait, there's more." Dominic paced across the room, passing by his mom's grand piano. "I was wondering about hiring a bodyguard for someone. My younger brother."

"Oh?" Max's tone was all seriousness. "What's going on?"

Dominic considered how much he should reveal. Max was not actually his friend. The man disliked him and hadn't made any secret of the fact.

Yet Max Bennett was one of the few people in the world willing to help him right now, even begrudgingly. Dominic had a feeling he and Max might have a few things in common, if they could ever get past the roles they'd been assigned.

"You'll probably hear about this from your law enforcement contacts soon enough. The Syndicate has a new leader. Charles Traynor. My uncle."

"And I'm guessing from your tone this is bad?"

"That depends on your perspective. But this might be one of the few times you and I will agree on something."

"What does that have to do with your brother?"

"I'd rather not spell it out. I don't even know who might be listening to this phone call or who might repeat what I say. But my kid brother, Raymond, he's in college right now. He has nothing to do with any of this. And I'd like it to stay that way."

"I can send you over some details on our personal protection services. Things can get a little complicated if your brother doesn't actually want protection, though. Believe me, I've been through that sort of thing before."

"I'm not sure yet." Dominic figured he needed to have a serious conversation with Raymond. But he also didn't want to freak his brother out. "But there's another issue. My finances are tight at the moment. Very tight."

"I'm sure we can work something out. Just look over the info I send you and have a chat with your brother. Then let me know what you have in mind."

"Thank you, Bennett." Dominic didn't speak with utter sincerity to someone like Max very often. But this, he truly meant.

"Don't mention it."

The rest of the day, Dominic kept listening for the door, wondering when Sylvie might arrive. But she didn't show.

By the time night rolled around, he was so wired he couldn't even lie down, much less fall asleep. Dominic just kept staring at the security panels, sometimes the one by the front door, sometimes the one upstairs. Watching the status shift from off to on and back again. Wondering if Sandford would keep his word and give him time. Or if Uncle Charles was plotting, even now, to finally take him out.

Chapter Seven

"Crane says I made a mistake with his install? I don't make mistakes."

Sylvie was in Max's office again. She had a major case of déjà vu. Here she was, arguing about whether she had to go to Dominic Crane's house. And Max was sitting behind his desk, squeezing his stress ball, and not having any of it.

"You're saying the man's lying? I assume half the things he says aren't true, but why would he lie about this? I even checked. His housekeeper called our techs on more than one occasion."

"Yeah, I heard. There was no problem on our side."

"But he seemed really worried about it. That's why I've asked you to go and check out the system. Make sure there's nothing going haywire."

"If there is, it's Crane's fault. He did something. This is some tactic of his."

"To what, get you to come visit him? I wouldn't put that past him either, but he didn't even want you to follow up on this. He asked for anyone else *but* you. I think maybe he's intimidated."

"A murdering crime boss is intimidated by me?" She suppressed a laugh. That was so not likely.

Max rolled his eyes. "Don't you think 'murdering crime boss' is overstating things? Even the DA's office is willing to dismiss that charge in exchange for his cooperation. Though you didn't hear it from me." Lana had probably told him. She was the Assistant District Attorney of West Oaks, second in command of that office.

But if Crane truly didn't want her to come back, Sylvie was surprised. Didn't the guy want to toy with her more? Wasn't he just the kind of conceited bully who would pick a target and keep going after it? Wasn't that his sick idea of fun?

Unless I was wrong.

Max sighed, even though Sylvie hadn't said anything else. "I've got enough on my plate today. I'm supposed to be downstairs at some training thing that was technically my idea. So, I don't have any more time for back-and-forth with you."

"Okay. I'll go to Crane's and take care of it."

"So go take—Oh. Well. Great." Max paused a second, like her sudden acquiescence had been a shock to his system. Then he jumped up. "Get to it."

They both headed downstairs.

If Crane didn't *want* to see her, that put a whole new perspective on this second visit. She was instantly in a place of greater power and control.

This time, she'd be ready to handle him.

And if there really *was* something haywire with the system she'd installed, Sylvie wanted to know about it. She was a perfectionist and hated the idea that something might've gone wrong.

When she returned to her desk, the workroom was deserted. Even Priyanka was nowhere to be found. *Oh,* Sylvie remembered. *The training Max mentioned. Right.*

She went down to the lower level. Their entire bodyguard

team had congregated in the gym, where a martial arts expert was doing a workshop.

Sylvie spotted Priyanka hovering by the door. She tugged on her assistant's sleeve, nodding for the girl to follow her out into the hall.

"What is it?" Priyanka hissed.

"I need you and Tanner. We have to go back to Crane's house. He says there's something wrong with the system I installed." Sylvie made a face, trying to convey just how absurd that idea was.

"But we can't leave now. This teacher is some Israeli Krav Maga master, and Tanner's going to help him demonstrate. And they said *I* could pretend to be a victim they're protecting. Do you know how cool this is going to be? You can't make me leave. Please."

Crap. Tanner wouldn't want to miss this. And if she dragged Priyanka away from this opportunity to ogle the men in their workout clothes, Sylvie would take the title as the world's most uncaring boss.

But what did she need a bodyguard for, anyway? Crane had mocked her for bringing Tanner along last time.

Do you need to call your bodyguard back inside to protect you from me?

Forget it. She could deal with Crane herself. And she was more than eager to prove that to him.

"Never mind," she said to her assistant. "Have fun. I'll be back later."

Another glance into the gym told Sylvie that a lot of their techs and sales team were watching the training, too. Which meant nobody would be looking for her over the next few hours.

She grabbed an equipment bag, checked her makeup in the mirror, and went to her car in the parking garage.

Crane was going to be sorry he'd ever messed with her.

She was going to show him that Sylvie Trousseau wasn't anyone to be trifled with.

SYLVIE PULLED up to Crane's house. She made another quick glance over herself. She'd worn her usual high-waisted jeans and boots, as well as a cropped tank top with a cardigan over it. After a moment's hesitation, she left the cardigan on the passenger seat and got out.

Maureen opened the door. "Sylvie, so lovely to see you again. I was just making lunch."

They went inside. Sylvie braced herself to see Dominic again, but he wasn't in the living room or kitchen. "I hear you've had a problem with the security system?"

"Oh, here and there. We appreciate you making a trip to check on it. I'm sure it wasn't your fault. Probably some button or other I pushed that I shouldn't have."

"Did you really push a button? Or are you trying to make me feel better?"

The woman's hand paused on the refrigerator door handle. "I guess it's the second one."

Sylvie laughed. "I appreciate the honesty."

Maureen described how the system had been glitching. Sylvie wondered what could explain it. Odd that they hadn't detected this issue at Bennett Security headquarters when accessing Crane's system remotely.

"I should get started." She was eager to plug in her laptop.

"But won't you have a seat and visit for a moment? We don't get many guests here." Maureen lowered her voice. "And Dominic has been especially antisocial lately. I'm desperate for some conversation."

"All right. A few minutes." Her afternoon schedule was wide-open, anyway. Sylvie lowered her bag to the ground and took one of the bar stools.

Maureen pulled containers from the fridge. "You hungry?"

"No thanks. I already ate. But I can help if you want."

"Would you? Aren't you a dear. Dominic likes cold food at lunch. Lots of chopping." She set up Sylvie with a wooden cutting board to slice cucumbers, celery, and tomatoes.

Sylvie cut a grape tomato in half. She didn't like that she was prepping Crane's lunch. But on the other hand, she didn't mind helping Maureen. The woman had good energy, like she didn't get too worked up over anything. Sylvie hoped some of those relaxed vibes might rub off, because she'd been wound too tight lately.

"You're from Louisiana, aren't you?"

Maureen beamed. "That's right. Baton Rouge. You're familiar?"

"I grew up in Texas, but my father's got Cajun roots."

"Well, well. Whereabouts in Texas?"

"It's a tiny place in the Hill Country. Mostly cattle ranches and Baptist churches."

Maureen seemed to be waiting to hear more, but Sylvie didn't feel like discussing her family. She didn't want to get into their estrangement, nor did she want to act like they were close. It would be a white lie, yet it would take something out of her, too.

"How did you end up in West Oaks?" Sylvie asked.

"My daughter moved out to Ventura, so I followed. Her father's never been in the picture. But she's grown, so now I have Dominic to take care of."

"Isn't he a little old for that?" Then she shook her head. She didn't mean to disrespect the woman's job. "Sorry, that sounded rude. But I hope he pays you well."

"Dominic isn't nearly as ferocious as he'd like people to believe. He's more of a pussy cat than a tiger."

Sylvie snickered, and Maureen grinned. "I mean it. Get to know him, and you might be surprised."

"I'm just here for a house call on the security system. I doubt I'll have time for that."

"A shame. I was planning on making crawfish étouffée for dinner, if you happen to stay." Maureen took the pile of vegetables from Sylvie's cutting board.

"Crawfish étouffée?"

The woman nodded, eyes knowing. "That's right. I order my mudbugs from a supplier in New Orleans. They ship 'em on dry ice for me."

"And you just so happen to be making them tonight?"

"Just so happens."

Sylvie couldn't help laughing. "I'll think about it." She couldn't remember the last time she'd had real étouffée.

Maureen held out a plate of vegetables, cheese, bread, and hummus. "Could you make sure Dominic eats some of this? He's so bad about skipping meals."

"I am *not* going to do that." But she did accept the plate that Maureen practically shoved into her hands. The woman took her by the shoulders and steered her into a hallway.

"He's just right down there. Go on, hun. Don't be shy."

Sylvie looked behind her, but Maureen had already disappeared.

Classical music came from the closed door at the end of the hall.

She did need to talk to Crane. He was the client, after all. She'd check in with him briefly, then take her laptop to connect to the panel.

I can do this. I'm cool. I'm fine.

He didn't hear her knock. She pushed open the door, plate of food held out in front of her.

"I'm not hungry, Maureen." Dominic was sprawled over a huge sectional sofa, reading a dog-eared book.

The room was just as fancy as the rest of the house. Decorative moldings on the walls and ceiling, expensive light fixtures. There was a grand piano on a raised platform at one end of the room, and large windows overlooking the back patio and the ocean.

"I'm not Maureen."

Crane looked over at her, eyes widening. He dropped the book, scrambling upright. He wore soft-looking stone-washed jeans and a plain white tee. His face was clean-shaven compared to the first time they'd met, but his hair was equally messy.

"Sylvie. I thought you weren't coming."

"I know. Max told me you asked for *anybody* else. But I'm afraid there's only me."

"I was just trying to do you a favor. I figured you'd rather avoid me after last time."

He reached over to the stereo and turned down the volume on the Debussy Nocturne he'd been listening to. Sylvie knew her classical music.

"Why? What happened last time?"

His eyebrow lifted.

She crossed the room, handing him the plate of food. "Been *dying* for your call inviting me back. Moody emo guys wearing ankle jewelry are my jam."

"That's an improvement over what you called me last time. I guess I'll take it." He plopped back onto the couch and set the plate on the coffee table.

Sylvie felt herself smiling. She'd caught him off guard. Crane was nowhere near as smooth as a few weeks ago. He looked anxious and unsettled.

I'm totally winning, she thought.

But the more she studied him, the more she wondered if there was some other reason for his change in demeanor. Redness rimmed his eyes, like he hadn't slept.

"Are you okay? You look like a vampire that just got staked."

"How kind of you. Probably just in need of food."

"But I thought you weren't hungry."

"Maybe I am after all." He shrugged and grabbed a carrot. "So you're here to fix the system you messed up?"

"Wasn't me who messed it up. But yeah, I'll fix it."

He leaned back against the couch, one foot up on the coffee table, regarding her. "Then where's your bag with all that...internet stuff?"

"Internet stuff? Is that a technical term?"

"Best I can do."

"Isn't the Silverlake Syndicate supposed to be a modern, sophisticated operation? You sure you were in charge of it?"

The corner of his mouth quirked. "That's what they tell me. But honestly? I'm not so sure."

She didn't know what that meant. "My 'internet stuff' is in the kitchen. Maureen recruited me to help make your lunch and serve it to you."

"You didn't have to do that."

"You *could* say thanks."

"You're right. Thank you."

He'd spoken more softly than she'd expected. He'd even sounded sincere.

Sylvie wandered around the room, hands on her hips as she examined the space. "Actually, I think Maureen might've pulled a bait and switch. She's probably in my car halfway to Vegas by now. You're stuck with me. Sorry."

"I can think of worse things," he said in that same soft voice.

Her heart rate jumped.

She really should've been working on the panel by now. But she was actually enjoying their chat. Probably because she was still *winning*. If Crane was going to play with her, at least she could be a tough competitor in his little game.

Sylvie kept walking around the room. The man had all kinds of musical instruments on the wall behind the grand piano. Guitars, banjos, violins. Trumpets and clarinets. Some looked antique. It was quite a collection.

"Do you play any of these?"

"Nope."

Dominic's voice was much louder now. He'd snuck up behind her. How did he do that? She hadn't even heard him get up.

Seems like a tiger to me, Maureen.

"I never had the discipline to learn when I was growing up." He pushed air through his nose. "Or now, I guess. This all belongs to my mother. She plays the piano and the strings. Not the others, but she likes collecting rare, expensive things."

Sylvie didn't want to glance at him because she'd be looking up, and that felt like a concession. But the warmth of him glowed against her side. "Does she come here often?"

"Not in the last few years. She lives in Norway with her new husband. Some kind of banker, I think."

"What about your dad?" Sylvie didn't even know why she was asking. She was supposed to be acting superior and aloof. Any minute, she expected Dominic to scoff at her show of interest.

But he just said, "He has early dementia. My mom left before that happened, and she didn't feel enough pity to come back. Can't blame her. But that's also why my brother Warren took over the family business in his place."

He'd said all that so casually. "And then you were up when Warren went to prison?"

"Yep. Then it was me. To everyone's great disappointment and regret."

Was he serious? Or was he messing with her?

She couldn't resist any longer. She looked up at him.

Dominic was staring at the instruments on the wall, his profile contemplative and melancholy. "You've got my life story now. Want to tell me yours?"

His eyes flicked down before she was ready. Long lashes, those near-black irises that almost blended into his pupils. His gaze hit her right behind the belly button. Pure longing, both in his eyes and in her response.

God, this was bad. She had to do something before she wound up a puddle at his feet again.

Sylvie reached for one of the violins. "May I?"

"Sure. Touch all you want. I won't stop you."

He'd taken a step back, and she heard the humor in his voice. But she wasn't so sure he was laughing at her anymore. He almost seemed...*shy*.

She gently gripped the instrument to keep her hands steady, then picked up a bow from a nearby shelf.

"You play?" he asked.

"You don't think I can?"

"I didn't say that."

Sylvie plucked the strings, taking her time with tuning it. Nobody had touched this poor baby in so long. But she was going to make it sing.

She placed the violin below her chin and the bow against the strings.

Chapter Eight

*D*ominic sat on the piano bench, waiting for Sylvie to draw the bow across the instrument. If she didn't know how to play, she was certainly making a good show of it. But he wouldn't put anything past this woman.

Maybe he'd won their first round a few weeks ago, but today he was off his game. He was still reeling from Sandford's call yesterday. Maybe that explained it.

He hadn't been able to reach Raymond, and now that Sandford was against them, he didn't know how to get a message to Warren. He'd thought he was in limbo before, but this was so much worse.

Did he need to find a new attorney? But wouldn't that just piss off Uncle Charles? Would his uncle view that as a potential sign Dominic was flipping—an act of war?

Sylvie was proving a very welcome diversion from his problems. When she'd first stepped into the room, he'd had a fleeting worry that she could be in danger if his uncle chose today to strike at him. But he'd dismissed the thought. Charles had given him some time before he had to make a decision. There was no real reason for concern and every reason for him to try starting over with her.

Sylvie didn't like him. She'd made that clear. But he was Dominic Crane. He'd been the head of the Silverlake Syndicate. A man who'd been feared. Who'd been *wanted*.

He was far from powerless.

Plus, he enjoyed listening to her talk. She kept saying surprising things. Making him smile. And making *him* talk, in a way he rarely did. In a matter of minutes, he'd told her about his family—leaving out Raymond, because that subject stung too much.

And this, right now, what she was doing? Even more surprising.

Sylvie had just started to play. Damn. She had skills.

She was playing Debussy's Claire de Lune. The bow moved with fluid grace across the strings. The hypnotic melody sent chills to Dominic's nerve endings.

Sylvie's version was expressive. Tender. The softness of her touch proved she'd studied the instrument well. He watched her biceps flexing while her torso swayed slightly.

She'd worn a tight, cropped tank, which showed off both her perky little breasts and the tattoos that covered the backs of her shoulders and the top halves of her arms. All black ink, clearly by a single artist. Beautiful work. He had an urge to strip her bare and study them more closely, like she was a museum piece.

Her tank rode up at the waist, revealing taut stomach muscles.

Her volume increased with the pace. Building toward a crescendo. He'd never heard this arrangement of the song before.

Fuck. It was like sex.

And his body was responding in kind. His pulse matched the beat of the music. His eyes roved shamelessly over the curves of her body as she played. Delicious zaps of pleasure ran along his spine and into his balls.

He wouldn't let himself get hard because he doubted

Sylvie would appreciate that. But he was starting to sweat from the effort of keeping himself in control.

So much of his life was ugly. And here she was, filling his day with beauty.

Suddenly, she stopped. The bow and violin lowered to her sides.

"Why didn't you finish the song? You were just getting to the best part."

She shrugged, replacing the instrument on the wall. "I proved my point."

"Okay, so you can play. I'd love to keep listening."

Sylvie's grin was devious. "I'm sure you would."

Oh, that burned. And after his asshole stunt last time? He completely deserved it.

"How'd you learn to play like that?"

She opened her mouth, and Dominic could already tell she was going to deny him again. So, he cut her off. "No, let me guess. Your parents were folk singers. You grew up at the feet of Joni Mitchell and John Denver in their glory days."

"I'm not *that* old." But she was still smiling. He kept going.

"But you were a rebel and only enjoyed music written at least a century ago. You entered a music conservatory in Vienna at the tender age of thirteen. Then…you were rescued by the American military from a war-torn country during your world tour, and that's how you ended up indentured to a philistine like Max Bennett. You're working off your debt."

"That's quite a story. And makes absolutely no sense."

"Then tell me the real version." *Who are you, Sylvie?* He was dying to know.

"It's so much more boring than any of that, I promise."

He gestured around him. "I'm short on entertainment these days."

Her smile vanished. Shit, he'd said the wrong thing.

"I'm not here to entertain you." Sylvie walked toward the door. "I should take a look at the system now."

"Wait."

She opened the door and strode out to the hall. Dominic trailed after her. In the kitchen, Sylvie picked up her equipment bag. Maureen wasn't here.

She went over near the front door, pulled a laptop from her bag, and plugged it into a port on the side of the alarm panel. "Could you tell me again what the system's been doing?"

"Sylvie, can we just go back to—"

"I'm here to do a job. Either you help me with that, or I can leave. Those are the two options."

He didn't want her to go. Not yet. "Fine. It's been switching itself on and off. Either Maureen or I keep the alarm set pretty much at all times. But at night, I'll walk by and see it go to 'unarmed.' Then it flips back again, even though she and I haven't touched it."

"Huh. And does it make any noises? Any sirens?"

"Nothing like that. I only noticed it in the first place because the light was flashing from red to green."

"Does it happen during the day, too?"

"Sometimes? I think. But mostly at night. I'm up a lot."

Her eyes slid toward him, then away again. "Let me see what the code looks like."

A window appeared on her laptop screen, filled with seemingly random gibberish. "You know what that stuff means?"

"I should hope so. I wrote it."

He hovered behind her. She was quiet for a long time, scrolling through the window of code. He should've been bored, but he wasn't. Her very presence—her scent, the sound of her breathing, the little unconscious hums she made—were fascinating to him.

It took effort not to run a finger down the vertebrae at her neck. Her skin looked soft. Kissable.

"My code looks just as it should be. I'll run a debugger just in case, but I don't see the problem. And I haven't seen this glitch myself."

"You don't believe me? You think I made this up?"

"No, I believe you. I'm not done yet. I'll check your network next. Maybe you picked up some malware? I would've thought our software could withstand the average virus. But I don't know what kind of weird porn you download."

He scoffed. "I only subscribe to high-end adult entertainment sites." Though he doubted he could pay those monthly fees much longer.

She scowled at him over her shoulder. "Ew. I don't need to know that."

"You were the one who brought it up."

And now he was having some vividly dirty thoughts about Sylvie stripping down and touching herself as he watched. He'd watch her do pretty much anything.

In fact, just watching her work was doing it for him. Dominic braced one arm against the wall, angling his body toward her.

"What are you doing?" she asked, not looking up.

"Looking at you. Is it bothering you? Should I stop?"

Normally, he wouldn't be creeping on some random woman who'd arrived at his house to do a job. But Sylvie wasn't just anyone. She'd shown definite interest before. Her verbal jabs at him were just another form of flirting. And she'd obviously been trying to impress him with the violin thing. Damn, it had worked.

"You don't have to stop," she murmured, so low he almost couldn't hear her.

Desire flooded his veins.

He wanted this woman. Every minute he spent near her, he wanted her even more.

Chapter Nine

*D*ominic was merciless, all right. The way he was staring at her, his breath on her neck… She was so aware of him she struggled to concentrate on the code in front of her.

He was just trying to get back at her for the violin. But she didn't have the same stamina he did for fucking with somebody's head. This tension was unbearable. She'd done a decent job of pretending in the music room that she didn't want him, but her willpower was cracking. Any minute, and she'd give herself away.

He was a client. And a mobster under house arrest for a murder charge. Completely off limits in every logical way.

But with each insult that passed her tongue, she somehow only wanted him *more*.

He should just get it over with. Either leave her alone or pull her into his arms and kiss her. Yet she couldn't bring herself to stop playing his game, either.

Sylvie's fingers were getting sweaty on her keyboard.

"Is there a table I could set my computer on? I want to run some more diagnostics and antivirus software." She had some special programs she'd written that might identify if Dominic had sophisticated malware on his network.

"How about upstairs? There's a workspace you could use that's close to the other panel. It's nice and quiet. I can show you." His tone was full of innuendo. Yet there was something boyish about him, too. Like he half expected her to say no and was holding his breath, hoping she wouldn't. Like his feelings might actually be on the line.

"Sure. Upstairs is fine."

Upstairs. Where the bedrooms would be.

What the hell am I doing?

This was such a bad idea. Right? But then, why did the thought of going upstairs with him make her skin flush and her belly swoop in the best possible way?

She grabbed her bag and the laptop and headed toward the staircase. He gestured for her to go first, as if she had any idea where they were going. As Dominic followed, she felt his eyes all over her, and she wished she didn't like it so much.

Sylvie went to the upstairs security panel she'd installed the last time. There shouldn't have been any differences from the one downstairs, since they worked together in a unified system, but she went through the motions of plugging in her laptop once again. She was just stalling at this point.

"Do you need to leave it plugged in?" he asked.

"Not really. I could just use the Wi-Fi."

Dominic pointed at a doorway. She unplugged the laptop and joined him.

They went into a game room. There was a round table with four armchairs circling it, probably for playing cards. A foosball table stood in a corner, plus a gigantic TV and several video gaming systems that looked untouched.

A couch dominated the center of the room. Another oversized sectional, with plenty of space for someone as tall as Dominic to lie down comfortably and still allow a second person beside him. Which she should not be thinking about, because her heart rate had just spiked once again.

Dominic shut the door, then sat on the couch and stretched his arms along the back.

I am not going to end up on that couch with him. It's not happening. Though her inner voice would've been a lot more convincing if dirty images weren't already flitting through her imagination.

Like going onto her knees in front of him.

Oh. My. God. Stop.

She set her computer on the table. "You don't have to stay here."

"I know. But I keep hoping you'll answer my questions from earlier. Don't think I forgot."

It probably wouldn't hurt to tell him more about herself. She just needed to get her mind off the overpowering physicality of him. She always found it easier to deal with a situation when she was fully inside her head. It was one of her strengths, and likely the source of her pleasure problem.

Whenever she felt insecure or didn't know what to do, she retreated to her mind. That was part of why playing an instrument was so good for her. It forced her mental talents to work with her body, instead of separating the two.

But she didn't practice anywhere near as much as she should as an adult. She was usually far too busy with work.

Her finger tapped a key, and a new window opened on her screen. "I started violin lessons in elementary school. My third-grade teacher knew how to play and had some instruments of her own, so she offered private lessons. I lived in a small town. There weren't a lot of opportunities for musical training otherwise."

"A small town? Where is it?"

"Central Texas. I grew up on a cattle ranch."

Dominic grinned wide, but she didn't get the sense that he

was laughing at her. "I wonder what they think of you, with your tattoos and attitude?"

"They don't think much of me at all." Whichever way he interpreted that sentence, he probably had it right. "See? I'm really not very interesting."

"Oh, I disagree. Tell me more. How'd you end up stuck as Max Bennett's underling?"

The guy was bored, and it was no wonder. He was just passing the time with whoever happened to be near. And right now, that was her.

"I really don't see why you care."

"I find you intriguing."

"*Really*. And what do you find intriguing about me?"

"Your tattoos. Your obvious intelligence." His voice had dropped lower, and his tone was intimate. "The skin at the back of your neck, the shape of your mouth when you're annoyed... Should I keep going?"

Oh, boy. Her whole body was blushing and tingling. "That won't be necessary."

It annoyed her that he could coax such a strong reaction from her with just a few compliments. Okay, more than a few compliments. Being the focus of Dominic's attention was a heady experience.

She wasn't looking at him, yet every inch of her was aware of him. The way he crossed his legs. Tilted his head.

"You didn't tell me how you ended up working for Bennett Security."

"It's just a job. I was looking for more responsibility, a challenge, so I applied."

"You're in charge there?"

"Of my department? Yep. Max is the only person I have to report to. But that also means I have a lot to do."

Sylvie forced herself to ignore him while she set up her diagnostics to run on the laptop. And he just sat there watching her work, with that same smoldering intensity in his gaze. Like he would sit waiting for her all day if needed.

"I keep thinking about the day we met," he said. "I assumed you hated me."

Her fingers stilled on the keyboard. "What makes you think I don't?"

"If you do, you're being nicer about it. Which I appreciate."

"I wouldn't want to be predictable."

Dominic laughed. "No, you're not that."

"But I'm not here to entertain you."

He groaned. "That was stupid of me. A lame joke. What I really meant is, we could entertain each other."

She snorted. "Oh, can we?"

"Yes. I'll bet you don't mind that idea." His grin was back. "Even if you hate me, I'm pretty sure there's *something* you want from me. And it has nothing to do with my security system."

"What do you think I want?"

"You're from the uptight security company, and I'm the degenerate criminal. But I see the way you look at me. You want what you're not *supposed* to want. Just like I do."

She shrugged, as if his words—and the sexy rumble of his voice—didn't make her blood course faster through her veins.

"So? Doesn't mean I'll act on it."

"You *never* do things you're not supposed to? You're missing out."

A tiny whimper snuck out of her throat. Her clit was so swollen that her every movement rubbed her jeans against it, jolting her with another surge of arousal.

"I break rules all the time," she said.

"Then you know how fun it can be."

Yes, her body whispered. It was fun. And it was *hot*.

That was the reason bad boys did it for her, wasn't it? The

knowledge that they *weren't* good for her. That she was doing something she shouldn't.

Her brain could deny it all day, but she'd been fantasizing about Dominic for weeks. She'd walked into his house wanting this to happen. Wouldn't it be a relief to give in? To just admit it?

Her diagnostic was running happily. No more excuses.

Sylvie pushed back her chair and stood up, her heart thumping. Dominic's eyes widened slightly. Like he hadn't expected her to make a move.

She started toward him and stopped in front of the couch, standing between his knees. For once, he was looking up at her instead of the other way around.

"You're right. I do want you." A sense of power raced through her at owning her desire this way. "Even though I don't like you."

Dominic's eyes moved over her like she was already naked.

"Then you have a decision to make," he said. "Will you be a good girl and do what you're supposed to? Or will you come a little closer and see how much fun it is to be bad?"

When he put it like that…

Nobody at Bennett Security would ever—*ever*—know. No one in the world would know, except maybe Maureen. Sylvie had the feeling the housekeeper wouldn't be too surprised. Maureen had worked for Crane for a while, after all.

Sylvie didn't want to date the guy. This was the exact opposite. They didn't like each other, and they both knew it.

She just needed to get him out of her system. Fool around with him, then move on. The faster, the better.

And there was an eager part of her that kept thinking… *What if he's the one?*

Whenever she was really into a guy, Sylvie felt the same naive optimism that he could give her what she'd been craving for so long. Not that her pleasure was the man's sole responsibility. Not at all. But Sylvie had tried so many things already to break through that barrier.

She couldn't even say *why* she couldn't climax. No number of therapists had been able to enlighten her. But maybe there was some special alchemy that she'd been lacking with her previous partners.

Maybe Dominic would be different.

She'd never been with anyone this forbidden. She was already overheating with need, and the man hadn't laid a hand on her yet.

She knelt on the couch in between his knees. His grin turned downright wolfish.

"That's not nearly close enough." His arms circled her hips and pulled her onto him. She straddled his thighs, not yet close enough to feel his hard-on, though she could see its prominent outline.

I'm in Dominic Crane's lap. His hands are on my ass. So, so bad. But so good.

He had the same smell she remembered from before. Salt and sex. The urge to lick his neck was almost overpowering, but somehow, she held onto her control. She didn't want him to know how much he'd gotten to her.

"I was telling you all the things I find intriguing about you." He touched the frame of her glasses. "Like these. Can you still see without them?"

"Up close." The words came out breathy.

Dominic slid the frames away from her face. He was a little blurrier. She inched forward to see him better, which was perhaps the whole idea. His scent was even stronger in her nose, drawing even more desire from her belly. Her pelvis rocked slightly against him.

His features weren't as flawless close up, yet they were somehow even more arresting. Dark eyebrows and ample lashes, a small hump in the bridge of his long, sloping nose. She ran her finger down it, then touched his cheek. There was a hint of stubble already growing in. His eyes were gentle and thoughtful as they studied her right back.

"You're pretty," she whispered. "As you already know."

"Not as pretty as you."

"Liar."

"Sometimes, yeah. But not about this." He kept glancing at her mouth.

"Wait." Hesitation surged through her, forcing her to pump the brakes. Her body was in charge at the moment, but her brain was very insistent on a few points. "I have ground rules. Ones I won't break."

This was really a conversation they should've had a few minutes ago. She needed to rein herself in before she did something not just forbidden, but *stupid*.

He nodded. "Tell me."

"I'm not ready to get naked with you." She didn't know Dominic Crane, and she didn't really trust him. Not enough to give him that much access.

"If you're concerned, I tested clean a month ago. The government was nice enough to allow me a doctor's visit."

"I'm clean too, but that's not what I mean. I'm not up for oral sex, or genital-to-genital contact."

"Okay."

She exhaled, relieved he'd agreed so readily. If he hadn't, she would've used some of her self-defense moves and gotten out of there.

"Can I kiss you?" he asked.

"Yes."

"And I can touch you under your clothes, right?"

"Yes." *Oh, please, yes.*

"I can work with that. I happen to find consent very sexy. Even when we're otherwise being bad." The corner of his mouth raised. "Now come here."

She braced her hands on either side of him against the couch. Her body rocked forward again, this time meeting the bulge in his jeans. He gripped her hips, stopping her forward motion.

"Tell me about your tattoos."

She grumbled. Now *he* was tapping the brakes, and it annoyed her.

"I started on them when I moved to L.A. I was nineteen." She pointed at the black silhouette of a dove with outstretched wings on her bicep. "This was my first. The symbolism is far from subtle, but I still like it."

He touched the dove. "And what about these?" His fingertip moved over patterns of thorny vines, flowers, and leaves. Tingles of pleasure spread over her skin.

"Sometimes I ask for a specific image. Sometimes I'm just the canvas." She trusted her artist completely, so she didn't always have anything particular in mind. The surprise was part of the fun, waiting to see what he'd come up with. Somehow it always matched her mood and personality.

"What's this one?"

Her newest. "A heron."

"You sure? I think it's a crane."

She scowled. "It's a *heron*."

His eyes danced. "If you say so." His fingers strayed beneath the straps of her tank. "Wish I could see the rest of them. But maybe another time." Dominic leaned forward to kiss her shoulder. The touch was soft, softer than she'd imagined he could be.

Sylvie sighed, tipping her head back.

Then he sat up and cupped the back of her neck, those dark eyes hooded and intense.

He brought his lush mouth to her lips. And those last threads of rational thought disappeared. Her mind checked out completely.

Chapter Ten

*S*ylvie was perched on his lap. Everything about her was so sweet, from her ripe pink lips to the blush in her cheeks. And those blue irises, now that they were out from behind her glasses—the girl was stunning. He'd admired her looks before, but now he couldn't pull his eyes away from her.

Dominic had always gravitated toward beautiful things. Art, music. But she wasn't just outwardly attractive. He *liked* Sylvie, though he'd implied that her dislike for him was mutual.

He felt lucky to get even this much of her. Sylvie wasn't like any other woman he'd met. He couldn't imagine her growing up in a small town full of cows, like a tropical flower growing amidst a field of wheat. There was nothing wrong with wheat, necessarily. But Sylvie was so unexpected, and that only increased her value in his eyes. Like a classically trained opera singer busking on an otherwise unremarkable street corner.

He'd meant to wait longer to kiss her, but then he just couldn't resist.

Dominic touched his tongue to the seam of her lips. Sylvie opened up to him, deepening the kiss. Her mouth was as plush as velvet. His dick had been swelling before, but now he was rock hard.

Slow down, he told himself.

Dominic was trying to pace himself so this experience could last all afternoon. He'd show her how much he could accomplish with just his fingers. After he was done, she'd be begging him to fuck her. It could be a power trip, getting a beautiful, intelligent woman into his bed.

But from Sylvie? He wanted more than that. She was obviously attracted to his body, but with her, the real challenge was winning over her mind.

If he did this right, she'd spend more time talking with him after today. Even—gasp—start to like him. Sylvie's attention felt like a gift, and he wanted to earn more of it.

Orgasms were the best place to start.

Dominic lay Sylvie back against the couch and stretched out on his side, facing her. While they kissed, he pressed his palm flat to her stomach, teasing his fingers just under the edge of her shirt, grazing the bottom edge of her bra. His hand moved to her arms, then down her side to her waist and hip. Tracing her outline. His fingers roved over the black denim of her jeans, thumb rubbing the seam from the inside of her knee to her inner thigh.

Sylvie bent her leg and let it fall open slightly, making room for his hand to travel further up. An invitation. He didn't accept just yet.

Instead, he sucked her tongue into his mouth. She moaned, rolling toward him, placing her hands against his chest.

Slowly, he dragged his fingers along her thighs again until he reached her crotch. He drew a light circle against the seam right over her core. She made a needy sound and her hips lifted, seeking firmer contact.

"Tell me what you like, Sylvie. Do you want me to touch you gently? Should I go slow?" He kissed her just the way he'd described, letting his mouth linger on hers. "Or do you want my fingers to be rough and fast and dirty?"

Sylvie grabbed his face and pulled him down to kiss her again. She thrust her tongue past his lips. Dominic's thumb kept rubbing against her. She was so hot beneath his hand.

"Slow at first," she panted. "Then fast. Definitely dirty." She reached for the button of her fly and popped it open.

Dominic buried his nose in her hair. "Do you want my fingers inside you?"

"God, yes."

"One finger? More?"

"Would you shut the fuck up and put your hand down my pants?"

Sylvie lowered her zipper. Smiling, Dominic put his hand on her stomach and started sliding it downwards. He stayed above her panties, lowering his fingers until he could cup her crotch. The fabric of her panties was damp.

Sylvie practically growled. She yanked his hand back up, then shoved it down, this time inside of her underwear. Dominic couldn't help laughing.

"So many rules and demands. I can hardly keep it all straight."

"I'm sure you'll manage."

"I think I'll do better than that."

He slid his fingers down again and finally felt the center of her. So hot and slippery. He nudged his fingers between her folds and gently rubbed around the edge of her opening.

She gasped so loudly Dominic worried Maureen would hear it downstairs. But then he quickly dismissed any concern. Maureen could probably guess what they were doing.

Dominic found her most sensitive spot. He pressed the nub lightly, not wanting to overstimulate her. But Sylvie's answering moan and a thrust of her hips told him that she was already primed for more. He dipped his middle finger into her wetness again and used the lubrication to massage her clit.

"Oh, yes. Right there." She opened her legs, giving him better access.

At the same time, Sylvie reached for his zipper. He'd wanted to make her come at least once before his dick came out to play, but if she was that eager, why not?

He diverted his attention from her for just a second so he could pull himself out of his pants. They both moaned as she closed her grip around his shaft.

Sylvie stroked his cock while Dominic returned to playing with her clit. Her touch was confident, her grip firm around him. Without a little more intensity, it wasn't enough to make him come yet. But he was still having trouble concentrating. He had to bring the focus back to her.

Dominic curved his long finger downward, not stopping until he'd penetrated her tight channel. His thumb kept up the stimulation of her clit. Sylvie bucked against his hand, humming and moaning in a sweet, high voice, pretty as music in Dominic's ears.

"*God.*"

"How's that?" he murmured.

"More." She wiggled her pants down further, so he could reach her even better. He added a second finger. He could tell she was almost there.

Sylvie was barely stroking his cock anymore, she was so distracted, and he was loving every second.

Any moment, and he'd have her right where she needed to be.

Chapter Eleven

*D*ominic's fingers were pumping inside her, stroking her clit. Playing her body like an instrument. Sylvie had never felt anything so fucking good.

It was going to happen.

She was going to come.

God, she could feel it. So close. So close.

He knew it, too, if that naughty grin was any indication. She felt his erection against her hip. It had slipped out of her hand. But what if his cock was inside of her instead? Wouldn't that feel even better?

No, she had to focus on this moment. She'd said no getting naked for a reason.

Don't get distracted.

His fingers were all she needed. His talented, long fingers. Tension was building inside of her, begging for release.

Yet she'd been here before. So many times. And it had never worked.

Stop thinking that.

Sylvie closed her eyes, trying to concentrate. Was she taking too long? Was his hand getting tired?

"Ow."

"Sorry, is that too much?" He slowed down.

"It's, um…" Shit. She'd gone dry.

Dominic pulled his fingers away and sucked on them, then replaced them just as fast. She felt the extra moisture, but her body wasn't cooperating anymore. The friction had suddenly turned painful. Like some switch had flipped.

"Want me to get lube? I have some in my bedroom."

Embarrassment rushed through her, drying her out even more. "No. It's okay. I'm done." She wrapped her fist around his cock again. "I almost forgot about you."

"But you're not finished."

"I'm good. It's fine."

"*No*, it's not." He kissed her neck. "We can take a break, but don't worry. I'll get you there. I'm not in a hurry if you're not."

"I'm getting sore. It's not your fault."

"Give me a chance." He licked the corner of his mouth. "Couldn't we bend the rules and take off your jeans? I could do so much better with my tongue."

Gah. That idea made her breath catch. But it wouldn't work. Nothing would work.

He must've seen the agony on her face. "You're right, I shouldn't have said that. You made your rules clear."

Sylvie sat up, tugging her jeans back into place.

"Whoa, wait a second. Come back. I'll behave."

"I'm not in the mood anymore."

"Sylvie."

She walked over the table, eyes stinging.

He was adjusting his clothes. "Can we *please* start over?"

"I'd rather not. This was a mistake."

"Okay. I'm not sure what just happened, but if you don't want to do this, then we don't have to." Dominic stood, rubbing his hands against his jeans. "Not like I go around forcing myself on women." Annoyance was sneaking into his voice.

"I told you, it's *not your fault*. Nobody was forcing anyone. You've been perfectly nice."

"I wasn't really going for *nice*."

"You're right, my apologies. No one should ever accuse Dominic Crane of being nice."

"Did you just now remember who I was? You forgot you were fooling around with a degenerate wearing an ankle monitor?"

"Trust me, I didn't forget that for a second."

Why wouldn't he let this go? She'd been trying to give him a hand job, and she'd had every intention of finishing him off regardless of her own limitations.

Sylvie checked the programs running on her laptop. The diagnostic hadn't finished yet. Dammit. She couldn't leave.

He crossed the room, going after her. "Was that the whole point of this? You wanted to even some score between us?"

She whirled on him. "Jesus, how conceited are you? How many times do I have to say it? This is *not about you*."

"Then what is it?"

"*Nothing*."

"Would you just tell me what I did?"

"I can't have an orgasm," she shouted.

Oh my god. I just said that out loud.

"You can't…" He blinked at her. "Really? You're serious?"

She covered her face with her hands.

"Okay," he said quietly. "I think I get it now."

"I promise you *don't*."

"I do have *some* experience. I know it's not as easy for women as it is for men. It's not a big deal." Dominic had followed her to the table. She felt the warmth of him just inches from her back.

"I decide what kind of deal it is. It's my problem, not yours."

"Who said it's a problem? Not everyone's built the same way." His hand rested on her arm, kneading the muscle. "Why don't you show me how you touch yourself? Show me so I can learn. I think that would be hot. I could touch myself, too."

In spite of her embarrassment, her blood heated again at his suggestion. But there was no point. Sylvie shrugged away from him. "You don't understand. I can't have an orgasm. Not with anyone."

"Not even... Are you saying you've *never* had an orgasm?"

"That's what I've *been* saying."

Sylvie sat in one of the hardbacked chairs by the table. She begged her computer to hurry up so she could get the hell out of here.

She didn't even know this man, and now he was privy to intensely private information about her. Even Ethan had no idea about her issues.

"It's nothing to be embarrassed about. You could've told me earlier."

"I was hoping..." She shook her head. "Hoping it wouldn't be an issue. With you."

"Oh." He pulled up the chair next to hers. "Then maybe it's better I didn't know. That's a lot of pressure." He smiled tentatively.

"Exactly."

In Sylvie's experience, most men didn't care if she came. They didn't seem to notice. But a couple of times, she'd admitted to boyfriends that she didn't climax with them. The guys always got self-conscious about it. Just like Dominic was doing right now.

"But you *were* enjoying yourself with me? And at some point, you stopped?"

She really didn't feel like petting his ego. "Don't ask me to explain. I don't understand why I'm like this, either."

"Have you experienced...trauma?"

"Nothing like that."

"Have you seen doctors? Could it be physical?"

"I've seen plenty. They tell me the problem is in my head."

"Sex therapists?"

"Seen those, too." They'd told her to try different devices
and masturbation techniques. No luck. "It didn't work for me.
But I really—" She was going to say she didn't want to discuss
this. But he was being pretty low key about it. Maybe talking it
through wasn't the worst thing. The more they discussed the
problem, the more her immediate mortification was fading.

He rested his arms on the table, humming as he thought.
"You said you're from a small town. Were they really conserv-
ative about sex? Could it be a guilt thing?"

"Don't psychoanalyze me. It's rude."

"I don't mean to be. But if it's not a physical barrier, there
must be a mental solution. That's a good thing, right?"

That was the same hope she'd been clinging to, despite all
the evidence to the contrary.

She raised her eyes to meet his. She didn't see any judgment there. His smirk hadn't made a reappearance.

"I want there to be a solution. But I don't know how to
find it."

"Then you need more data. I could help with that."

"More data is usually good. But you don't strike me as a
scientifically minded person. No offense."

He clutched a hand over his heart. "That's harsh. Maybe
I'm not usually into science stuff, but I *do* like to experiment.
I'll try anything once."

Now the smirk was back, but he was looking at her like he
was already dreaming up ways they could gather this "data."

Dominic's legs nudged hers beneath the table. He reached
for her arm and dragged his fingertips across her skin. "So
you've tried touching yourself, and it hasn't worked?"

She nodded. How did he do that? Keep his voice so even
and soothing. Hypnotic. She was getting turned on again.
Desire had rushed back to all her sensitive parts.

He kept stroking her arm. "Have you been with women?"

"I don't have any sort of issue with my sexuality."

"Have you tried porn?"

She opened her mouth, then hesitated. "Occasionally."

He leaned forward to whisper, his lips brushing her ear, his cheek against hers. "What makes you get hot when you think about it? Do you want a man to dominate you?"

She squeezed her legs together. He was lighting up every one of her nerve endings. "I like communication."

"We're communicating right now." Dominic's hands moved to her thighs, gently massaging, while he kissed along the line of her jaw. "Come back to the couch. I want to make you feel good. No expectations."

"I can make you feel good, too." That was something she enjoyed. Making a man come apart for her.

He took her hand and brought it to his crotch. She felt the hard length of him tucked against his fly. "You turn me on, Sylvie. Let's see how close we can get to the edge without going over. How long we can make it last."

Now, she knew she was in trouble. She'd worried she couldn't trust him before, and maybe she still shouldn't.

But she had the feeling he could convince her to do anything if she gave him the chance. Her clothes weren't going to stay on for long if he kept talking like that. It wasn't like her to surrender so much control. Yet she didn't want to say no, either.

He led her back over to the couch and tugged her down into his lap. Dominic kissed her, taking long pulls from her lips.

Sylvie unbuttoned his jeans. "Can I touch for a while?" She'd been so distracted earlier she hadn't even gotten a good look at him.

His smile was lopsided. Dominic reached for his zipper.

Then her computer dinged. She almost ignored it, but the laptop rang out again with another notification.

Sylvie groaned. "I should check on that. One of my programs is mad about something."

"Do you have to?"

"I'm supposed to be working."

That thought made her feel sheepish. Max probably wouldn't appreciate the way she'd been spending her workday. Which had made this tryst all the hotter, but still.

She went over to the table and paused, expecting to see a notice about her diagnostic. Maybe the program had detected the source of the problem with Crane's security system.

But it wasn't the diagnostic.

Sylvie stared in horror at the screen. It showed an old-school, 8-bit animation of a dragon breathing fire. Something she'd thought was funny when she coded it for the firewall she'd designed for this machine. But she wasn't laughing.

Alert the villagers! the notice window read. *The castle is under attack!*

"Oh, fuck."

Downstairs, Maureen screamed.

Chapter Twelve

*D*ominic jumped up from the couch, buttoning his jeans. Maureen had just cried out downstairs. He ran for the closed door to the hall, then stopped to look back at Sylvie. Something was wrong with her computer, too. He didn't understand what was happening.

"I need to go check on—"

"Yeah. Go." Sylvie barely glanced at him. Her fingers flew over her keyboard.

He threw open the door and dashed down the back staircase. Maureen was in the kitchen. She saw him and pointed toward the front of the house.

"I saw a man outside in the front yard. He has a black ski mask on. I was going to call 911, but I can't find my phone."

"I will." Dominic took out his device with one hand and wrapped the other around the woman's shoulders. "Sylvie's in the game room. Go upstairs. Both of you need to hide."

It's my uncle, he thought. *That fucker.*

Maureen screamed again. "Look!" Through the blinds of the kitchen window, a dark shape loomed into view.

"Get down." Dominic dragged the woman to the tile floor

just as a shot tore through the kitchen, thudding into a cabinet beside the Sub-Zero refrigerator. "Stay there. Don't move."

He crawled toward a cabinet door and threw it open. A Glock 19 was duct taped to the underside of the sink.

Dominic peeled the tape away and aimed the weapon at one window, then another. At the first sign of movement, he squeezed off a shot. A bullet hole appeared in the glass, webbed with cracks. The figure darted out of view.

"Upstairs," he commanded to Maureen.

"Is the security system on? The doors are all locked, but if they try to break in—"

"I'll check. Just go."

Maureen hunched over and ran for the back staircase.

Dominic edged toward the patio doors. He couldn't see anyone out on the deck. He confirmed that the doors were locked, then continued through the living room.

It wasn't hard to imagine what was happening. Apparently, his Uncle Charles had denied his request for more time. Dominic should've expected this, yet the abrupt violence of this attack had blindsided him. He'd thought their family connection would be enough to buy him at least a few weeks of peace.

But it hadn't, and now Maureen and Sylvie were in danger because of him. Guilt closed around his throat. Dominic couldn't let anything happen to them.

Watching the front windows, he dialed 911. "Yes, my name is Dominic Crane. Someone's trying to kill me in my home. No, I can't hold. Just send help. Patrol car, SWAT team, anything."

He gave them his address, hung up, and dialed the number for Bennett Security next. Not Max Bennett, but their emergency line, which Dominic had programmed into his contacts. He'd been worried something like this could happen eventually.

But not with Sylvie here. Not in broad daylight.

He wished she'd brought along that burly bodyguard from her last visit. But Dominic had mocked her for that, hadn't he? He'd been such an idiot, pretending that he was the greatest threat to Sylvie in this house.

If someone hurt her, it would be on him.

"Sir, I don't see an alarm activation. Did you hit your panic button?"

"I don't even know if my system is working."

Beside the front door, the panel for his security system was blinking red. He didn't know what that meant.

"Sylvie Trousseau is here with me. I'm guessing she's your boss. So send some of those trained bodyguards with guns to my home address *right fucking now*."

If nobody could get here in time—or if they didn't care to bother—Dominic would turn himself over to save the others. But only after he put up a fight. The rest of the Syndicate might think he was weak, but he wasn't going to just roll over.

Keeping his back against one wall, his gun ready, Dominic inched closer to the door. His insides felt like everything had spun around and switched places. Since he was a teenager, violence had been a part of his life. Yet he'd never gotten used to it.

I'm going to protect Sylvie and Maureen, he swore to himself. *Whatever it takes.*

As he watched the window in the door, a shape darted across the front of the house. He pulled back.

Then something red smeared across the glass.

What the fuck?

His nausea rose. It was blood. They were smearing blood on his door.

A warning. But whose blood? *Whose?*

Dominic waited for someone to try breaking in. The glass in the windows of this house was tempered and strong, but it would shatter under enough pressure. He couldn't tell if anyone was coming.

But what if they climbed onto the upstairs balconies? What if they breached the upstairs windows instead?

Dominic ran for the staircase.

The door to the game room was closed. "Who's there?" Sylvie said from inside. She must've heard his footsteps.

"It's me. I'm coming in."

"Wait. I'm unlocking it."

When she opened the door, Sylvie held a Glock at her side.

"Did you bring that with you?" He shut the door behind him and locked it.

"No, it's yours. Maureen got it for me." Sylvie gestured at the couch. "She knew where you'd hidden it."

"Don't mention it to Max. These guns are all unregistered." He had weapons stashed in other parts of the house too. In his line of work—well, former line of work—one never knew. He'd certainly get his bail revoked if the DA found out, but he had bigger problems.

Maureen's face had taken on a pale shade of green. "The police are sending help?"

"I hope so. We'll see." He pointed at Sylvie's computer, which lay closed on the table. "What was going on with your laptop?"

"Someone was trying to hack my machine. They nearly succeeded. I had to shut down the internet connections. But I can't access anything now. Not headquarters, not our network, not your security system. I'm blind. I turned off my phone, too."

"What about that man who shot at us?" Maureen asked.

"I don't know if they're still here." His nerves were on edge as he listened for noise from downstairs. He didn't know how many men there might be, what they were planning. Whether they just wanted to warn Dominic or had other intentions.

Sylvie peeked through the closed blinds. "The attempted

breach on my laptop cannot be a coincidence. I've seen this
kind of thing before. A cyberattack at the same time as a physical one. The Syndicate, right?"

"Probably. So you know how to shoot?"

"Yeah. Max makes all his employees spend time in the gun
range."

"That's smart." Dominic dragged the heavy couch over to
block the door. "You both should stay down, in case they get
upstairs and start shooting."

"What about you?" Sylvie asked.

"I'll give them something else to aim at."

She frowned but took Maureen to a corner, where they
crouched down together.

Dominic stayed in the center of the room, aiming his gun
at the barricaded door. Still nothing from downstairs.

In his peripheral vision, Maureen was trembling slightly.
She'd known about his role in the Syndicate since not long
after he hired her. He'd made sure she understood that his life
—and therefore hers—could be in danger. She'd confirmed
she could keep quiet and out of his business, so long as he
didn't bring his work home and paid her an above-market
rate.

But it was different facing something like this in reality,
rather than in the abstract.

Sylvie was completely calm and collected. He had no idea
what was going through her head. If she was scared, in shock.
Angry.

He wished he could hold Sylvie's hand to reassure her.
And maybe himself.

Sweat trickled down his sides.

In the eerie silence, Dominic allowed himself to think
about what Sylvie had confessed—that she'd never had an
orgasm before. At first, when she'd pulled away from him, he
was the one who'd been embarrassed. Satisfying a woman was

one of the few things that Dominic could usually get right. And yet, he'd failed.

He was willing to experiment with her. In fact, he'd been looking forward to it. They could do whatever she felt comfortable doing, and they'd both probably learn from the experience. Not to mention having a hell of a lot of fun.

But this attack, whatever was really going on, had put a damper on those plans. He couldn't imagine that Sylvie would be able to forget who he was ever again.

After today, she'd probably want nothing more to do with him.

"What was that?" Sylvie asked.

Maureen squeezed Dominic's arm. He held his breath.

There was the crash of something heavy against an exterior door. The splintering of wood. Maureen gasped. Dominic's arms ached as he pointed the Glock at the barricaded doorway. His heart drummed against his ribcage. Somebody was in the house. But who?

A shout came from downstairs. "Police!"

Sylvie crawled toward the window and peeked between the blinds. "I see a SWAT van. And half a dozen squad cars are just pulling up."

Dominic closed his eyes for one brief moment of relief. But he wasn't out of danger yet. He pulled the magazine from his Glock and hid both items under a cabinet. "I need to hide your gun."

Sylvie yanked the magazine. "I'll do it."

"Could you call the police back now? Tell them where we are?"

Dominic held out his phone. She accepted it. "Why can't you?"

He knelt on the carpet. "I'm going to lie down on the floor with my hands spread so the SWAT team doesn't shoot me on sight."

Chapter Thirteen

"We don't have to do this right now. We could wait until morning." Max stood in front of his desk with his arms crossed. He must've had a client meeting today because he was wearing a suit, though he'd discarded the tie.

He'd already put his jacket around Sylvie and brought her a cup of coffee, but she couldn't stop trembling.

"No. I need to." She rested her head against the cushion of Max's couch. It was ten o'clock at night, and the windows were dark. She was exhausted and starving. And she still had so much work ahead of her.

A storm of emotions kept rolling through her. Terror at being under attack—both her person and her computer. Shame that she'd left herself vulnerable. Dismay at seeing Dominic yanked from the floor by officers in SWAT gear, as if he were the one who'd threatened them.

"Okay, then walk me through what happened earlier. Because I still don't understand."

Even she was still struggling to make sense of it. Sylvie forced herself to back up to the beginning.

"It started with my computer. I was on Crane's network, running diagnostics on his security system. I hadn't been able to identify any anomalies in my code, and a scan for known malware hadn't turned up anything either. Then notifications started going off. My firewall had detected suspicious packets, information it didn't recognize, trying to get into my system."

Sylvie had written the firewall herself. It was unique to her machine, not something that would run on the typical Bennett Security laptop. She preferred an extra sense of security, even with the headaches that came with it.

And thank god she did, because otherwise her computer wouldn't have detected the intrusion.

"When exactly was the first sign that something was wrong?"

"I'll have to check my logs. I'm not sure. I might've been…distracted."

Max eyed her. "By what?"

"It's not important." She was never going to admit how monumentally stupid she'd been.

She'd have to create a mirror of her hard drive for analysis. She needed to uncover exactly what sort of code had invaded her system. But she suspected a bundled attack, one that could've compromised the Bennett Security intranet once she returned to the office. It would've been a disaster, and she'd only narrowly avoided it.

If the attack had come a few minutes later, she would've been caught in an even worse position with Dominic. Maybe even naked and underneath him. She might've ignored her computer altogether.

"My best guess? Someone installed a back door in Crane's home network that affected the security system. He said the problem occurred mostly at night. Maybe that's when they were accessing his network, tracking what he'd been up to. But when I connected my laptop, it must've triggered some sort of a notification on their end. They tried to load their malware onto my system."

"You think this could've been an attack on us specifically? On Bennett Security?"

"Probably." If these people had access to Dominic's security system, they could've seen her on the video. There were cameras on the front door, inside the entryway, and along the exterior sides of the house.

"Our network here at headquarters would be a very attractive target," Max said. "Especially for people like the Silverlake Syndicate."

"Exactly what I was thinking." As Bennett's resident cyber security expert, Sylvie had all sorts of useful tools black-hat hackers would love to get their hands on. Not to mention sensitive client information.

Max stopped his pacing and stared at her. "Wait a minute. Could Crane have had something to do with this? What if he made up the story about these 'glitches' to lure you—or some other employee—to his home so this malware could get onto our network?"

Nausea twisted through her. She didn't want believe it.

If he'd truly lured her there to gain access to her laptop, then he'd been trying to seduce her as a distraction. Every single thing he'd said and done would've been pure calculation. But if Dominic had been playing her? She'd made it easy for him.

She'd claimed to hate him. But before the attack? She'd actually been starting to like the guy.

"Sylvie. I need an answer. Do you think Crane had something to do with this?"

What else could explain the perfect timing of this attack?

"It's possible Crane set us up."

And there was the shame again, crashing over her and threatening to pull her under.

Max closed his eyes. "Fuck. And I walked right into it."

"So did I."

He gripped the skin between his eyes. "Okay. Back up.

What about the physical attack on Crane's house? Clearly the timeline means something."

"It has to. The Syndicate's used similar techniques before. So we have to assume the same people were trying to gain access to my laptop and attack Crane's house. They *did* try to shoot him." Which weighed on the side of Crane having nothing to do with it.

"But did you see that happen? Did you see the gunman aiming for Crane?"

"No. I was upstairs with my laptop. They exchanged gunfire in the kitchen."

"So you don't actually know who shot at whom. Or if it was all just staged."

"But that would mean that Maureen, his housekeeper, was in on it. I can't see that happening."

Yet Maureen had handled the whole thing pretty calmly. She'd barely seemed frightened at all. In the moment, Sylvie had assumed the woman was tough. She'd worked for Crane for two years, including the time he'd ruled the Syndicate, so she'd have to be.

But what did Sylvie truly know about either Maureen or Dominic? Almost nothing. All she knew was they'd both been kind to her today, though in extremely different ways. But kindness could be faked.

Which made her feel even sicker.

Now that the seed had been planted in her mind, it started to spread. Maybe the guy who'd fired into the kitchen intentionally missed. Even if Maureen was innocent of any deception, that didn't absolve Dominic.

Max tapped his fingers against his desk. "At this point, we have to examine all possible explanations, including whether Crane's behind it. But whoever's responsible, I want to know what they were after and how much damage this might've caused."

"I'm going to get onto my machine and start investigating.

I'll study every log, every packet of data, every clue they might've left behind. I'm going to find out who these people are and where they came from. You can be sure of that."

She blew out a heavy breath. Her hands fidgeted, eager to be at her keyboard working so she didn't feel so powerless.

Max came over and sat on the arm of the sofa. "I can bring someone else in on this if needed. I know this day's been really rough."

She didn't want to dwell on the fear, or even on the uncertainty she felt about Crane's motives. She just wanted to dive headfirst into her computer and find those bastards who'd tried to attack her inner sanctum.

"I don't trust anyone with this but myself." Not because she thought her team wasn't loyal, but because their skills couldn't rival hers. That wasn't cockiness, it was just true.

From somewhere deep inside, she conjured a smile.

"All I need is that mirror drive, a secure internet connection, and your permission to use the company expense account. Because I'm going to order a shitload of takeout to get me through the next few hours."

AFTER SYLVIE FINISHED WITH MAX, she called her cousin Ethan.

"Hey, what's up?"

Ethan had no clue anything unusual had happened today. Sylvie often worked long hours, sometimes not getting home until the middle of the night. So her cousin had no reason to suspect anything could be wrong.

She'd managed to hold herself together while she talked to Max. But now she felt her composure slipping. "I was wondering if you'd had dinner yet. I was going to order Chinese, and I could really use a friend here with me." She bit back a sob.

"Sylvie, honey, what's wrong? What's going on?"

"I'd love to explain it to you. But I can't come home. That's why I was hoping you could come here and share some pork buns with me?"

"Of course I will. But are you sure it's okay? Are you supposed to let outsiders into your fancy secure building?"

Ethan had only visited the public areas of their headquarters. But Sylvie was in no mood to deal with restrictions. "I'm the boss of almost everybody here. And I don't think even Max Bennett will deny me today."

"Wow, that bad of a shitstorm?"

"Get over here so I can tell you."

Half an hour later, they were eating fried rice, beef and broccoli, and steamed buns in the breakroom. Ethan had barely touched his serving. He'd been too shocked by what she'd described. And she hadn't even mentioned anything that happened between her and Dominic before the attack had started.

"So now you have to figure out who did this?" Ethan asked. "How?"

"By tearing apart that hard drive and finding every bit of code that doesn't belong." She was going to send as much info as she could to her friends in the hacktivist community.

She'd made a lot of contacts over the years, though none of her friends shared their real-life identities. Yet she still trusted them completely. Her friends would track down the people responsible. Not just because they were loyal to her, but because they used their abilities to right the moral wrongs in this world whenever possible. Sylvie was sure the people who'd come after her were on the wrong side.

Was Dominic one of them?

Ethan pushed a slice of beef around his plate. "I'm so sorry this happened."

"Me, too."

Sylvie's cousin had the biggest heart of anyone she'd met.

Ethan was an unassuming guy. He wore wire-rimmed glasses straight out of the nineties and had a closetful of chinos. People had commented that the two of them seemed mismatched, especially when they went out together and people assumed they were a couple. But Sylvie didn't think anybody in the world understood her the way he did.

"Do you ever think the way we grew up, how oppressive it was, messed us up?"

Ethan wrinkled his brow. "That's a sudden change in topic."

"It's more connected than you realize."

"Okay, well… 'Messed up' could mean a lot of things."

"I mean about sex."

He nodded, thinking. "I doubt it's possible to grow up with people telling you your very existence is wrong and not be affected. But I moved past it. It wasn't easy, and there's a voice at the back of my mind that sounds a lot like my mother's. But I haven't heard it for a long time."

"Thank goodness for that."

"But I'm guessing you're not asking about me, because we've had that conversation plenty of times before. What's really on your mind?"

She set down her fork. She'd never told Ethan about the orgasm thing. And she didn't want to now. But she did need her best friend's advice.

"I met someone. I'm *definitely* attracted to him, but I don't think I can trust him. And even if I could, I'm worried I have too many hang-ups."

"Is he pushing you farther than you're willing to go?"

"The opposite. I was able to tell him things I could never express to anyone else, even though I hardly know him. And he seemed to accept it without much thought."

In some ways, it made more sense that Dominic had been faking.

Ethan was nodding. "And even though you want that

acceptance, you feel like you can't trust it? Because it's so different from what you're used to?"

"In a way." She exhaled, not wanting to get bogged down in the sordid details. "In the past, the guys I've been with didn't seem to mind the barriers I kept. But this new person—it's like he can see straight past them."

Here was the part that really freaked her out: if Dominic had been lying to her, why did she still want him?

It wasn't just that he was sexy. Whether or not his motives were genuine, Dominic had *seen* her. He'd offered things no man had before.

I want to make you feel good. No expectations.

Sex with Dominic was probably a *terrible* idea. If he'd manipulated her, set a trap, made her feel threatened—it was unforgivable.

So why was her heart racing as she remembered his kiss?

Ethan reached for her hand across the table. "When Luis and I first got together, I had a hard time just being myself with him. It was scary, opening up to someone so much. And that voice I mentioned? It kept telling me there was no way he was for real. But I just listened to my heart. I know how cheesy that sounds, but it's true. I had to trust him, that he was who he said he was, and the risk was worth it."

She wished she could do the same with Dominic. But it wasn't just her heart at risk. It was Bennett Security.

They finished eating, and Sylvie put the leftovers in the breakroom fridge. The bodyguards would probably have it polished off by tomorrow morning.

"I have a long night ahead, just my laptop and me. You should probably head home."

Ethan nodded. "Before I go, I found that letter Faith sent. The one you supposedly threw away?"

"I guess I should've been less obvious."

He shrugged. "You know I like to borrow your stuff. Next time, don't put it in the drawer where you keep your best pens.

I was thinking, I know Faith hurt you. But maybe she's looking for the same thing we were just talking about. Someone to see her and accept her for who she is. No matter how scary that might be."

"Maybe. I could give that some thought. But not until I have more time."

Ethan gave her a hug. "I hope you find your Luis."

"I hope that, too." Someday.

Later that night, as Sylvie was working, a text came in on her phone from an unfamiliar number.

Sylvie, it's Dominic. I hope you don't mind that I tracked down your number. I wanted to make sure you're okay.

Her chest tightened at the thought of him. The memory of his hands on her, his lips brushing her ear as he whispered dirty things. Even with the terrible ordeal of that afternoon, arousal still rushed to her core.

She wanted to demand explanations. What had really happened? What was the truth? But she had no reason to expect it.

Sylvie: I'm fine. Thank you. How about you and Maureen?

Dominic: We're in one piece.

Sylvie: In a safe place?

Dominic: Safe enough.

Sylvie tapped her fingers on her desk, contemplating her next reply.

Sylvie: What about the blood on the door? What was that from?

Dominic: Just pig's blood.

She made a sound of disgust. Had that been theater for her benefit?

Those men who'd smeared that blood, who'd shot at the house—they'd likely been Dominic's allies just months ago. She could barely wrap her head around that fact.

If the attack had been real, it must've served as a warning to Dominic. But of what?

Dominic: I'm so sorry you got caught up in my shit.

Sylvie: It happens.

Dominic: What about your computer?

Her thumbs paused on her screen, and a cold thread of anger wound through her insides. Was he fishing for information? She had to be careful.

Sylvie: What about it?

Dominic: There was some kind of intrusion, right? Did they cause any damage?

Sylvie: We haven't determined yet.

She thought that was a vague enough response.

Dominic: Is there anything I can do to help?

Sylvie: How could you help? I thought you didn't know anything about computers.

There was a pause. Three small dots appeared, then

disappeared, several times before Dominic's response came. But it was a complete change of subject.

Dominic: You probably never want to see me again.

She debated another moment.

Sylvie: Maybe it's for the best if I don't.

She waited for him to tell her she was wrong. But he didn't respond, and Sylvie placed her phone facedown on the table.

Chapter Fourteen

*D*ominic woke on a cold, hard floor. His head was fuzzy, and his stomach was in knots.

He would've spent most of the night prowling the hallways, but Maureen had asked him to sleep on the floor beside her bed. He'd offered to put her up in a hotel after the police finally left, but she'd refused.

There had been a small chance he could get permission to stay somewhere else himself, despite his bail restrictions. But nobody had seemed to have the answers or any interest in seeking them out.

The officers hadn't arrested him for the weapons they'd found, either. So maybe they'd split the difference by just letting him stay put.

He'd called an emergency repairman to secure the door the SWAT team busted in, and he and Maureen had barricaded themselves in her bedroom.

Dominic had slept with another gun under his pillow. The police hadn't found them all.

He kicked off the blanket and got up, stretching his back. Maureen was still asleep. But she sat up as soon as he started moving the armoire he'd placed in front of her door.

"Dominic?"

"Sorry. I need to go to my room. I should get cleaned up."

"You go ahead. I'll do the same, and then make breakfast. We'll do better if we keep to our routines." She waved him away.

Dominic didn't know exactly what this day would bring, but he was sure it wasn't going to be pleasant.

At least he'd gotten in touch with Raymond and knew his brother was safe.

When Dominic had first seen the blood painted on that door... He shivered at the memory. He hadn't even allowed himself to face the possibility that the blood belonged to his brother.

Thankfully, a forensics team had quickly determined the blood came from a pig, rather than a human.

Of course, he hadn't told Raymond about the blood during their phone conversation. He hadn't even mentioned that someone had tried to shoot him. But he'd reminded his brother to be careful and not trust anyone, not even people who claimed to be family.

Dominic had never had much control over his own life, not really. But this uncertainty was worse than anything he'd experienced before.

And then the texts with Sylvie last night—those had really driven the knife in. He'd predicted she'd probably want to stay away from him. But it hurt to know for certain. She hated him. That hadn't changed.

He'd sounded like an asshole, pretending he could help with the computer thing. She'd seen right through him. But the real life threat had been so much worse.

If those men had wanted to get into the house to hurt Sylvie or Maureen, they could've done it. They'd simply chosen not to. The attack was proof they could do whatever they wanted to the people he cared about when he least expected it.

But Dominic still didn't even know if Uncle Charles had been behind it, or what the man might want from him.

All he could do was wait to find out.

HIS FIRST VISITORS arrived around ten in the morning: two prosecutors from the West Oaks District Attorney's Office.

Maureen answered the bell. Dominic walked in from the living room, where he'd been nervously flipping through cable channels.

The DA, Stephen Abrams, walked into the entryway, followed by Lana Marchetti, his second in command. Lana nodded at him. They'd spoken several times, though not in person.

He'd flirted with Lana in the past, shamelessly, but he'd been putting on a show, pretending that nothing really got to him. Better to seem like a jerk than let them guess how freaked out he'd been over the arrest and what happened after. But Dominic had helped Lana, too, so he hoped she might be willing to hear his side of things.

But Dominic was far less encouraged to see his former attorney, Aaron Sandford, stroll in behind them.

"What are you doing here?"

Dominic had been looking at Sandford, who just a few days ago had threatened him on his Uncle Charles's behalf. But it was the district attorney who answered.

"We have a lot to discuss," Abrams said. "Is there some-place we could all sit down?"

Dominic led them into the living room. Maureen went to make coffee and find cookies in the pantry. But Dominic could hardly focus on being hospitable.

What the hell was Sandford doing here? He didn't repre-sent Dominic anymore, did he? That was what he'd said on the phone. Yet Sandford was smiling at him sympathetically, as if he actually cared that someone had tried to kill Dominic yesterday.

Lana sat on the edge of a chair, crossing her slender legs. She wore a gray pantsuit, and her brown hair was swept into a bun. "We've heard about the latest attempt on your life. I'm glad you and your housekeeper are all right. But next time, you might not be so lucky. If you're willing to testify, we could arrange with federal authorities to get you into a safe house. Is that something you'd want?"

Before Dominic could answer, Sandford spoke over him. "My client and I have already had a chance to speak. Mr. Crane tells me he won't be intimidated by these people and has no intention of abandoning his home."

Dominic glared at him, but Sandford's cold gaze warned him to keep his mouth shut.

"That's not advisable," Lana said. "Next time—"

Sandford's eyes didn't leave Dominic's. "We're confident there won't be a next time. Isn't that so, Mr. Crane?"

Dominic cleared his throat. He could almost hear the threat hidden in Sandford's words: *Step out of line, and next time it'll be Raymond we go after.* "I hope not."

Stephen Abrams accepted a mug of coffee from Maureen. "Unfortunately, there's the matter of the weapons found in your possession during yesterday's incident. They aren't registered, and your bail conditions expressly forbid you from possessing firearms in any case. We're not going to file new charges at this time, but that could change. It depends."

"On what?"

"On whether you seem interested in turning over a new leaf." Lana tilted her head. "Dominic, do you really want to remain loyal to people who are trying to kill you? Or are you willing to do what's right, so you can put your past behind you?"

Sandford was still glaring, but even if he wasn't, Dominic wasn't dumb enough to respond to Lana's questions.

"Agree to testify against the Silverlake Syndicate," Abrams said, "and we'll wipe your slate clean. I've already been consulting with the US Attorney on this since any case against the Syndicate would likely be brought in federal court. She's agreed you would have immunity on all federal charges as well. And they're offering to protect you."

Sandford laughed. "It's all well and good for you and the US Attorney to make grand promises. But Dominic is the one who'll suffer if you fail. I doubt you actually care about that."

Lana narrowed her eyes at the man. "I assure you, we do. We take care of our witnesses."

"My client has nothing to say about any Syndicate. He's never been involved with any such organization. And he doesn't know who's been targeting him."

"Is that true, Dominic?" Lana's tone conveyed that she already knew the answer. So there was no point in lying to her. But he certainly couldn't tell the truth.

He said nothing.

As the two district attorneys were leaving, Lana stopped to shake his hand. "Take care of yourself. I hope you'll change your mind." She'd placed a piece of paper against his palm. Dominic stuck it into his pocket.

Sandford stood beside him while the others drove away.

As soon as they were gone, Dominic turned and grabbed Sandford around the throat. "It was you, wasn't it? You think I'm just going to sit here like a fucking lapdog and wag my tail while you shit on me?"

Sandford clawed at Dominic's hand. "Your uncle," he wheezed. "Not me."

He gave the man's neck another squeeze and dropped him. Sandford stumbled back into a porch pillar, coughing. Dominic wasn't worried about any neighbors seeing. The houses up here in the hills were too spread out. Privacy was paramount.

"It was a message from your uncle. And when he hears about what you just did to me——"

"Like Charles gives a fuck about you. You're replaceable." Dominic had never killed anyone with his own hands, but right now he was tempted.

"His people are watching you on video right now. So go ahead, show them how defiant you are. They'll send those same men who were here yesterday, only this time they won't just scare you. They'll finish the job."

Dominic glanced up at the plastic eye above his door. "So it was you causing the problems with the security system? You're the one who told me to install a Bennett alarm in the first place. Did you do something to Sylvie's computer, too?"

Sandford was loosening the collar of his shirt. "Believe it or not, your uncle doesn't tell me everything he's planning. I take orders just like everyone else. But he made it clear to me that you'd better sit here and stay quiet. You've seen how easily Charles could take you out. His men aren't like the amateurs who went after you before. And just imagine what a piece of cake it would be to walk into Raymond's dorm."

Dominic flexed his hand, longing to take out his anger and frustration on this man.

Sandford was backing away from him toward the street. "And as for Sylvie Trousseau, we saw you two together in the entryway of your house. Camera in there, too, remember? Charles's men would *love* to pay her a visit, I'm sure. Too bad you're stuck at your house and couldn't join in. You'd probably be into that."

Dominic took two long strides forward and slammed his fist into the lawyer's nose. Sandford screamed. Blood spurted over his tan suit.

Shaking out his hand, Dominic went back inside and shut the door.

～

IN HIS BATHROOM, Dominic took out the paper Lana had given him. It was a cocktail napkin Maureen had set out with the cookies.

Lana had written, *If need to speak privately, no Sandford, send message through housekeeper. I will arrange.*

So she could tell that all wasn't well between Dominic and his lawyer.

He was tempted. He liked Lana and respected her. It was much more pleasant having her on his side than against him.

But for now, Dominic had no choice but to do what Sandford instructed: sit and be quiet. Not unless he wanted to risk Raymond, or even Sylvie, getting hurt. God, he hated that she'd gotten pulled into this mess.

The further she stayed away from him, the better. Good thing she already knew that.

Dominic tore the napkin into tiny pieces and flushed them down the toilet.

Chapter Fifteen

*S*ylvie walked into the conference room. Lana was already sitting at the table. "Hey Sylv, how are you?"

"Tired. But I've made progress." She hadn't slept yet. Instead, she'd been subsisting on fancy coffees from the machine in the breakroom, plus the leftover fried rice the bodyguards hadn't annihilated. Her bed at home was calling her, and as soon as she'd finished here, she planned to sleep for as long as possible.

But she worried she might dream of Dominic. She'd been keeping busy enough to avoid thinking more about him, and she dreaded the places her mind would go once she slowed down.

Max closed the door. "I thought it would make more sense if we go through this once, since you both have things to share?"

Sylvie and Lana nodded.

"Let's hear an update on our security situation first," Max said, taking his seat.

Sylvie opened her laptop. "I've learned a lot about the attack. They were definitely trying to infiltrate Bennett Security."

"Were you able to tell where it came from?" Lana asked.

Hackers routed their IP addresses through proxy servers to mask their identity and location. But it hadn't taken Sylvie's friends long to zero in on the source of that malicious code.

"The attack came from a group of hackers operating in Russia. They're guns for hire, and they don't come cheap. They work with organized crime, warlords in Third World countries. The worst of the worst."

"Such as the Silverlake Syndicate?" Max had brought his stress ball with him and was crushing it in his fist.

"That's what it looks like."

"But that's a big step up for the Syndicate," Lana said. "Their previous cybercrimes activity wasn't this sophisticated."

Max nodded. "Dominic mentioned his uncle's taken control. I assume he wasn't lying about that?"

Lana rested her elbows on the table. "His uncle's name is Charles Traynor. I've been in communication with the gang division in Los Angeles. Their informants say he was the head of one of the warring factions, but he's managed to get most of the splinters to unite behind him. He's known for his brutality, and he's got a lot of money of his own. That could explain how he's funding this new group of hackers."

"But what about Dominic?" Max leaned back in his chair. "If this guy is his uncle, that has to mean Crane is working with him, right?"

"That's where it gets interesting. Stephen Abrams and I went to Crane's house this morning, along with Crane's lawyer, Aaron Sandford. And I got the distinct impression that Sandford was putting words in his mouth, forcing him to refuse the offer of a safe house. I think his uncle is afraid Crane will flip on the Syndicate. Which would explain why they shot up his house."

Sylvie took a deep breath. She felt weak with relief at

hearing this small amount of proof that Dominic hadn't set her up. But her relief didn't last long.

If his uncle was trying to silence him, that meant Dominic was in terrible danger. So was Maureen.

"Unless Dominic refused the safe house because he simply doesn't need one," Max pointed out. "If there's no real threat at all."

Lana inclined her head. "True."

Which Sylvie didn't like to hear. Her stomach had twisted up yet again.

Max crossed his arms. "Here's something that doesn't fit. Crane mentioned wanting a bodyguard for his younger brother, Raymond, a college student in L.A. Maybe he's truly worried, and Charles Traynor is the reason."

Raymond? Sylvie thought. Dominic hadn't mentioned a younger sibling.

"But on the other hand, if this uncle is so much more ruthless and better funded, wouldn't he have succeeded if he wanted Dominic dead?" Max rubbed his chin. "If Dominic's not working with them, if he really could flip, there must be some reason his uncle still wants to keep him alive."

"It's possible his uncle needs Crane to accept him as the new leader," Lana said. "The Crane family has been in charge of the Syndicate for decades. Dominic could have sufficient remaining allies to make him dangerous."

Max was nodding along. "Which means that Dominic might still try to reclaim his position as head of the Syndicate. Maybe this cyberattack on Bennett Security was part of his plan. He wanted to prove he's more resourceful than his uncle."

And once again, they didn't know if they could trust him. They didn't know which side Dominic was on. Sylvie's nerves were getting whiplash from this conversation.

"I passed Crane a note offering to speak to him without Sandford," Lana said. "Technically, I'm not supposed to do that, but if he's under duress, it's an extenuating circumstance. He hasn't tried to contact me yet."

Sylvie tapped a few keys on her laptop, cycling through windows to check for updates from her hactivist friends. "We don't know if Dominic is working with his uncle or against him. But the Russian hackers—whoever's really in control of them—still have that back door into Dominic's network."

Which could give Bennett Security a potential way in.

"Do you think our other clients are vulnerable, too?" Max asked. "If these Syndicate hackers have broken into Crane's system?"

"It doesn't work like that. They may be able to control the security system at Crane's house to some extent, but they can't access my encrypted code and use it against our other clients. But if they truly want to come after us, they're not going to stop. There will be more attempts. Ones I might not see coming."

No matter what was happening with Dominic and his uncle, Bennett Security could still be at risk.

"Then what do we do?"

"I'm trying to get to that, boss." Her tone was heavy on the sarcasm. "If you'll let me?"

Max held up his hands. Lana smirked.

"Here's my point. Their back door into Crane's network could also give *me* a way to get to them. A door swings both ways if you can forgive the clunky metaphor. I could send my own malware to them. A rootkit will get me access to their system, which I'll bundle with a payload to get whatever we want. Their keystrokes, screenshots, their communications with the Syndicate. The list is pretty endless."

Max stood up, stress ball still creaking in his grip. "You're saying you could go on the offensive. I like it."

Lana was grimacing. "Here's where I should probably tell you to contact the federal government. They'll want to be involved. The DA will also want to know why he wasn't informed."

Sylvie understood exactly what Lana wasn't saying. "So, we might want to stop discussing this in front of you?"

Because there was no way she'd invite the Feds to their party. They wouldn't give a shit about Bennett Security's interests. Sylvie wanted to protect her employer on her terms, using all the tools at her disposal. Legal and not so legal.

Lana got up. "I have another appointment anyway." She kissed Max on the cheek. "See you at home?"

Max waited until his girlfriend was gone. Then he leaned his hands against the table, a calculating expression on his face.

"How do we get this malware of yours to the Syndicate's hackers?"

"I have to write it first." But that would be the easy part. "Then I'll have to upload it onto Dominic Crane's computer."

"Can you do that remotely?"

"Maybe, but I'll have way more options if I do it in person."

Max sighed, closing his eyes. "I knew this plan sounded a little too easy."

"Don't pull the 'overprotective Max Bennett' routine on me. It's so tired."

"But the last time you went to Crane's house, gunmen showed up and the SWAT team got called in. You could've been hurt or killed. What about one of our bodyguards? If all they have to do is plug something into a computer, even a knucklehead like Tanner could handle it. Right?"

"It's nowhere near that simple. And Crane... It won't seem that strange to him if I go back there."

Max fixed her with a scrutinizing glare. "Why is that?"

"He thought he could manipulate me. I can manipulate him right back." She wasn't going to confess any more than that.

"All right. If you truly want to do this and there's no other way, then we'll use your plan. But I'm going to send a bodyguard with you. That is nonnegotiable."

"I agree. That's a good idea." She'd bring Tanner with her. After what happened during her last visit, Crane wouldn't think too much of it. And she knew Tanner would agree to keep a respectful distance and not get too nosy.

"And I'm going to assign a detail to keep Crane's residence under surveillance. If anybody starts rolling on that house while you're anywhere near, I want our people there protecting you. But I'll tell them to keep a wide perimeter, so they don't trip any alarms—either with Crane or the Syndicate."

"No arguments here. I can't let Crane suspect what I'm really doing."

"Then what are you going to tell him? Checking up on his security system isn't going to get you very far. Don't you think?"

"Just leave it to me. I'll get close to him and get this taken care of."

When she got back to her desk, she stared at her computer screens, guilt already burning in her stomach. Even though she knew Crane had most likely deceived her.

She'd told him they couldn't see one another. Now, she had to act like she'd changed her mind…which wasn't all that far from reality.

She *did* want to talk to him. She wanted to talk to the Dominic she'd spent time with, who'd kissed her so fiercely and made her feel beautiful. She'd been surprised to find him more sincere than she'd expected. If that had been an act, he was good.

But who was the *real* Dominic Crane?

Was he the arrogant womanizer she'd met the day of the install? Was he a ruthless mobster intent on reclaiming his throne? A follower, doing as his uncle instructed?

Or a sweet, sexy guy who'd been trapped in a life he didn't want? Who'd been misunderstood?

Ugh. This sucked.

But this was her job. She was protecting Bennett Security from a serious threat. She'd just have to break this project down into steps, like any other, keeping the end goal in mind.

Sylvie took out her phone and pulled up her texts. She had Dominic's number from when he'd written last night.

Sylvie: I know I said before we shouldn't see each other...

Now what? How was she supposed to handle this?

Sylvie: I've been thinking of you. Wanted to say hi, see how you're doing.

Which was so true it made her chest ache.

Now, she'd just have to wait and see how he responded.

Chapter Sixteen

*P*leasure sang through Dominic's body as he read Sylvie's text.

Sylvie: I've been thinking of you. Wanted to say hi, see how you're doing.

He almost wrote back. Then he wondered if Sandford and his uncle had access to his cell phone, too.

Sandford had threatened her. Dominic wanted Sylvie to move on and forget about him. Then maybe his backstabbing lawyer would do the same and forget about her. Sandford could focus his ire directly on Dominic instead.

So he couldn't write to her. He had to let her go.

That night, he paced the house and watched the doors, both thinking of Sylvie and wondering when his uncle's next attack might begin. Maureen kept a stoic demeanor, going about her daily tasks. But she didn't smile nearly as much as usual, and the two of them barely spoke.

The next day, he broke down and asked Maureen to pick him up a burner phone on one of her shopping trips. There was a small risk his uncle's people might find out, but Dominic told her to buy it at a drug store along with a bunch of toiletries. After he got it and pulled the phone out of its clamshell packaging, Dominic entered the number for Sylvie's phone.

Hi. It's Dominic.

Sylvie: Hi back.

He lay on his bed, feeling like some idiot teenager texting a girl from school. When had he ever felt this insecure about a woman?

Dominic: Other phone isn't good. Long story. Sorry I couldn't write back before.

Sylvie: How are you and Maureen?

Dominic: It's been quiet. No more SWAT team visits.

Sylvie: That's a relief. Any other news about the attack?

He didn't want to tell her about his uncle. That wasn't Sylvie's problem.

Dominic: Nothing of note. What are you doing right now?

Sylvie: What else? Working. I'm dull like that. What are you doing?

He could almost see her in front of her computer. Chunky pink glasses, a pout of concentration.

Dominic: Just talking to you. Best part of my week so far.

There was a long pause. He worried he shouldn't have

confessed that. He wasn't even sure what they were doing. Flirting? Did she still hate him, or not?

Sylvie: Is that really true? Or are you bullshitting me?

Dominic: What do you think?

She didn't write back, and he wished he'd said something else.

Usually in his life, others had gravitated toward him because they wanted something. His money or power, his looks, his access to the family business. He didn't know how to make friends with someone like Sylvie in this kind of context.

What did Sylvie want from him? Was it just sex, or something more? Whatever it was, he suspected he'd give it to her if she asked. Or at least he would try.

THE FOLLOWING DAY, he tried texting her again.

Dominic: Are you around?

Sylvie: I'm at work. Big surprise, right?

Dominic: Guess where I am.

Sylvie: Disneyland?

Dominic: Totally where I'm going the minute I get out of here.

Sylvie: Are you a Space Mountain guy? No…Teacups.

Dominic: You already know me so well.

Sylvie: You're not that hard to figure out.

Dominic: No? I'm disappointed in myself.

Sylvie: Why? You'd rather keep me guessing?

Dominic: If it keeps you interested, then yes. Are you? Interested?

Sylvie: I'm writing to you, aren't I?

Dominic: And I'm still wondering why. I was afraid I'd lost any chance to see you again.

Sylvie: I keep going back and forth on that. Undecided.

Dominic: I've thought about you pretty much constantly since that day. How I wish we could finish what we'd started. Just putting that out there.

Sylvie: You're always this up front?

Dominic: No. Most of what people say about me is probably true. I'm not a good person. Or honest, most of the time.

Sylvie: Is there a 'but' after that?

Dominic: But...you make me want to be nicer.

Sylvie: I don't think you're as dark and broody as you like people to think.

Dominic: Is that what I like people to think?

Sylvie: Seems that way to me.

Dominic: I'm more interested in what YOU think.

Sylvie: I think…maybe we could see each other again. If that's something you want.

Dominic: I want. But what I want has rarely been the determinative factor in my life.

Sylvie: How dark and broody of you.

Dominic: If you come over again, what about your ground rules? We could collect more data without them. Just a thought.

No response.

~

SHE DIDN'T WRITE BACK until yet another day had passed.

Sylvie: Tell me something you've never told anyone.

He was on the couch in the music room. He thought carefully about his response.

Dominic: I watched two seniors have sex under the bleachers when I was a freshman. They didn't know I was there.

Sylvie: Damn. You had to go straight to the dirty talk.

Dominic: Not what you wanted? I just assumed.

Sylvie: That I'm always horny because I can't get off?

Dominic: Not what I was thinking, but now that you mention it…

Sylvie: Very funny. Mine's not dirty. Still want to hear it?

Dominic: Of course I do.

Sylvie: I stole Rachelle Miller's cowhide wallet in ninth grade. Took it right out of her gym locker after she made fun of me for the drawings on my arms. And I don't regret it.

Dominic smiled.

Sylvie: Tell me another.

Dominic: I took a hundred-dollar bill from my older brother's wallet once. Gave it to a homeless guy.

He didn't want her to say that was sweet or generous. It had been a pathetically small gesture.

Sylvie's next reply took a while, but he waited patiently.

Sylvie: My best friend chose our oppressive small town over me, even though she'd said a million times she couldn't wait to escape. I was so hurt I burned all the pictures she ever drew for me and all the notes she ever wrote. But I wish I hadn't. I wish I still had those memories of her.

This was far more than he'd expected. She couldn't despise him if she was sharing things like this, right?

He wished she hadn't gone through that. Yet somehow, he knew Sylvie didn't want sympathy. Maybe because he didn't either.

Dominic: The first time I saw my father kill someone, I couldn't stop vomiting afterwards. I told my mother I had food poisoning. She fired our cook.

That one was a test—to make sure she hadn't forgotten who he was. What he'd come from, what he'd done. Even though he wasn't ready to tell her most of it. If she was starting to like him, he didn't want to fuck that up.

Sylvie: Okay. I've got one about throwing up, too. But this involves eating all my cousin's Easter candy.

He snickered.

They kept sharing secrets, mostly without comment. But he thought he understood why this was so cathartic. Maybe not just for him, but for her.

They weren't supposed to like each other. And it was fun to break the rules.

Dominic fell asleep with the phone in his hand.

THE DOORBELL RANG AFTER BREAKFAST. Dominic saw Sandford and someone else through the window.

This couldn't be good.

He gave Maureen a hand signal that meant, *Lock yourself in your room and don't come out until I say so.*

Then he went to answer the door.

Sandford had a new suit and a butterfly bandage at the bridge of his nose. Two black eyes had almost faded. "Mind if we step inside?"

Dominic widened the door and gestured for them to enter. "Be my guest. I love having friends over."

Sandford's companion eyed him as he passed. The guy was some roided-out Neanderthal, obviously brought along to keep Sandford safe. Or perhaps deliver the beating that Sandford no doubt thought Dominic had coming.

"This is Alexi." Sandford pointed a thumb at the Neanderthal. "If you come near me, if you even think about raising a hand, he'll take it out on your nut sac."

Dominic looked the bodybuilder up and down. "You never know. I might be into that."

The guy didn't react.

Dominic's breakfast churned in his stomach, though his inner alarm bells didn't ring out just yet. He'd lived through unpleasantness before. And for now, his uncle seemed to want him alive. The beating wouldn't be too severe, if it came at all.

Dominic showed them into the living room. "I'm guessing you have another message for me?"

"Not exactly." Sandford took a tablet computer from his bag and set it up on the coffee table. "Your uncle would rather speak to you directly."

Sandford hit a few buttons. A window opened, and after another minute, Charles Traynor appeared on the screen.

Uncle Charles had served as a captain in their organization since before Warren took power. He was in his fifties, but he looked younger. His hair was still the same shade of black it had been when Dominic was a child. He didn't know if Charles dyed it or if it was natural.

Uncle Charles had always been athletic and youthful. Dominic remembered him playing touch football with the kids at holiday gatherings, though Dominic himself usually sat on the sidelines instead of taking part.

"Nephew, it's been far too long. How are you?"

"I'm alive."

Dominic had seen his uncle smile and laugh at the Christmas dinner table. But he'd also seen Uncle Charles gouge out a man's eyes with his thumbs. Dominic was under no illusions about what kind of man Charles Traynor was. This man wasn't calling to listen to his nephew whine. That would only be a show of weakness, and Dominic's reputation was damaged enough as it was.

"I've heard about your legal trouble. Unfortunate that they

haven't dropped those charges yet. I keep hearing you're innocent."

Another potential trap. His uncle didn't give a shit if he was innocent or not. In fact, his innocence would no doubt be a strike against him. "It's a little dull around here most of the time," Dominic said. "I've never minded a vacation, though it would be more pleasant if I had better companions to choose from."

"But you've had some very pretty visitors lately, haven't you?"

Shit, Dominic had walked right into that one. He'd meant to distract the Syndicate *away* from Sylvie, not remind them of her.

"I'd rather talk about work. Sandford tells me there have been some changes?"

"I'm glad you brought that up because it is an awkward subject. Isn't it? The last time we spoke, I was reporting to you. But with your legal difficulties on top of Warren's prison sentence, the business needs someone at the helm. We've had a few petty skirmishes. People outside the family trying to take advantage of this time of confusion. I couldn't let that happen."

"You want to make sure the business stays in the family."

The man's eyes were hard, seeing everything. "That's exactly right. I'm glad that you and I are of the same mind. That's quite a weight off my conscience. Family is everything."

"It is."

Charles picked a piece of lint from his sleeve. "Since you acknowledge the importance of keeping our family together, I'm sure you won't have any problem sending a message to the captains? Making it clear that you accept my authority as the acting head of the business?"

Dominic felt the presence of Sandford's Neanderthal behind him, though he couldn't see the guy. "I'm open to that.

But I was hoping for more clarity. What would be my role going forward?"

In other words, *How do I know you won't arrange a convenient accident for me as soon as I give you my endorsement?*

"As soon as we can resolve your legal troubles, I'd love to have you back at my side. But Dominic, we both know you've never relished the burdens and responsibilities that come with power. Let's be frank. Before Warren left us, you preferred to spend your time on more enjoyable pursuits than running this business."

Dominic wasn't about to disagree.

"I know you'd rather promote your nightclubs or...whatever it was you kept yourself busy doing. My leadership will be better for all of us in the long run. And far better for the business."

Dominic could only nod. If he opened his mouth, he was liable to say something that would get him killed. He didn't truly want to be in charge of the Syndicate. He never had.

But there's always someone worse, Warren had taught him.

"I can't tell you how glad I am that we agree. Take care of yourself, nephew. Oh, and perhaps take it easier on Sandford? I know he can be frustrating, but he's only the messenger. He has a few more instructions for you. Bye, now."

Sandford turned off the tablet screen and replaced it in his bag. Then he turned around with a smug, closed-mouth grin.

"As your uncle said, there's more that we expect of you. You can draft that message to the captains at your leisure. I'm sure you'll want to take your time getting the wording just right. But your uncle needs a more affirmative act on your part to confirm your loyalty to this organization and this family."

"You don't know a damn thing about my family."

Sandford went on as if Dominic hadn't spoken. "We've been aware of your...let's call it 'friendship' with Max Bennett for a while. And now you're even closer to his employee, Sylvie Trousseau."

Acid rose in Dominic's throat. He waited for Sandford to mention the burner phone, the conversations he and Sylvie had been sharing every night the past week. But thank god, the man moved on. So he didn't know.

"It's time we exploit those connections. If the Syndicate is going to gain a foothold in West Oaks, we need to neutralize Bennett Security. They've been causing problems for us, and your uncle wants to know that won't keep happening. If you can deliver Bennett Security to us, then all will be forgiven. Your uncle will know you're still as loyal as you claim to be."

Dominic bit the inside of his cheek. "How am I supposed to do that?"

Sandford took something else from his bag—a tiny flash drive with a USB connector. Dominic hardly knew anything about computers, but he knew what that was for.

"This drive has a specially written program on it. It's a more updated version of the one we tried to get onto Sylvie's laptop the last time she was here. I don't know all the technical aspects, but apparently the experts we hired had more trouble breaching her system than they expected. But if you get this onto her hard drive, our computer friends will be able to take care of the rest."

Dominic sat back against the couch, crossing his arms. He was working very hard to keep his expression neutral. "You're overestimating how much Sylvie trusts me. After the last time, I doubt she'll ever come near me again. Much less let me plug things into her computer."

Sandford's smirk was lascivious. Dominic wanted to punch it off the guy's face. "Don't sell yourself short. I have the feeling Sylvie Trousseau will let you plug anything into her *hard drive* you desire. All you have to do is seduce her. You're probably most of the way there. Or maybe you've already had her? And she'll be eager for more?"

Dominic stood rapidly, fists at his sides. Sandford shuffled back, sending a panicked glance at his Neanderthal body-guard. "I wouldn't do that if I were you. Because then Alexi will have to punish you, and you'll have to explain your performance problems to Sylvie. Just do what we say. Make your uncle happy. And you won't have to find out what Charles will do if you fail."

Dominic said nothing more to Sandford, just showed him and his muscle to the door.

There was no way he'd trick Sylvie into coming back here so he could use her. He wasn't going to betray her that way or put her in any more danger.

Uncle Charles hadn't mentioned Raymond again. Nor had Sandford. Dominic still worried about his brother's safety. But if Charles really wanted to unite the Syndicate and have the express support of the Crane family, then he wouldn't harm Raymond.

Right?

But either way, Dominic wasn't trading his brother's safety for Sylvie's welfare. There had to be some other way to make his uncle leave him alone. He'd give his endorsement, even lick the bottoms of his uncle's boots if that was what the man demanded.

But Dominic was leaving Sylvie out of it.

Chapter Seventeen

*T*anner pulled up to the curb in front of Dominic's house and shifted the truck into park.

"You sure about this?" he asked.

Sylvie grabbed the bag nestled between her feet. "Max already asked that earlier."

"But Max doesn't know about you and Crane, does he?"

She tilted her head to look at him. "You don't either."

Over the past week, her text conversations with Dominic had morphed into friendship territory. Yet she still didn't truly know the man she'd been talking to.

Was he real? Or a lie?

It was like Sylvie had two different people in her head: the woman who genuinely liked Dominic, who wanted to know more about him. Who'd even shared her secrets—true secrets —with him. And then there was the Bennett Security employee who was actively plotting to betray him.

Now here she was, right outside his house. Desperate to see him again and dreading what she had to do.

She'd never been so confused.

"I know what Priyanka told me," Tanner said. "How you

looked ready to either slap Crane, or strip him naked the first day you met?"

"Since when are you talking to Priyanka? I told you to steer clear of her."

"I'm steering clear. But she likes to gossip in the breakroom."

Damn it. Sylvie's assistant would need another talking-to. "Don't worry about me and Crane. I'll handle it. Come on."

She had her custom-designed bundle of programs ready to go, loaded onto a USB flash drive. She hadn't actually seen any of Dominic's computers during her previous visits, but he'd mentioned those fancy porn sites. Clearly, he had a device some-where. She'd find it. And if it didn't have a USB connector, that wouldn't stop her. She had plenty of adapters at her disposal. She could probably even work with his phone if need be.

Wrestling with the moral implications of her plan had presented more of a challenge. But she had a job to do.

Sylvie and Tanner approached the front door. The bell rang, and she heard it echoing in the entryway. Her fingers tightened around the strap of her bag as her nervousness grew.

No matter what else she thought of Crane, he'd been outwardly sweet to her. Made her feel comfortable in a way that no man had before. After their conversations, assuming he'd been genuine, she could even consider him a friend.

And he was still the most attractive man she'd ever seen. So yeah, there was that, too.

In the past week, Sylvie had gone back and forth a dozen times on whether she thought Dominic had lied to her. She kept coming to the same conclusion: even if—*if*—he'd done nothing to intentionally deceive her, she still couldn't trust him to remain neutral.

If the Syndicate was threatening his life, he might be willing to make all sorts of compromises to ensure his own safety. Whether he wanted to get his leadership position back or not, Crane had no reason to show any loyalty to Bennett Security. Sylvie's priorities were incompatible with his.

She had to protect the company and the people she cared about. It was as simple and as crucial as that.

This was going to be shitty. No way around it.

Maureen opened the door. "Sylvie, what a pleasant surprise. And you're Tanner, isn't that right? Lovely to see you again." She stepped out onto the porch and pulled Sylvie into a hug.

"I'm sorry I haven't gotten in touch before now," Sylvie said. "How have you been?" Dominic had mentioned Maureen in some of his texts, but Sylvie hadn't spoken to the woman directly.

"Oh, I'm fine. It's been a bit nerve-racking, sticking around this place. But it seems that's what's in the cards at the moment."

Sylvie wondered how much Maureen knew about the attack or the Syndicate's new leader.

"What can I do for you today?" Maureen asked.

"I was hoping to take another look at the security system. We'd better make sure there won't be any more problems." This was the story she'd decided on to get in the door. Of course, once she and Dominic were alone, she had a different explanation for what she was doing at his house.

When she'd texted about seeing each other again, he'd seemed to be in favor. Yet he'd resisted all her attempts to set a firm date. She'd resorted to this surprise visit, thinking he wouldn't refuse.

But to Sylvie's disappointment, Maureen frowned. "That's not necessary. Dominic said he's not concerned about the security system anymore, and I suppose that's his decision."

"Could I talk to him about it? He might see things differently if I could explain…"

"I'm sorry, Sylvie. Dominic doesn't want to see anyone

right now. He made that clear to me. But I sure hope that you and I can visit another time?"

Before Sylvie could say anything else, Maureen had pushed the door closed. The lock snapped into place.

"That didn't go well." Tanner stuck his hands in his shorts pockets and rocked back on his heels.

"I know. I don't need the commentary." They had to assume the Syndicate was watching through the porch camera.

Shit. What was she supposed to do now? She'd assumed that Dominic would want to see her. In fact, she'd assumed he'd be eager.

She'd had this image of him pining for her, pulling her into his arms the minute they were alone. As if he'd been just as conflicted, longing to kiss her again, the way she'd been longing for him. Even though that fantasy also made her guilty as hell.

Now she felt like a dumbass. And she had no Plan B.

But they hadn't texted last night. She'd assumed Dominic had something else to occupy him. Was he tired of her? Or was something *wrong*?

"Should we go get fish tacos instead?"

She leveled a glare at the bodyguard. But Tanner had a point. What else were they supposed to do? Maybe she could come back and try again later.

They started back toward Tanner's truck. But then Crane's front door opened, and Dominic himself stepped out onto the porch.

He wore his usual white T-shirt and jeans, his feet bare. His ankle monitor peeked out below the hem.

"Sylvie? What are you doing here?"

She turned around and walked back toward him, her chest getting tighter with every step. Even with all her planning and preparation, all her debates about whether she should do this or not, her heart still lifted at the sight of him.

Her story about the security system died on her tongue. "I missed you. I wanted to see you."

He smiled, though the expression didn't quite reach his eyes. She saw hesitation there, and something more she couldn't decipher.

Could he be feeling some guilt of his own?

Dominic looked over at Tanner. "The bodyguard's back?"

Tanner waved.

She shrugged one shoulder, her bag shifting. "After last time, I thought it wasn't a bad idea."

Dominic laughed, and this time his eyes lit up. "Around here, a bodyguard's not a bad idea at all. Why don't you both come in?"

They went into the kitchen, where Maureen was setting out a cheeseboard. "Glad Dominic changed his mind. I hated turning you away. Tanner, could I interest you in a snack?"

"You must be psychic, Ms. Maureen, because you just read my mind." He pulled up a stool at the counter while the housekeeper blushed.

Sylvie felt Dominic's fingers circle her wrist. He tugged her down the hall and toward the music room. They went inside, and he shut the door. Once they were alone, he let go of her and took a step back.

"I wish you hadn't come."

"You said in your texts you wanted to see me."

"I *do*. But the last time you were here, you could've been hurt."

"I wasn't, though."

"What about your computer? The attempt to access your system? You never told me what happened."

That again. She'd thought he had dropped that subject. Why was he suddenly so concerned? "My firewall took care of it. They failed. Everything turned out fine."

"No, it *didn't*." He pressed a hand over his eyes. "Sylvie…"

"What's wrong?"

Tell me about your uncle, she thought. *Tell me the truth. About everything.*

Through all their conversations via text, Dominic hadn't mentioned his present role with the Syndicate, or his lawyer Sandford, or Lana's offer to talk privately. Which had to mean he was hiding things. But how much?

He perched his hands on his hips, staring at his feet. "When we first met, I didn't like that you called me out for who I am. But it was fair."

"You mean, when I called you a degenerate?" And worse.

"You know I associate with some very unsavory people, even though it's not completely by choice. I don't want them anywhere near you." His eyes lifted. "I just want to keep you safe. Around me, you won't be."

It was like there were two different versions of Dominic Crane, too: the man who'd ruled an organized crime ring, who could've seduced her in order to undermine Bennett Security... And the man she'd been talking to lately. This man, right in front of her. The one who wanted to protect her. Who honestly seemed to care.

The alternate sides of Sylvie matched the different versions of him.

And it was tearing her apart.

"I can handle myself. Plus, I've got Tanner with me."

"Yeah, what's *that* about? Does he know..."

"About what happened between us before? Not specifically. But he's my friend. I've done him plenty of favors in the past. He's my wingman, I'm his wingwoman."

"So you two haven't ever..."

"You're not jealous, are you?"

"I don't get jealous. But if you have a threesome in mind, I should probably know now so I can prepare. He's a *very* big guy."

"Oh my god." She swatted his chest with the back of her

hand. "I'm not interested in Tanner like that. But if you are, don't let me stand in your way."

"I'm kidding. I'm not jealous. But I'd rather not share you if I can help it."

Her body flooded with warm feelings.

In one sense, she was playing a role. Getting close to him, even *lying* to him, to find the hackers who were targeting her company. But this tenderness—she didn't have to fake it.

Yet it slashed her heart down the middle, not knowing if they were both acting. If this was just layers upon layers of betrayal.

But wouldn't it be better if this *wasn't* real for him? Because then she wouldn't have to feel so shitty about what she was doing.

She wished she knew which version was the real Dominic Crane. And which was the real Sylvie.

"So there's no other reason you're here?" he asked. "I saw you on the camera. I thought you were saying something to Maureen about the security system."

"That was an excuse to be near you. But I could work on the system if you like."

"I don't think there's any point."

"You're not worried about people coming after you again? Trying to break in?" She carefully watched his reaction.

"I am. But if they really want to get to me, I don't think I can stop them."

"That's awful."

"But I told you. That's my life."

"You don't have any other choice?"

Instead of answering, Dominic backed her up against the closed door and kissed her.

His tongue teased her lips open. Dominic's hands moved along her sides. Was he trying to distract her? Avoid answering the question? Avoid something else? It was working. This man had more influence over her than Sylvie wanted to admit. If she wasn't careful, she could get lost in him, just like she had on her last visit here. Which had nearly ended in disaster.

He smoothed the hair back from her face. "Spend the night," he whispered. "No expectations. No pressure. We'll just see what happens."

Anxiety swelled in her chest, half excitement and half sorrow. She'd have all night to find his computer and upload the malware. It was going to be easier than she'd thought. But that only made her remorse more acute.

"I'd like that."

She'd expected to see satisfaction on his face. But instead, she saw a mirror of her own regret.

Chapter Eighteen

They wandered into the kitchen. Tanner raised an eyebrow at Dominic, but Sylvie's friend didn't remark on the fact that they'd been missing.

Dominic smiled back at Tanner, meeting the man's curious gaze. He wondered what the bodyguard was really thinking.

"I was just telling our guest what I'm making for dinner tonight." Maureen was pulling ingredients out of the fridge and freezer. "Crawfish étouffée, just like I promised Sylvie the last time she visited, though I certainly hope tonight's dinner is more successful."

Sylvie sat down at the counter next to Tanner. "I was sorry I missed your crawfish before. I was afraid you might've used up your supply."

"Oh, no chance of that, dear. Dominic and I didn't get around to much fine dining that evening."

They were all laughing and joking about the fact that they'd nearly been murdered the last time Sylvie was here. Maybe that was better than dwelling, yet again, on how terrible that day had been. Or how Dominic deserved the blame.

Yet if Sylvie knew what was good for her, she *would* be

scared. She would've run away from this place and never come back.

But then, she'd started up those text conversations, and he'd kept them going, as if he had any business dragging her deeper into his life. And now, here she was.

Dominic hadn't even meant to invite her inside. When she'd arrived on his doorstep a few minutes ago, he hadn't intended to meet with her at all. But then, he couldn't resist seeing her, talking to her. And the moment she'd said she had missed him, there was no way he could turn his back on her.

But what the hell am I doing? he asked himself. His uncle's spies would've seen Sylvie come into the house. They'd know she was here and assume he was working on Sandford's instructions. But he'd already decided he wasn't going to install that stupid program on her computer.

He still had that little flash drive stashed in a cabinet upstairs. Why hadn't he just thrown that fucking thing away when he had a chance?

He was starting to sweat. "I'll be right back," he said to the others and spun on his heel.

Dominic went into the bathroom and splashed cold water on his face. He looked at himself in the mirror. It was the same face he'd seen there for years, the lines around his eyes gradually getting deeper, and the set of his mouth growing harder.

Could he seriously be considering this? Inviting Sylvie into his home, into his bed, just so he could give Uncle Charles what he wanted?

Fuck. He didn't want to do it.

But if his uncle would leave Dominic alone... Leave Raymond alone...

Why else would he have invited Sylvie to stay the night if not to have this chance?

No. I can't.

But was he capable of it? Of course he was.

Just like he knew he was capable of killing a man with his bare hands if he had to, even though he'd never done it before. Dominic's uncle might think he was nothing but a hedonist, interested only in pleasure. But he was a survivor. That was how he'd lived through his membership in the Crane family and the Syndicate. He'd tried to hold onto his humanity at the same time so he could face his own reflection in the mirror, like he was barely able to do right now.

He *was* capable of betraying Sylvie. But would he?

He couldn't say for sure.

Dominic washed his hands and left the bathroom. He passed through the entryway, where Sylvie had left her bag. He knew her laptop would be inside. It had to be if she'd been offering to work on the security system.

He was staring at it when Tanner walked into the entryway. Dominic's eyes darted up to the other man's.

Tanner cocked one hip. "Sylvie said we're going to be staying the night. Did you know that invite included me?"

"I figured. I'd rather have you here looking out for her in case there's any trouble."

"You expecting trouble?"

Dominic shrugged. "No, but it usually finds me. Sylvie is willing to take the risk. It's her choice."

Tanner nodded. "Just so you know, I don't have a problem with you. Or with whatever you've got going with Sylvie."

Dominic wasn't sure what to say to that. He was glad Sylvie had a friend like Tanner around her, someone who had the training and the size not to be intimidated by anything. But then again, if Tanner were an even better friend, he never would've let Sylvie come over here in the first place.

"But if you hurt her, in *any* possible way, then there will be a problem. Just so we're clear," Tanner added, matter-of-factly. Then he ambled over to the bathroom.

Dominic went back to the kitchen, forcing himself not to look at Sylvie's laptop bag along the way.

Sylvie and Maureen stood beside the stove, chopping fragrant vegetables. "The foundations are the holy trinity—that's onion, bell pepper, celery—and the roux. You've got to get it nice and dark, but not burned."

Sylvie turned and smiled at him. Immediately, he felt like a monster for the thoughts he'd been having, the temptation to take advantage of her visit.

She'd come here to see *him*. Against all odds, she actually seemed to like him.

When was the last time he'd met someone like her? Someone intelligent and thoughtful and down-to-earth, who gave him a hard time when he deserved it and yet was so sincere? Who was beautiful outside and within?

His last girlfriend had been the exact opposite. Vapid, shallow, interested in how Dominic looked and what he could provide for her in terms of status and sex and money. Lots of people had wanted him for those reasons. But being attractive was essentially meaningless, a chance of fate. Same with having the "Crane" last name. It was all just genetics, not really *him*.

Dominic was pretty sure Sylvie liked him for the small pieces of his true self he'd been able to show her.

Well, okay. She was here for his body and the promise of sex, too. He was well aware of that. She thought he could help her with her orgasm problem. And he was perfectly willing to try. But in exchange, she was sharing a part of herself with him.

He would forget about that flash drive. It wasn't going to happen. He exhaled, glad the issue was settled in his mind.

"Need any help?" Dominic asked, joining the ladies in the kitchen.

Maureen waved a spoon at him. "Oh no, keep him away. That man is a menace around a stove top."

"That's not true. I'm helpful."

"Au contraire. What about the time you added a table-spoon of cayenne to my jambalaya instead of paprika?"

"They're both red."

"Nearly singed my nose hairs clean off."

Sylvie giggled. Dominic slid his arm around her waist and kissed her head. Maureen lifted a brow at them. "None of that in my kitchen, either. You're liable to knock over the flour canister like that *other* time. I thought it had snowed indoors in July."

Sylvie looked up at him. "What other time?"

Dominic steered her toward the balcony instead. "Nothing you'd want to hear about." He didn't want to talk about ex-girlfriends with her.

Not that Sylvie had interest in being his girlfriend. He was in no position to be seeing anyone seriously, and she'd be a fool to want anything serious with him. Sylvie was no fool.

They were having fun. Enjoying one another. Maybe they were even friends. But it couldn't be more.

He slid open the glass patio door. The sky was full of color, oranges and reds and pinks. The ocean reflected the sun in fragments, spreading the sunset across the surface of the water.

"This is a nice place," Sylvie said. "I'm guessing most people under house arrest don't have such a sweet view."

"Probably not. But I doubt I'll have it for long."

She looked at him sharply. "Why? What's going on?"

Damn. He hadn't meant to bring this up. "Just family stuff. I don't actually own this house. The Crane family trust does. And according to rumors, they're thinking about cutting me off."

He wondered if there was harm in mentioning his uncle. He knew the Syndicate couldn't be listening. Dominic had an electronic detector to find listening bugs, and he did regular sweeps of the house. His uncle had to resort to using the cameras in the security system to spy on him, but there were none out here.

"My Uncle Charles took charge of the family business. The Syndicate," he forced himself to say. He wanted to be honest with her.

"And he's cutting you off? Do you think he's the one who sent those people after you?"

Dominic nodded. "He wants me to endorse him as the new leader to prove I'm out of the way."

Sylvie gripped the railing, looking down at the water. "And is that what you want? Or do you want your old position back?"

"It's not a question of whether I want it. It's whether I should."

"I don't understand."

And how could she? How could he ever expect her to? "It's not important. Not important right now, I mean." He stood behind her and wrapped his arms around her waist. "You're here to enjoy yourself, and I'm being depressing."

Sylvie spun around in his arms so she was looking up at him. "Max said you have a younger brother."

"I do. Raymond. He's not in the Syndicate. I never wanted him to be."

"But you're worried about him?"

Dominic had decided to drop the request for a bodyguard for Raymond. It would just piss off his uncle more. "Yeah. I don't want him to end up like me." Dominic blinked as he looked into the sunset.

"Well, I haven't spoken to anyone in my family except my cousin for over a decade. My parents disowned me."

She'd hinted at this in their text conversations but hadn't said it specifically. "Why would they disown *you*? You're perfect."

"Not perfect enough. See? You're not the only one with

problems." She ran her hands down his arms. "If you could be anything, what would you be?"

"You mean a job?"

"It could be a job. Or an identity, or an animal, a mineral or…anything."

He laughed. "I don't know. What would you pick?"

Sylvie glanced away. "I'd be exactly my true self and never have to be anyone else."

"I like that. I'll pick that, too." Maybe then he'd know who the heck he really was.

"You can't copy me! You have to choose your own."

He scoffed. "Pretty sure I can do what I like. But… I guess I'll be a racehorse out to stud. All I'd have to do is eat oats and fuck all day. I could go for that."

Sylvie's eyes turned molten at the mention of fucking.

He leaned forward to kiss the corner of her mouth. "What's the status on those ground rules of yours? No getting naked…"

"I'm considering revising them." Her fingers started sliding up the inner seam of his jeans toward his crotch. "Because I don't think I can resist you."

Then Maureen called them in for dinner. Dominic gritted his teeth, telling his cock to calm down. He grabbed Sylvie's hand, and they walked back inside together.

Dinner was good, as usual. He always enjoyed Maureen's cooking. Afterward, he and Tanner shared dish duty. It was strange, having double the number of people in his house suddenly. Maureen clearly loved the extra attention and Sylvie's ample compliments on the food.

But Dominic's mind was straying again to the flash drive.

He didn't know what Charles would do when—if?—Dominic failed to deliver Bennett Security. His uncle might still go after Raymond to punish Dominic. Or what about Maureen?

Or even Sylvie herself, as Sandford had threatened?

A blow to Max Bennett's company was only financial. It wasn't the same as someone losing his or her life. Raymond, Maureen, Sylvie... Dominic's dinner rose in his throat just contemplating the risk.

But he couldn't go upstairs and sleep with her if he was going to sneak away and install that program afterward. Even Dominic Crane wasn't that much of a sleaze.

God, he hated this so damn much. This fucking choice was no choice at all.

Either way, he would lose.

Chapter Nineteen

*S*ylvie paced across the guestroom. She couldn't keep still.

She'd already changed into flannel pajamas. Maureen had provided them, along with some toiletries for her to use. The housekeeper hadn't specified where these items came from, but Sylvie could guess she wasn't the first female guest to stay overnight unexpectedly.

Tanner was in a room somewhere else in the house. He seemed to have had a perfectly nice evening, as if he wasn't bothered at all by their true mission. She didn't know how Tanner could be so easygoing. Just smiling and accepting Maureen's hospitality, while knowing he and Sylvie were here for an entirely different purpose.

He'd be keeping an ear out, while another of Sylvie's team —someone she trusted to keep this sleepover quiet, not Priyanka—would watch Dominic's security cameras to make sure no uninvited Syndicate guests turned up.

All evening, every time Dominic had smiled at her or brushed her hair affectionately, she'd nearly been sick. Either Dominic was a monster, or she was.

Max was counting on her. This plan had been her idea,

and she didn't know any other way to get back at those Russian hackers.

She couldn't go through with this. But she *had to* go through with it.

Sylvie forced herself to breathe. She needed to think.

Everything Dominic had said or done tonight spoke to his sincerity. Was she just that gullible? Or had he been telling her the truth, all this time? If Dominic hadn't lied to her, then… what? Should she call this off?

If the Syndicate was now his enemy, then taking them down would be a good thing for him too. Except he'd suggested he might reclaim his place as its leader. Not because he wanted to, but because he "should." Whatever that meant.

He'd called it "the family business." If Sylvie helped destroy the Syndicate, how would he react? Would he thank her for freeing him? Or would he hate her for interfering?

Her mind was spinning in circles trying to track the different possibilities, and it was leaving her dizzy.

A soft knock interrupted her thoughts. She opened the door and found Dominic in the hallway. He'd changed from his jeans into a faded pair of sweatpants. His white tee was the same, snug over his toned upper body.

"Can I come in?"

Flutters of anxiety spread through her insides. "Of course." She stepped aside.

Dominic glanced over like he'd heard something strange in her voice. "You okay? You had fun tonight?"

"Definitely. I had a great time. I don't think I said enough thank-yous to Maureen. She's an amazing cook."

"She is. I'm lucky to have her. She made tonight special, without me even having to ask." He walked over to her bed and sat on the edge of it. Sylvie sat down next to him, gripping the bedspread beneath her hands.

"It was almost like a date," he said, "except I couldn't take you out because I'm legally barred from leaving my house.

And my dates don't usually bring bodyguards along with them. Though maybe they should."

She laughed, and the sound was too high-pitched.

"You sure nothing's wrong?"

"No. Er, yes. Nothing. Maybe I'm just…nervous."

He turned those intense dark eyes on her. "*I* make you nervous?"

"A little. That can't be a surprise."

He leaned toward her. "You always surprise me." His voice was breathy. But instead of kissing her mouth, he kissed her forehead. "I hate to do this. But would you mind if I take a rain check on the rest of tonight? The experimenting. I'm not in the right headspace. I'm sorry. It's nothing to do with you, I promise."

Half the tension left her body. There was no way she could've slept with him knowing what she was really here to do. She would've made a terrible spy.

"It's totally fine. You don't have to apologize." But she also didn't know what to think. If Dominic had truly wanted to manipulate her, wouldn't he be eager to sleep with her?

"I know that's why you came over here." He raised his eyebrows. "So you could use me for sex."

Sylvie almost choked as she coughed. "That's not the *only* reason."

"Most of my friends, ex-friends now, would've been pissed if I ended the party too soon. I was supposed to keep the good times rolling at all costs."

She studied him. "You don't have to do that with me."

"I know that in theory. But it's old habits." He smiled sadly. "I'll let you in on a secret. I don't actually want to be the racehorse out to stud. That's what a lot of people would expect me to want, and sometimes I forget the difference."

"What *would* you be?"

"Maybe I'd do something related to art? I've always liked

photography. How it can be stark or rich, quiet or expressive. But it's always got a piece of the truth."

She was trapped in her thoughts. *If...if...if...*

"Sylvie? You sure you're okay?"

"I was just thinking. About what you said before." She touched his cheek. "I don't want to use you, Dominic."

If she could only see into his soul. Know the truth. Tears stung her eyes and nose. She swallowed them down.

"My brothers just call me Nic. You could call me that, too."

"Okay."

"You don't have to sleep over if you'd rather head home."

"No, I like being here." Every word was a blade she was plunging into her own heart. "With you."

His hand reached for hers. "I mentioned my younger brother before. Raymond. You asked if I was worried about him, and I didn't really answer. I didn't want to tell you. But I'm *very* worried. I'm afraid my uncle is going to hurt Raymond to get back at me."

"What are you going to do?"

Dominic squeezed his eyes shut. "I don't know. I feel like I have no good options. No matter what I do, somebody's going to get hurt. Maybe not physically. But they'll feel betrayed."

The lump in her throat was becoming a boulder. This man sitting next to her, he couldn't be faking. There was just no way. She refused to believe it. Which meant...

There was only one liar in this room, and it wasn't him.

"Couldn't you talk to Lana in the DA's Office? She has all kinds of contacts. I know she wants to help you."

His gaze was wary. "But I don't think she can. Nobody can. So, what do I do?"

Sylvie was asking herself that same question. "You're not going to kill anyone, are you?"

He huffed a laugh. "No."

She'd been ready to tell him not to do anything illegal,

either. But who was she to make such demands? She broke laws all the time when she hacked into government databases or private networks.

"Then choose whichever course will cause the least harm," she said, "while protecting the people you care most about. Even if someone feels betrayed, that's better than having lives threatened."

The Syndicate threatened lives all the time, especially now that his uncle was in charge. Dominic had just admitted it. If she had an opportunity to stop the Syndicate, she had to take it. No matter how much it pained her.

"That's what I'm thinking, too," he said. "But I still hate it."

Me too. So much.

They held each other for a while before saying goodnight.

Sylvie got under the covers and stared into the dark. She'd already glanced around this floor while she was supposed to be getting ready for bed. Dominic had a laptop in an office down the hall. Once the house was quiet, she'd sneak down there and plug in the flash drive.

It would be over with soon enough. Maybe once it was done, this guilt wouldn't be consuming her from the inside out.

Or maybe this feeling would just get worse.

I have to protect the people I care about, she reminded herself. Yet Dominic was starting to become one of those people.

She'd been so wrong about him.

But Sylvie had to be tough. She had a responsibility to Bennett Security. If she didn't install that malware on Dominic's network, then the Syndicate hackers would take advantage of her weakness. Dominic's uncle could hurt countless innocents too, not just Bennett Security and its clients. She had to stay strong.

But maybe she could help Dominic in some small way.

Sylvie kicked off the covers and grabbed her phone to send a text to Max.

Sylvie: Put a bodyguard detail on Dominic's younger brother, Raymond Crane. Danger from Syndicate is real. But please keep discreet. Must be very unofficial.

Max wrote back immediately, which didn't surprise her. He was usually working late.

Max: Where are you? Have you completed your task yet?

She hadn't told Max she was spending the night at Dominic's, nor did she intend to. She'd already sworn Tanner to keep his mouth closed.

Sylvie: I'll get it done, boss. But please do what I asked?

Max: On it. Keep me posted.

Sylvie went to her door and listened. Everything was quiet in the rest of the house. She opened the door a crack and peered into the dark.

No footsteps, no light. Dominic was probably asleep by now.

She had to do this. If she let her feelings for Dominic get in the way, then she'd failed.

Sylvie went back to her laptop bag and got the flash drive from a zippered pocket. She stashed it in the back pocket of her pajamas.

Her feet padded silently along the carpet.

When she got to Dominic's office, she closed the door almost all the way. The room was nearly pitch black, so she used her phone as a light. She snuck over to the laptop and pushed open the lid.

A password window appeared, but that wasn't a problem. Her program was designed to bypass the need for a password altogether.

Sylvie pulled the tiny rectangle of plastic from her pocket. It was so lightweight, yet it held such power. Days' worth of work and cleverness. She was proud of this bundle of programs. And she also despised what it would do. Not the part about tracking down the hackers or harming the Syndicate.

But once she loaded what was on this device, there was no going back. Not where Dominic was concerned.

She found the USB port on the side of the laptop.

She inserted the drive.

Her fingers drummed against the desk as the laptop restarted, opening into safe mode. A tiny window appeared, and her code started scrolling. A status bar blinked to life, a counter marking rapid progress.

Thirty-eight percent. Thirty-nine.

Cold sweat broke out all over Sylvie's body. Her breaths were shallow. Her pulse thrummed violently at her neck.

Seventy-two. Seventy-three.

Her throat kept constricting tighter and tighter.

Ninety-seven. Ninety-eight.

What am I doing?

With a curse, she grabbed hold of the flash drive and yanked it free. The status bar froze at ninety-nine percent.

Cancel? it asked her.

Hands shaking, she hit yes and then went through the steps of erasing any evidence of the aborted download from the computer's RAM. She shut it down and restarted. When the password request appeared, she closed the laptop and backed away, shocked by what she'd just done.

She'd lost her fucking nerve. She might not get another opportunity to access Dominic's computer. And Max was already getting impatient.

She could restart the loader right now, but the more she screwed around with this, the more likely the people monitoring Dominic's network would notice some anomaly.

Yet even as these thoughts spun through her mind, she knew that she wasn't going to try again.

Many times, Sylvie had hacked her way into places she wasn't supposed to go. But the rules she broke, the privacy she violated—the people affected—had always been anonymous, and she'd known her activities wouldn't cause them any irreparable harm. In fact, she'd been convinced she was serving the greater good.

But she couldn't use Dominic this way. He trusted her, and she couldn't violate that. Even though she knew she was making the wrong choice, and people might get hurt because of it.

Somehow, the idea that she'd hurt Dominic was worse. She was choosing *him* over her friends. Over Bennett Security. What kind of person did that make her?

A tear ran down her cheek, and she swiped it away.

She had to go tell Max she'd fucked up. They'd come up with some other plan to go after the Syndicate. At least, she prayed they would.

Sylvie pulled her sleeve over her hand and wiped off the laptop and its keyboard, just in case. The flash drive returned to her back pocket.

She rushed back out into the hallway. There was no way she could sleep tonight, but at least she could spend the hours until daylight brainstorming how she was going to make up for this.

But halfway back to her room, she collided with something solid in the dark.

"Sylvie? What are you doing out here?"

It was Dominic.

Shit.

More lies and excuses flew to her lips, but she wouldn't let them out. She couldn't bear it, not anymore. "I thought I had to do something. But I changed my mind. What are *you* doing?"

"The same."

He reached over and switched on the light. His sharp gaze studied her. Dominic looked past her shoulder, as if trying to puzzle out where she'd just been.

"Were you in my office?" A quirk of his mouth suggested he was kidding, but his eyes said otherwise. "Were you spying on me, Sylvie?"

She took a step back. Then another. If she yelled for Tanner, how fast could he get here?

Was she honestly worrying about whether she needed her bodyguard right now?

"What's wrong?" His eyebrows drew down. "Jesus. Are you afraid of me?"

"Should I be?"

He drew his hand across his eyes and leaned into the wall. "God, no. I'd *never* want you to be afraid of me. I don't care what you were doing."

She pushed out a guilty breath. "You sure about that?" Sylvie wasn't afraid of him. But maybe she did want his anger. She deserved it.

Her fingers went to her back pocket and took out the flash drive. She held it up.

Dominic stared at the piece of plastic. But he didn't do any of the things she'd expected. He didn't grab it away from her, didn't demand to know what it was. Instead, a look of profound sadness passed across his face.

Then he laughed.

Dominic stuck a hand in his own pocket and pulled out another USB flash drive.

Her stomach flipped. "What the hell is that?"

"Show me yours, I'll show you mine?"

Chapter Twenty

Sylvie grabbed his arm. Dominic let himself be dragged down the hall into her room. She pushed him inside and closed the door. "Are you sure we can talk freely in here?"

"Pretty sure. It's not bugged. But I can't discount my uncle's people using parabolic microphones."

"There are more Bennett Security bodyguards patrolling the neighborhood. So that's doubtful."

"Of course there are."

Dominic pulled up a classical playlist on his phone to add background noise, just in case Sylvie's friends were listening in, too. He didn't want anyone overhearing this conversation.

They each set their thumb drives on the dresser. His was black. Hers was red.

"Explain," she demanded.

"You first."

"No."

She'd been in his office. He was sure of it. She'd probably been messing with his computer. The situation was dripping with irony, and he'd never liked those kinds of books. The dark dramas where people do terrible things to each other, all under the mistaken belief that it's necessary.

Maybe because his regular life too often fit that description.

A few minutes ago, he'd snuck out of his own room and come to Sylvie's after he was sure she'd be asleep. He'd confirmed her lights were off and soundlessly opened the door. He hadn't even glanced at her bed to see that she was there, just reached immediately for the laptop bag where he'd seen it when he said good night.

He'd had her laptop in one hand, the USB drive in the other. But then, his limbs had stopped cooperating. He just couldn't plug the damn thing in. Couldn't do it. So he'd quietly replaced her computer, backed out of her room, and carefully shut the door.

Then who did he run into in the hallway but Sylvie herself?

Apparently, she'd had more balls than he did.

"What did you do?" he asked.

"Nothing."

"Neither did I."

"Bullshit."

"Right back at you."

Sylvie leaned on the edge of the dresser. She spun one of the flash drives around like a top. "I'm curious. Is your uncle really threatening your brother? Or was that just a new lie to manipulate me into trusting you?"

"I would *never* lie about Raymond."

"Just about yourself? I know you must've faked that murder attempt. Maureen's screams? The blood on the door? What a touch of drama."

"Are you kidding? They shot at me. You know that. You were here."

"Yes, very conveniently. After you insisted I come back to fix your supposedly 'glitchy' security system."

"Hey, yesterday you showed up at *my* door. Claiming you missed me? You wanted to see me? I should've known better." He felt pathetic to have imagined she liked him.

"I did want to see you, and I felt terrible about hiding my ulterior motive. I hated lying. But you clearly had no problem with it whatsoever. Pretending you liked me in your texts? Asking me to spend the night? 'We'll see what happens?'"

His gut twisted with shame. "I know. I'm sorry. But later, I practically hinted that you should go home because I didn't want to do this. I tried to tell you the truth, that I had no decent choices and didn't want to betray someone and hurt them."

"Right. Blame me for not interpreting your veiled warning. Why not try air traffic control signals? I wouldn't have understood those either."

This argument was pointless. They were wasting time. Sandford had threatened her.

Dominic dug his hands into his hair. "Sylvie, I need to know what you did. If my uncle and the people he's working with find out you're trying to mess with them, they won't hesitate to kill you. They have no scruples."

"Unlike you?"

"If you think I'm the worst there is, then you're fucking naive."

"I didn't do *anything*. I chickened out because I felt bad about betraying your trust. I was under the momentary impression you deserved better. Shows how stupid I am."

"You didn't use whatever's on that flash drive?"

"*No.*"

He closed his eyes, sinking on the bed. "Thank god. Neither did I."

"Well, I stopped the loader before it was finished."

"Wait, you what? You *plugged it in*? These people are watching everything that's on my computer. They might've seen what you were doing."

She made a face. "No, they couldn't. I'm not some amateur."

"What does that mean?"

"It means I have skills. Those assholes aren't going to catch me. If I'd loaded that malware onto your laptop like I'd intended, they still wouldn't know about it."

"What malware? What does it do?"

"Probably the same kind of thing you have on your flash drive. You were supposed to load it onto my computer, right? A rootkit to install a back door in my system, bundled with a payload that would steal my info. Maybe bots to spread onto the Bennett Security network. And of course, it would report everything back to the people who made it, all while staying perfectly hidden."

"And that's what you were going to install on *my* computer?"

"To go after the black-hat hackers who work for your uncle. *You* were trying to give them access to Bennett Security. After Max trusted you and tried to help you."

Dominic clenched his teeth together.

"Weren't you?" she demanded. "That's what you wanted. To hurt Bennett Security."

"I never wanted this. I had no clue about the first attack. And the thing tonight—I wanted nothing to do with it."

"But you were still going to help your uncle."

"No wasn't an option. I didn't go through with it."

"But you considered it."

"So did you. You plugged your drive in. *I* didn't do that."

"But at least I'm on the right side of things! I was trying to work *against* the Syndicate. You're still working *for* it. And you always will, won't you? Because it's the 'family business.' Because you're Dominic Crane."

He shot up to standing and advanced on her, forcing her back up against the wall. "You think I want to be? You think I like being defined by my family name? Trapped by their expectations? I've never been good enough, but they won't let me go, either. All my life, nobody except my brothers has cared about me as a person. Everyone else has only wanted what they could use me for."

Sylvie had said earlier that evening, right to his face, that she didn't want to use him. Liar.

She must've been thinking the same thing because she averted her eyes. "As a kid, I felt trapped by my family, too. So I left. I started all over again. It was scary, but I did it. I didn't just sit around making excuses."

Dominic braced his arm on the wall over her head. He glared down at her. "Then I guess you're stronger than me. You're lucky I managed to find the willpower not to fuck you earlier."

"Because you felt too guilty? You're right. That does surprise me."

"I still thought about it. I was tempted." He brought his other hand to the wall at her side, caging her in. "If I'd been willing, would you have fucked me? Even with what you were planning later?"

Sylvie's gaze lifted to his. Her chest heaved as she tried to catch her breath. Her plump mouth was slightly open, and she smelled like heat and anger and desire.

Sylvie thought he was the bad guy? Fine. He would be.

He lowered his head until his lips were an inch from her ear. Close enough she'd feel his whisper against her skin. "Admit it. You still want to fuck me right now, even knowing what I am. Even though you hate me. You want me just as much as I want you."

She grabbed his face and crashed their mouths together.

His tongue pushed in, battling hers, trying to reassert control.

Her teeth bit hard into his lower lip, making him grunt with a mix of indignation and lust. Dominic pressed her to the wall, maneuvering his thigh in between her legs. His dick felt

long and heavy in his sweatpants, not even all the way
hard yet.

Her fingers dug into his hair and yanked, forcing his head
back. Then Sylvie put her hands to his shoulders and shoved.
His legs hit the bed. Another shove forced him to sit on the
mattress.

Her eyes were wild with fury. He thought she'd had
enough, that she might even slap him.

But instead, she went to her knees in front of him and
yanked down the waistband of his sweats, uncovering his
growing erection.

His brain was still trying to process these new develop-
ments when her lips closed around his shaft and sucked.

"Fucking hell."

Oh, yes. This is happening.

Her mouth was rough and aggressive, like she was trying
to punish him by devouring his cock. It was right on the edge
between pain and pleasure. Her tongue pushed into his slit,
and he braced his hands behind him on the mattress as light-
ning bolts of heat traveled up and down his spine.

Sylvie lifted off of him, and her fingers took hold of his
length instead, her tongue moving down to lap at his balls.
Dominic almost came when her mouth closed around his sac.

"Shit," he moaned. "Stop. I'm going to…"

"This isn't what you wanted?" Sylvie stroked him a few
more times, like she was daring him to come, before backing
off. She stood up, her lips swollen from sucking him. Her
glasses were askew on her nose.

"I'll show you what I want." His fingers wrenched open
her pajama top, sending a couple of buttons flying. Creamy
skin appeared, rosy-tipped breasts. So beautiful. He teased one
nipple with his teeth while he tugged the other between his
knuckles.

"*Yes*. Just like that." Sylvie dug her hands into his hair
again and pulled.

He didn't want to think about what they were doing, or why. Dominic didn't want to be her enemy. But if this was the only way he could have her—savage and angry—then so be it.

Sylvie couldn't stand him, but she wanted to fuck him. He'd happily oblige.

He pushed her pajama pants and her panties over her narrow hips. She stepped out of them. Dominic shucked off his sweats the rest of the way and kicked them aside.

Sylvie fisted the edge of his tee. His arms lifted as she pulled the shirt over his head. They were both naked now. Her eyes went molten as she looked at his body. He looked right back.

Some might've called her figure boyish, but to Dominic, it was all soft femininity. The long slope of her stomach, a slight flare where her hips curved into her thighs.

"My turn." She straddled his lap and pushed him back onto the mattress. He let her kiss him until they were both breathless, hips grinding together. He used one hand to cup the back of her thigh, fingers sliding toward the juncture between her legs. So wet. He loved how turned on she was.

"I need you up here so I can taste you." Dominic lifted her by the hips, encouraging her to crawl upward. He kept moving her up his body until her knees were spread to either side of his face. Fuck, yes. One of his favorite views. Gorgeous pink folds, right there within easy reach. The scent of her was musky and primal, calling to some wild part of him deep in his chest.

"Hands on the headboard."

"You're bossy." But he saw her take hold of the top of the bed.

Two of his fingers spread her even wider. Then he shoved his tongue inside her.

Her answering moan send thrills of pleasure to the base of his spine. He backed off a bit, kissing her inner thighs.

"Did I say you could stop?" She was angling her pelvis toward his mouth, obviously ready for him.

Dominic smiled and lapped at her with the flat of his tongue. He nibbled and sucked at her, not worrying if she was headed toward an orgasm, just following her gasps and shouts.

"You'd better be quiet up there, unless you want your bodyguard to think you're being mauled."

Sylvie pushed herself against his mouth in reply. He fucked her with his tongue, and she made little high-pitched panting noises. Dominic's cock was achingly hard, leaking all over his stomach.

Suddenly she sat to one side. "Wait. We should—"

Dominic got up to his knees and cut off her words with a fierce, messy kiss. He didn't want her to reflect on how much she despised him, how they shouldn't be doing this. He couldn't stand to hear the contempt in her voice. Sylvie melted against him, gripping his shoulders as he lowered her back to the mattress.

Her thigh rubbed his erection. He rutted against her, desperate for the feeling of her skin. The thought of being inside of her, fucking her with that same savage intensity he'd seen in her eyes, sent jolts of need through his body.

"Tell me you want me," he murmured. He really hoped she had a condom.

"Ye—wait, no. *No*." She pushed him off her.

Damn. She'd come to her senses a lot faster than he had.

"We need to talk. We can't just fuck like all the other stuff didn't happen."

"We can't?" His massive hard-on begged to differ.

"*No*, Dominic. We can't." She scrambled up against the headboard, pulling the blanket partway over her nakedness. "I need to know what your uncle will do when he finds out you didn't install that program. Will he hurt you? Or Raymond?"

He'd been trying not to think about that. "He won't

realize it till tomorrow, at the earliest. I'll figure something out."

"I want to help you."

Dominic crawled up to sit beside her, pushing his dick with his hand to calm it down. "You sure about that?"

"Of course. I don't hate you. I could never hate you now that I…know you."

"That's the nicest thing anyone's ever said to me." He only wished that were a joke.

"But we have to trust each other. For real this time."

He exhaled. "Then the answer's yes. My Uncle Charles will hurt me and Raymond once he realizes I failed to follow instructions. And Maureen. Sylvie, he threatened *you* as well." Dominic put his arm around her and drew her against him. "I'm afraid of what could happen." He couldn't bear to lose *anyone* he cared about, including her.

"I've got Tanner and the other bodyguards I work with. And I texted Max tonight about putting a detail on Raymond. They're going to stay hidden so the Syndicate doesn't find out."

Dominic closed his eyes as anxiety filled his stomach. His erection was gone. "Your friends are that good? If the Syndicate sees Bennett Security watching my brother, they'll blame me."

"They *are* that good. But it's only temporary because we'll get Raymond to safety. And you and Maureen. I'll make calls in the morning."

Dominic looked down at her. She sounded so confident. But how many times had he faked his way through, hiding the confusion that ate him up inside? "You're sure the rest of Bennett Security will agree with you?"

"I'll convince Max, and he's all we need. And don't worry about the flash drives. I have ideas for how to buy us some time. Do you trust me enough to let me handle this?"

"I trust you." If anyone could actually help him, he believed it was Sylvie. "If you can honestly say you trust me."

She caressed his cheek. Her blue eyes studied him. Sylvie pulled his head lower, so their noses touched. "I want to trust you. So I will."

Her lips met his, softly at first. Their tongues brushed. Their kisses grew hotter, deeper, more intense. Not angry. Not like before.

Dominic thought of the way Sylvie had played the violin. His hand traveled down her body, firm but gentle, relishing every inch of bare skin.

"Everything else can wait until morning, right?" he said. "Come to my room. Spend the night in my bed."

"I want that. Want *you*."

Arousal sped down his vertebrae.

It meant a lot to him that she'd said she trusted him, even if he hadn't given her much reason to. She trusted him simply because she chose to. He intended to live up to her show of faith.

He was choosing to trust her, too, because he couldn't bear the alternative.

To so many people, he was the bad guy. But he'd never wanted that. *Especially* not with Sylvie. *This* was his defiance of all the ugliness and cruelty he'd seen in his life—to be sweet and tender and real with someone else, and to get the same in return.

Chapter Twenty-One

They snuck down the dark hallway to a set of double doors. Dominic held one open. "Go ahead."

Sylvie walked inside. She was wearing her pajama top, and Dominic had put his sweats back on. He followed and switched on a lamp at his bedside, filling the room with a soft glow.

"This used to be my parents' room, but I gutted it and redid the whole thing when I moved in here."

All the furniture was constructed of pale wood in a modern, Scandinavian style. The walls were white, with gauzy curtains hanging over the patio doors that led out to a balcony. Black and white photographs hung in frames on every wall, many of them of tropical ocean landscapes and snowy mountain peaks. Two different kinds of extremes.

He went back to the doors and flipped the lock. "What do you think?"

Sylvie sat on his California king bed. A pale blue comforter was folded up at the end of it, and his white cotton sheets were tangled, like he didn't often bother to make them. "I was expecting a sex dungeon draped with black silk."

He snorted. "That's totally my usual vibe, but Maureen complained laundry day was hell."

The room was beautiful, almost austere in its simple coloring and clean lines. A dramatic contrast to the decorating style she'd seen in the rest of the house. But this room was also a place she could imagine curling up. A place she could relax and just be.

"I don't see how you ever leave this spot."

He sat beside her on the bed, folding his legs beneath him. "So you like it?"

She gave him a quick kiss on the lips. "Are you really asking if I like *you*?"

He gave her that soft, sweet smile that she was starting to enjoy even more than his wicked one.

"I do," she whispered. "I like you."

She couldn't describe her relief at knowing he hadn't lied. And knowing she hadn't betrayed him.

Sylvie glanced at her bag, which she'd dropped just inside the entrance to the room. It now held the two flash drives. She'd told him she trusted him, and she really wanted that to be true. Her heart was ready to take the risk, even though her rational mind was still a step or two behind.

There was no way this alliance would work if they couldn't be honest with one another. Thank goodness she hadn't done anything irreparable, and neither had he.

She still felt wary about the fact that he'd been working against Bennett Security. But he hadn't actually gone through with it. Wasn't that what counted?

"I like you, too," he said.

"For saying nice things to you instead of being mean?"

He shrugged one shoulder. "I'm easy that way."

She wished they'd been open with each other from the start. The man she'd been getting to know the past few days was the *real* Dominic Crane, and she wished she'd never doubted him.

But she still needed to get back to Bennett Security to inspect that program on Dominic's flash drive and find out exactly what it contained. She would need to send this latest info to her hacker friends to see what they made of it.

She already had several ideas to turn this around on the Syndicate and make their latest attempt work in her favor. But it would have to be creative and subtle. If the Syndicate's Russian hackers-for-hire were anywhere near as good as they seemed so far, anything less would raise their suspicions in no time.

Normally, the late hour wouldn't have stopped her from getting started on a project. But she couldn't safely inspect the program here, and she couldn't just take off in the middle of the night. The Syndicate would wonder why she'd left Dominic's house.

So her work had to wait until the morning. Like she'd said.

Or maybe those were all excuses. Maybe she just wanted this time with Dominic, and she was willing to set everything else aside for a little while to get it. She'd given so much of her life to Bennett Security. She wanted a few, impossible moments only for herself.

He came in for another slow kiss. "I'll show you how much I like you. I can be rough if that's how you want me."

"No, I like this Dominic better." Her fingers ran along his chin and down his neck, feeling the throb of his pulse just under the skin.

His smile told her that he approved of that answer. "But I have ground rules."

She pulled back. "*You* have ground rules?"

"Yep. Just one: no orgasms. For either of us."

"You're kidding." Sylvie rolled her eyes. "You don't have to hold back so I can keep up. That's like...a participation trophy."

"We're not running a race or competing. We're having an

experience together. Wouldn't you rather go at the same pace?"

She pointed at the erection once again tenting his sweat-pants. "You're already way ahead of me, and I've barely touched you in the last half hour."

"What, you don't think I can keep myself from coming?"

"I like the *idea* of it. But honestly? I don't."

"You think I'm too weak?"

"I'm not taking that bait."

"Then you must be issuing a challenge."

Sylvie looked over at him. "A challenge? But it won't be. You don't think I can *make* you come if I want to?" Maybe he couldn't do the same to her. But men weren't so difficult. Every man she'd ever been with, anyway.

"That's dirty. Challenge accepted."

"Fine, if you insist on turning this into a game... I'll make you feel so good you won't be able to stop yourself from going off."

He grinned as he kissed her. "Just watch me."

"We'll see."

Sylvie set her glasses on the nightstand. She moved higher on his bed, positioning herself with her back against his pillows. Keeping her knees together, she slowly undid the remaining buttons on her pajama top. But she didn't take it off, instead letting it fall open to either side of her. Next, she trailed her hand over her breasts and down to her core. She spread her legs just enough to allow her fingers to massage over her most sensitive parts.

"You'll have to do better than that," Dominic said.

She smiled at him, still taking her time. She remembered what he'd said when they were first fooling around in his game room. How he wanted to see how she touched herself. Sylvie hadn't done this in a while because it made her frustrated about her body's lack of cooperation. But it did feel good.

And it felt even better with Dominic's heated gaze running over her.

She let her knees fall open a bit wider, moaning as her fingers slid deeper into her center.

Dominic pushed his pants off, his erection bobbing. He crawled over the mattress to her. She'd been surprised earlier that he was uncircumcised, but it didn't bother her. She liked that he was different from every other man she'd been with.

Everything with him was different. Uncertain and reckless and a pure adrenaline rush. She didn't want it to end.

Dominic reached over to a drawer in his nightstand and pulled out a tiny bottle. "You already look wet. But this could make it feel even better."

She held out her hand, and he poured a dime sized amount of lube into her fingers. She brought it to her clit, loving the way the liquid made her fingertips glide against her skin. It was downright indulgent. She closed her eyes, her head falling back against the pillows. Her legs opened wider, unable to resist the urge to quicken the pace and turn up the pressure.

She heard the drawer of Dominic's nightstand slide out again. Sylvie opened her eyes to see him holding a short, thick, cylindrical vibrator. It was pointed slightly at one end.

"I was feeling a lot more optimistic about my love life when I bought this. It's new, never been used. Want to try?"

Sylvie held out her hand, but he shook his head, his grin widening. "Nope, this is mine. If you want it, I get to use it on you."

"Okay, but I get to pick the position. Lie down." She sat up and shook her pajama top the rest of the way off.

His eyebrows raised, but he did as she said, lying down across the middle of the mattress. Sylvie straddled his face like she had earlier in the guestroom, but this time, she was facing the opposite direction. His cock was right under her mouth, lying flat against his stomach.

She gave him a nice long lick, from his tip to his balls. A lusty sound rumbled from Dominic's chest.

Sylvie felt him rise up and brace his elbows against the mattress. His tongue lapped between her legs. She gasped. But she wasn't going to let him distract her.

She had a challenge to win.

Her fist circled his shaft, pointing him upright toward her mouth. She suctioned her lips around him and swirled her tongue across his slit, which he'd really seemed to like earlier.

A buzzing sound stole her attention just before she felt contact against her clit. She moaned around his cock. Dominic moved the vibrator in small circles. The lube kept the friction just right, not too intense.

"How's that?"

Fucking amazing. Delicious tension flooded her body. She didn't bother to answer. Instead, she took in more of his length. She worked him up and down with her mouth. His hips started to buck. Sylvie added a hand between his legs, massaging his balls. They'd tightened against his body.

For a little while, she forgot anything except how much she enjoyed giving pleasure. There was something so satisfying about making a man come. After all their battles, making Dominic lose control would be even better.

She wanted to taste his cum on her tongue. The vibrator on her clit just added to the experience.

Dominic was panting. Close. The vibrator kept slipping, like he could hardly concentrate.

Then his arms lifted her off him, and his cock fell out of her mouth. He dropped her onto the mattress. "Nope. We're done with that."

"Not fair! That's cheating. I almost had you."

"Exactly. I had to make you stop." He scrambled off the bed, reaching down to squeeze the base of his shaft. "Shit. I almost lost it. That was way too close."

She lay back against the pillows. "You're too far away. I miss you."

"I know what you're doing. I need to calm down first."

Sylvie picked up the vibrator and held it against her opening, teasing herself with it. "I wish you were the one doing this, instead of me."

"Now who's not playing fair?"

The pointed end pressed inside of her, stretching her. "Come over here and fuck me."

Dominic wiped sweat from his face, but his eyes were locked on the vibrator between her legs. The tip of his cock glistened, both from her mouth and his precum.

"Goddammit." He frantically searched inside the nightstand and grabbed a foil-wrapped condom. His fingers shook as he tore the edge of the wrapper and rolled the latex down over his length.

The cap on the lube bottle made a snapping sound. Shiny liquid poured onto his cock, and his hand spread it around.

Sylvie tossed the vibrator aside and heard it roll to the floor. Dominic knelt on the mattress. He held onto her thighs and yanked her lower, so she was lying flat on her back. He braced one hand on the bed, the other hooking below her knee and bending her leg.

Sylvie cried out as he entered her in one smooth motion.

"Not so loud. I don't want your bodyguard banging down my door."

She pushed her lips together, muffling her next moan.

He fucked her with lazy strokes, clearly in no hurry. And she wasn't either. She wrapped her legs around him and enjoyed the sensations as he filled her again and again.

Dominic wasn't overly muscled, but his arms and stomach were lean and defined. She gripped his biceps, feeling the strength coiled up beneath the surface of the skin. His chest was smooth, hairless, with pale pink nipples. Dark waves fell across his forehead and into his eyes. She reached up to brush the strands away and tuck them behind his ear. He smiled down at her.

"You're beautiful," he murmured.

"I think that was my line."

"I don't just mean on the outside."

"Neither do I."

Sylvie's heart was swelling in her chest. It scared her, what she was feeling right now—like she wanted a lot more with Dominic Crane than could ever be possible. They had a surprising number of things in common. But their lives and their backgrounds were fundamentally different. Incompatible.

Stop thinking about the end, she told herself.

"Can we flip over?" she asked. "I want to be on top."

He grasped the edge of the condom and pulled out. They changed positions, Dominic lying flat, and Sylvie poised over him. She spread her legs and guided him inside of her.

He made a humming sound. "That's so good."

She arched her spine, bracing her hands back against his thighs as she rocked back and forth on his dick. That tension was building inside of her again, pleasure that teased her and only made her long for more. Dominic held her hips, pumping to match her every thrust. He made her feel so sexy and so dirty.

"I want to feel your cock pulsing as you shoot every last drop of your hot cum inside of me."

His eyes rolled back. "*Fuck*, Sylvie."

She leaned forward to whisper to him. "Please, Nic? Come for me?"

"*So* not fair."

"I want to feel you."

She rode him hard. Dominic matched her intensity. His dick jerked as he started to come, shuddering as their bodies slammed together. Sylvie closed her eyes, reveling in every throb of his shaft inside of her. She didn't know how it would

feel to orgasm herself, but this had to be the next best thing—
feeling him come undone. And it had nothing to do with their
silly challenge.

Dominic pulled her down against his chest, stroking her
hair. "I don't think I've ever enjoyed losing so much."

She didn't think she'd enjoyed *anything* so much. Sex with
Dominic had been utterly satisfying. Sylvie didn't feel like
she'd missed out on a single thing. But she already knew how
much she'd miss him when he was gone. Because this couldn't
last. And no matter how long they had, it wouldn't be enough.

Chapter Twenty-Two

*D*ominic had thought Sylvie riding his cock by moonlight had been pretty damned spectacular. But Sylvie half asleep in his bed while morning sun streamed through the windows? Breathtaking.

He reached for her hand and brought it to his mouth, pressing a kiss to her knuckles.

She yawned. "What time is it?"

It was late enough that he didn't want to tell her. She'd rush off. "Around breakfast. We can stay here a while longer."

"If you say so." She put her arms around his neck and cuddled against him. Her eyes closed like she was dozing.

He pretended that she was just a girl he liked, and that he was just a guy. A guy who didn't have a stupid fucking ankle monitor attached to his leg.

She had called him Nic. He'd never asked another woman to call him that, not even his girlfriends. It felt intimate. Not in a sexual way, but deeper than that. More true. It was a name only people who cared about him had ever used.

Assuming Sylvie cared about him. He was fairly sure she did, and that was pretty amazing. It felt like winning the lottery on his birthday, nothing he'd ever expected or thought he deserved.

Some of his exes had called him "Dom" as a nickname, thinking he'd like it. That kind of a name went with the sex dungeon image, which Sylvie had laughed at because it was so ridiculous. He didn't have any problem with other people getting kinky. More power to them. But it just wasn't his thing. It didn't fit him, like clothes that belonged to somebody else.

Sylvie saw that. She saw *him*.

He had no idea what he was going to do to fix the mess he was in. But he liked to think Sylvie would stick around through the hard parts and then... What? He couldn't even imagine a life past the current crisis. His life had always been the Syndicate. But whatever it looked like, he wanted Sylvie to be there.

"What are you going to tell Max?" Dominic asked.

He didn't want to inject reality into the little fairytale they had going this morning. But it was getting late, and they'd have to leave the refuge of his bed before long.

"I need to explain about the flash drive Sandford gave you, and what he expected you to do with it. But there's something I need to know." She lay on her side to face him. "Are you planning to go back to the Syndicate?"

He chewed the inside of his lip.

"Planning on it? No."

"Dominic, I'm going to take down those Russian hackers, but the endgame is going after your uncle and the Syndicate itself. Max and I aren't working with law enforcement yet, but we will if we have to. And I'm going to tell Lana what Sandford's been up to. I'm not keeping any secrets for you."

"I know. I expected that."

"But you can't play both sides. I can't..." Sylvie sat up against the pillows, grabbing the sheet to cover herself. "I can't let how I feel about you cloud my judgment on this. The only way I can help you is if I know you won't interfere."

"How *do* you feel about me?"

Her eyes slid over to meet his. "Like I'd do pretty much anything to make sure you're safe. That's what scares me."

Dominic rested his head against her shoulder. She'd asked him serious questions, and he owed her serious answers.

Taking down the Syndicate... Every time that idea had crossed his mind before, he'd dismissed it. But maybe he'd been holding onto the idea of the Crane "family business" more than anything else. The Cranes hadn't been a real family since he was a kid. So there was nothing *real* for him to hold onto at all.

Dominic was afraid his older brother wouldn't forgive him for betraying the Syndicate, but what stake did Warren have in the business at this point? Once Warren got out of prison, Charles would probably put a hit on him. It might even start another war.

Dominic's father barely knew his own name because of the dementia. His mom had given up on their old life years ago. And Raymond was never going to get started on that path in the first place.

Sylvie had said she'd do anything to keep him safe. Had anyone ever felt something like that for him before? He doubted it. Not even Warren.

"We agreed last night that we'll trust each other," he said. "I meant it. I'm going to keep you safe, too. You and Raymond. Even if I have to destroy the Syndicate to do it."

"Does that mean testifying against them, like Lana wants?"

Nausea welled up in his throat, but he only hesitated a moment. "If that's what it takes, I will. I guess I'll need to reconsider that safe house she offered."

Sylvie cupped his cheek and kissed him. He pulled her down so that her body stretched over his. There were no sheets between them, nothing but skin and sweat and longing.

Their mouths were hungry for each other, hands desperate to touch and to please.

He'd never felt this kind of need for another person. It was like a live wire inside him, lighting him up but burning him, too. She was right here in front of him, but that wasn't close enough.

A phone rang. Damn it, no.

"Shit, that's mine." Sylvie jumped out of his arms. Dominic flopped back onto the pillows.

She dashed across the room and dug into her laptop bag. "It's Tanner." She answered it. "Yeah, everything's fine. I'll be down in a minute."

She turned around, a sheepish look on her face. "Tanner saw I wasn't in my room. Did you know it was almost ten o'clock?"

"That's still breakfast time, isn't it?"

"Not when I'm supposed to be at work by eight." She wiped her hand over her face. "I need to check my messages. Why don't you take a shower while I try to catch up on things?"

He kicked his legs off the bed. "You don't want to shower with me?"

A smile twitched at the corner of her mouth. "Of course I do. That's exactly why I can't. I have to get going."

DOMINIC JOGGED downstairs and went straight to the kitchen. His hair was still damp, leaving droplets of water on the shoulders of his white T-shirt.

Tanner looked up as he came in. The bodyguard was sitting at his usual stool by the counter. Maureen was emptying clean dishes from the dishwasher. "So you've decided to make an appearance. Tanner and I enjoyed our breakfast quite a while ago."

"She made beignets."

Maureen nodded. "Just like Café du Monde in New Orleans. We were going to save some for you, but you know how the saying goes."

"Snooze, you lose," Tanner finished with a laugh.

"Assuming all you were doing was snoozing?" Maureen lifted two skeptical brows.

"Have you two been practicing this comedy routine all morning?" Their teasing couldn't ruin his mood. He was too happy and sexually satisfied, even though he and Sylvie didn't get another round this morning.

Dominic was glad Tanner didn't seem weird about the sleeping-with-Sylvie thing. Generally, Tanner seemed like a good guy. He hadn't made Dominic feel completely worthless, so in his book, that qualified as a friendship.

But then again, the bodyguard had probably known about Sylvie's true mission here. And that meant he assumed Sylvie had slept with him in order to get close enough to install her virus thing on his computer.

So maybe Tanner wasn't as innocent as he seemed.

Maureen poured Dominic a cup of coffee and gave him a bagel, since the beignets were gone. Tanner wandered off, probably in search of Sylvie.

"You're rarely so chipper before noon. I assume you and Sylvie had a nice night?"

Dominic sipped his coffee, leaning against the counter. "We did." He didn't try to hide his grin.

"It's lovely to see you smiling."

"I can't even remember..." He didn't finish the thought. He knew Maureen understood. He was happier right now than he'd been in ages, despite the danger they were in.

Maureen finished with the dishwasher. She grabbed a towel to wipe off the countertops. "I just hope you two know what you're doing. It seems to me a little odd that Sylvie and her bodyguard would turn up here so soon after your lawyer did."

"What do you know about Sandford's visit? I told you to wait in your room while he was here."

She gave him a wry look. "And you think I do every little thing you say? I can hear a conversation in the living room from over in the hallway. I heard what Sandford asked you to do."

"I wish you hadn't." Dominic hung his head. He couldn't believe she hadn't said anything. "And you think I went through with it? I didn't."

"I'm not judging. I know you care for Sylvie, that's obvious. But this situation is as messy as mud season. I just don't want to see either of you getting hurt. I almost said something last night, but… It's been so long since you had a friend."

That made him feel pathetic. "I know my life has been really messed up for a while. But last night, Sylvie and I talked about everything. She knows the truth, and she's going to help me fix things."

Maureen glanced over her shoulder, checking that the others weren't close by. "But don't you think you've let other people control you for far too long already? Expecting Sylvie to fix things is the same as putting all the responsibility on her shoulders. All the *power*. Isn't it past time you were responsible for yourself?"

He set his cup roughly on the counter. Coffee sloshed over the side. "I like you, Maureen, and I'll let you get away with pretty much anything. But you're going too far. I *am* doing something." He dropped his voice to a whisper, though his tone remained harsh. "I'm going to testify against the Syndicate. I'm going to help take them down." He prayed that Maureen wouldn't disapprove. "And I'm going to make sure you and everyone else who's important to me is safe. Sylvie is trusting me. I hope you will, too."

She patted his arm. "Oh, Dominic. I've always trusted

you. And I've always known you were capable of so much more than you believed. But you prove your worth through your actions, not by making plans or promises."

She didn't think he'd go through with it.

He picked up his coffee mug and put it in the sink. "I'll prove myself. You'll see."

Maureen had it wrong. He wasn't putting all the responsibility on Sylvie's shoulders. He did need Sylvie's help and her support. That was the only path forward.

But in the end, Dominic was the one who'd have to face down his uncle and his former allies. He was the one who'd carry the burden of being a traitor.

Chapter Twenty-Three

*S*ylvie walked into the Bennett Security workroom, but she didn't make it as far as Max's office. Her boss saw her come in and hurried over to meet her. "Where the hell have you been?"

She nodded goodbye to Tanner, who was quickly making his way toward the elevator, probably hoping to avoid Max's wrath.

"I got held up. There's a lot to discuss."

"I sure hope so. Did you install your malware on Crane's network?"

Sylvie glanced around at her coworkers. They all appeared to be busy at their workstations, but she was sure they were listening. If this got a little too personal, she didn't want them to hear.

And damn it, she felt protective of Dominic now. She didn't like Max talking about him in front of everyone. "Could we go up to your office please? It would be better if we discuss things there."

Grumbling, Max led her up the open-riser staircase. She made sure his door was closed before she started to speak.

"I didn't install the programs I wrote."

Max had just sat down behind his desk, but now he rock-eted back up. "What? Why the hell not?"

Sylvie blinked slowly, trying to figure out how to say this. The same thing she'd been doing this morning while Dominic thought she was sleeping, and later, while Tanner drove them to headquarters.

"Nothing went wrong, exactly. But I couldn't go through with it." She raised a hand when Max opened his mouth. "A lot's changed, and this would be better if you'd just let me explain. Can you do that, boss?"

Max sank back down into his chair. "Fine. But please, for the love of all things holy, don't tell me you chickened out because you're sleeping with the guy." He'd obviously been joking, but he faltered when he saw the look on Sylvie's face. "Oh god, no. You're kidding, right?"

"Just let me get this out, and you can save the lecture for later."

Sylvie explained how Dominic had asked her to spend the night, and how she'd planned to get access to his computer during her stay. Max kept quiet, though a muscle at his jaw kept clenching.

"But I didn't know Aaron Sandford—on behalf of the Syndicate—had already ordered Dominic to install something on *my* computer. I haven't examined it yet, but it's supposed to be an upgraded version of the one they tried to hit me with the last time. The whole purpose was to target Bennett Secu-rity. Dominic didn't tell them 'no' outright because they were threatening him. But he didn't do it, obviously. Instead, he told me the truth." That wasn't the exact chain of events, but it was close enough.

Her boss leaned his elbows on the desk. "Thank god for that. But I still don't understand why you failed to complete your mission. If Crane didn't catch you, what was the issue?"

"It could've put Nic in even worse danger if his uncle found out. And…I didn't want to keep lying to him."

"*Nic?* Sylvie, do you have feelings for this guy?"

She pressed her lips together. But that was all the answer Max needed.

"Jesus, I can't have you involved with this. You aren't objective."

"So what if I'm not objective? Nobody's truly objective. Not even you. We can trust Dominic. He wants his brother protected, and he wants out of the Syndicate. For *good.*"

"You're sure about that? There's no way he's playing you?"

"Completely sure. He said he's going to testify."

"Has he told Lana that? Has he signed a plea deal?"

"No. He only just made the decision. And—"

"Then he hasn't committed to *anything.*"

"I trust him, Max. He's…" She searched for the words. "He's different than we thought. Dominic never even wanted to be head of the Syndicate. I know it sounds messed up, but he's been trying to do the right thing. Growing up in a family like his, it's amazing that he ended up being decent at all."

Dominic was kind and funny and more accepting than most people Sylvie had ever met. But she didn't want to gush too much in front of Max. She didn't want him to know just how much she cared for Dominic Crane.

"You don't understand how hard it is to grow up a certain way and figure out how to break free of that. It's scary. And Dominic actually had to deal with the threat of violence if he didn't go along. And despite all that, he's always tried to push back against it. Now he's finally ready to cut all those ties, and I know it's not going to be easy for him. But if he says he's doing it, then he will."

"I do understand something about messed up childhoods." Max ran his fingers through his hair. "But if you're vouching for him, then I'll take him at his word."

"Thank you." She hadn't realized until now how important it was that Max see the real Dominic, the way she did.

"But we need a plan of our own. What about those Russian hackers the Syndicate has working for them? What about everything we discussed before, about how they wouldn't stop coming after us?"

"I'm going to reprogram the Syndicate's malware and install it on my computer myself. But it'll have a stowaway along for the ride. When my supposedly stolen data goes back, I'll be able to infiltrate *them* myself."

"But if their program is on your machine, how will you keep them from accessing all of Bennett Security?"

"Because it won't truly be my computer. I'll create a decoy, set up to look like the real thing. And they don't know our protocols. I'll make them think that our system is so over-the-top secure that they can't get access beyond just my device. My decoy machine will have plenty of fake info to keep them occupied. It only has to fool them for a little while, long enough for me to get what I need on the Syndicate and for Dominic and his loved ones to get into a safe house. By the time the Syndicate realizes I've fooled them, our whole operation will be complete."

"Who's arranging the safe house transfer?"

"Lana and the Feds, I assume. Once they know Dominic will testify. But I'd appreciate if you helped."

"I'll talk to Lana and coordinate. I've already got guys on Dominic's younger brother, keeping their distance as you asked. But if there's any other way I can help make sure the Cranes get to safety, then I'll do it."

"Thank you, boss." Sylvie couldn't help herself. She went around his desk and gave him a hug. It was definitely a bad move according to those sexual-harassment videos, but she figured Max would understand where she was coming from.

He patted her on the back. "So you and Crane? I really didn't see that coming."

She laughed. "Neither did I."

Chapter Twenty-Four

*a*n hour after Sylvie left, Aaron Sandford called Dominic's phone. "I'm told by our computer experts that you haven't used that memory stick I gave you. What are you up to?"

Dominic was in the music room. He went over to close the door, glancing around the space, even though he knew there were no cameras here watching him. "We were a little busy last night."

"I'm sure you were. But even you can't go for *that* long. She was at your house over half a day."

"She's not stupid. She was going to notice if I started going through her things to mess with her laptop."

"Are you fucking with me right now? Do you think this is a game?"

Dread sat in Dominic's chest, squeezing his lungs, and making it hard to breathe. "I don't give a shit about you, Sandford. But I'm not messing with Charles. I wouldn't."

He kept his voice steady and confident. Sandford was used to him being defiant. If he started acting cowed at this point, the lawyer would get suspicious. But Dominic was out on a limb right now, further from safety than he'd ever been. One wrong step and he could fall.

"I'm lucky she was willing to see me again at all, after what happened before. You're the one who sent a gunman here and freaked her out."

"Yet she *did* come back. That's lucky."

"You told me to make it happen, and I did! Now you're acting like it's a problem?"

"She brought one of her coworkers from Bennett Security. You have to see why that raised my concern."

"The guy's her friend. He just sat in my kitchen the whole time and ate my food. Like you said before, getting women to like me is what I'm good at. But building trust doesn't happen in one night." He hated playing along this way, acting like he was just as despicable as some people believed. "I'm going to get this done, but you have to be patient."

"You don't tell Charles Traynor to be patient. He decides on what the timing should be, not you."

"But there's no point in rushing if it means she'll catch me in the act, right?"

A pause. "It's your job to make sure you're not caught. When exactly do you plan to get this finished? Tonight?"

He and Sylvie had already talked about this. She was going to need at least until tomorrow to finish her coding. "She can't come back today. But I'm planning to see her again tomorrow. I'll install the program then."

"See that you do. You've already witnessed how much patience your uncle has to spare for you. It's not much. If you don't deliver Bennett Security like you promised, then a lot of people are going to pay for it. You'll be wishing those thugs had finished you off when you were in jail."

Dominic punched "end" on the screen and tossed his phone onto the coffee table. He sank onto the couch, wiping his hands over his face.

What the hell am I doing? This is insane.

Ratting out the Syndicate? Going against Charles?

Why did I ever think I could do this?

But he'd told Sylvie he would. His word had never meant much, but she did. She trusted him. And Dominic knew this was the only way forward, even if it scared him more than anything had before.

He grabbed his other phone from the cabinet where he'd hidden it. The burner he'd been using to communicate with Sylvie. He needed to talk to Raymond. But could he risk it?

His thumbs moved over the screen.

Dominic: Hey kid, call me at this number when you get a chance.

Raymond would know it was him.

There was another person he needed to speak with today, too. Lana Marchetti. Sylvie had promised to pass along his burner number to Lana. So Dominic had to sit and wait for that call, too.

Sylvie was off doing all the work, and he was just sitting on his ass being useless.

He thought of what Maureen had said to him. That he was putting all the responsibility and power on Sylvie's shoulders. That he should be doing something to prove he could be responsible for himself.

Was she right?

No, she couldn't be. Testifying against the Syndicate would be doing plenty. If Lana would just call, then he could get the process in motion.

Before he lost his nerve.

∼

THE CALL finally came after lunch. His burner phone rang in his pocket. Not Raymond's number.

Dominic and Maureen were sitting out on the balcony.

Before he answered it, he nodded his head toward the patio doors. "DA's office," he whispered. Maureen understood and nodded. They went inside and up the stairs.

Dominic answered as they walked down the hallway toward the game room. "This is Dominic Crane."

"I think you know who this is," Lana said. "Can we talk?"

Maureen switched on the television and turned up the volume. Dominic was trying to take every precaution to keep the Syndicate from somehow listening in.

"Yes, we can talk."

"I have one of our investigators on the line with me. It's routine."

That made him nervous. But he said, "Okay."

"Does Aaron Sandford still represent you?"

"Not if I can help it."

"Then the first thing we should do is get you a new lawyer. I can arrange for a public defender. But we have to strike Sandford as your attorney of record so he can't make any more decisions for you."

Dominic was standing by the card table, and Maureen had taken a seat right beside him so she could hear most of the conversation. These decisions affected her safety too. Dominic had wanted her involved.

"That's a bad idea. The minute Sandford realizes I'm cutting him off, my uncle is going to come after me. It would be a declaration of war."

"So are you telling me that you're under duress, and you want to fire your lawyer but can't because he's threatened you?"

"Pretty sure I just said that."

"I have to be certain. Otherwise, it's unethical for me to be talking to you when you have counsel of record. But clearly, you're in a difficult position, and so am I. The offer the district attorney authorized me to make still stands. Full immunity if you agree to testify against your former allies in the Syndicate. Have you considered that offer?"

Dominic hated this kind of legal speak, where they kept talking around the issue. But at least Lana seemed to be getting to the point, even though she had to already know the answer.

"Yes, and I want to accept. I want to testify. But there's more I need in return. You mentioned a safe house before."

"That's right. Provided by the federal government. Nobody will be able to reach you there."

"I want my younger brother Raymond and my house-keeper Maureen brought with me as well. Sandford and my uncle have been threatening them."

"That can be arranged. But I'm also going to need a proffer of what you plan to testify to. So that my boss and I can be sure it'll be worth it on both sides. The US Attorney will want to make her own demands of you, too."

"I guess I can do that. But only after we're all in the safe house. I'm sure it'll take a while for me to go through every-thing I know." He felt sick at the idea of confessing his family's private information, everything he'd learned growing up as a Crane and then as a member of the Syndicate. It could prob-ably fill a book. And he knew he wouldn't come out looking good to anyone.

Once again, he'd be giving pretty much the entire world a reason to hate him, though for very different reasons. What would Sylvie say if she knew the full extent of the compro-mises he'd made? He'd done a few decent things, but could that wipe away even half the shit he'd failed to stop?

"Given the recent attempt on your life, I'm inclined to agree on arranging the safe house first. Especially now that we know it was Sandford's interference that kept you from going into protection before. But I need to be sure you're serious. This is going to be difficult, Dominic."

Maureen put her hand on his arm. He looked at her, and

she nodded her encouragement. *I've always known you were capable of so much more than you believed.* That was what she'd said to him that morning. He wanted to believe that, too.

"I'm ready. I want to do this."

"I'm very glad to hear that." He heard the smile in Lana's voice. The triumph. This could very well make her career, and he was happy at least one person could come out ahead from all of this.

"When do we get moved to the safe house?"

Lana sighed into the phone. "Well, time has passed since the attack on your house, so I'll need to speak to my contacts on the federal side of things to get everything arranged. There's a process. I'm hoping it won't be more than a week or two."

"A week or two? Do you have any idea how much could happen before then? My uncle is already impatient. Who knows what he'll decide to do to me in the next few days."

"If there's any reason to believe the Syndicate will make a move earlier, then we can speed things up. But nobody has touched you in almost two weeks. You haven't told me anything to make me think danger is imminent. And if we try to move you too soon, the danger will probably *become* imminent—because the Syndicate will be paying attention."

"That's true." Dominic thought of his plan with Sylvie to go after the Syndicate's Russian hackers. If the Syndicate realized what they were doing, then the danger was going to get extremely real. But Sylvie had also asked him not to discuss that aspect of their plan with Lana.

"So, you're saying if anything changes, you could move things up. Then I guess I'll let you know. If I see anybody charging at my door with a machine gun, I'll be sure to take a moment and give you a call."

"I know it's not ideal. If worse truly comes to worse, I'm sure Max could provide one of his own safe houses, though I'd have to get your bail conditions modified first to allow it."

And then Dominic would owe Max even more. "Maybe. I'll just take things one day at a time."

"That's wise. Let me get things moving, and I'll be in touch. This is a good number?"

"Yeah, until I let you know otherwise. And if Sandford talks to you—"

"Then I'll act like nothing whatsoever has changed. Don't worry, I can handle it. I'll also need contact information for your brother. Has Raymond agreed to go into protection?"

"Not yet. I'm trying to reach him, but it's not easy to make sure our conversation will be secure."

"Then get me his number, and I'll see what I can do. You believe he's in danger, and I assume you know what you're talking about. If he needs convincing, I can be pretty persuasive."

"I don't doubt it." Before she could hang up, he added, "Thank you, Lana. I appreciate this."

"I've been wanting to help you for a while after what you did for me. You might be surprised just how many people are willing to give second chances. All you have to do is ask."

Maureen squeezed his arm again.

"I'll try to keep that in mind."

Chapter Twenty-Five

*B*y the time Sylvie got home, she was an exhausted wreck. She'd spent hours poring over the code that she'd modified to trap the Syndicate's hackers. With the help of her entire team, she'd created her decoy hard drive, slightly altering the Bennett Security data so that nothing sensitive would be compromised.

Even by her standards, she'd gotten an insane amount done. But she still had more to do tomorrow before she returned to Dominic's house.

Despite all her anxiety about targeting the Syndicate, she still felt a thrill of eager anticipation to see him again. Not just to get naked with him, but to hold his hand and talk through everything they were both dealing with right now. She knew Dominic would listen. And he would share with her, too. Who would've thought he'd be so easy to talk to?

But Dominic was the same as he'd ever been. She was the one who'd been making unfair assumptions.

That made her wonder about other assumptions she'd been making. Including about her former best friend, Faith.

The birthday card was still sitting in her drawer, waiting to be opened.

Sylvie went through the door into the kitchen. Ethan was stirring a pot on the stove, and Luis was setting the table. Both men looked up and smiled as she came in. Between Dominic's house and the long hours at work, it felt like forever since she'd seen them both.

"Ethan, you're cooking? Did my birthday already come around again?"

Her cousin shrugged, but Luis barked a laugh. He'd worn his shoulder-length dark hair in a messy bun, and the sleeves of his white button-down were rolled up. "I'm the one who cooked. Ethan's just standing there stirring and hoping to take the credit."

"But I do make this part look good," her cousin said, posing with the spoon, which was all the more comical given his pleated khakis and polo. Stylish, Ethan was not.

Luis had made spaghetti Bolognese. Sylvie threw together a salad, and the three of them sat down to eat.

"Ethan tells me you've had some drama lately. You met someone?"

"And she spent the night at his place."

Sylvie passed the spaghetti. "I did meet someone."

"Is he special?" Luis asked.

She felt the smile inching across her face. "Yeah. He is." She thought about what she could say. "I feel good when I'm with him. Like I can say pretty much anything. We didn't get along at first, but that's because I didn't want to give him a chance. But he's won me over."

Luis and Ethan were both grinning, exchanging an amused glance.

"Sounds familiar," her cousin said. "So when do we get to meet him?" He bumped her foot under the table. "Or at least see a picture."

Sylvie figured she could dig up a mug shot of Dominic pretty easily, but no way was she doing that. She wasn't ready to reveal his identity to them yet. Not because she was embarrassed, but because it was all so new and uncertain at this point. And she didn't want them to see Dominic's past and make the same assumptions she had.

"I don't know. Things are a little difficult right now. He has a lot going on."

And she didn't even know if Dominic would want to meet her family.

They liked each other, but was this just a fling that would end as soon as Dominic was out of danger?

That was completely setting aside the possibility of some sort of witness protection. He could be moving across the country, and she'd never see him again. She didn't like to think that would happen, but it was far from unlikely.

"Actually, I've been thinking about my old friend Faith from high school. Ethan's been bugging me to open a birthday card she sent me. I think I should go ahead and do it." She got up and went over to the drawer where she'd left the envelope.

When she turned around, Ethan was rolling his eyes. "Now that's a deliberate change of subject. But I'll allow it. Go ahead and open your letter."

She sat back down at the table, cradling the envelope in her hands. Using the tip of her finger, she carefully pried it open along the top. She didn't want to tear the paper where Faith had drawn the balloons. She couldn't even say why. It just seemed like she should leave them intact, since Faith had taken the time to draw them.

The front of the card was a typical birthday message, a sweet one rather than the beginning of a joke. She opened it, and there was only Faith's handwritten message inside. As if her friend had chosen this card specifically to let her own voice speak, without the interference of words written by some impersonal card company.

Dear Sylvie,

I know it's been a really long time, and I probably don't even deserve a response from you. So don't feel like you owe me one. I just wanted to say I still think of you. I've never stopped, not since you left.

How's Ethan doing? Last I heard you two were still close, and I hope that's true.

If you're willing to talk, then I could tell you all kinds of things about why I stopped speaking to you. I'm not looking forward to that part because it makes me sound like a complete jerk and a coward. But it's the truth, and I owe that to you.

If you're willing to listen, you can text me at the number below. I don't expect anything more, not even forgiveness. But at least you'll know what happened, and that it's not what you probably think.

I'm going to hope you do write back, because hope is all I have going for me at this point.

Faith

Sylvie held up the card so Ethan and Luis could read it.

Ethan whistled. "Wow, I got a mention. That was nice of her." He wasn't even being sarcastic.

Sylvie dropped the card onto the table. "Then why didn't she bother to write you? She abandoned you as much as she did me."

"But she was *your* best friend. You were the real connection between us. And it's your heart she broke, not mine."

She squeezed her eyes shut so the tears wouldn't escape. "I don't see what explanation she could have that would justify not speaking to me for over a decade."

But maybe there were more factors at play in Faith's life than Sylvie knew. If Dominic had taught her anything, it was to give someone a chance. That taking the risk might be scary, but it was worth it.

She pulled out her phone.

"Are you going to write her?" Luis sounded hopeful.

"I think you should," Ethan added.

"Both of you chill. I'm doing it."

Sylvie: Hey Faith, it's me. Sylvie. I'm pretty busy the next few days but let me know when you're available, and we can find time to chat. Talk to you later.

She hesitated, then hit send.

Chapter Twenty-Six

"What are you doing?" Maureen stood in the doorway to his bedroom, staring at him skeptically.

Dominic got up off his hands and knees. "I was cleaning. Is that a problem?"

"Not generally. But it does make me concerned about the state of your mental health. I've never seen you clean anything."

"Which is a problem in itself, isn't it?"

Usually, Maureen was the one to tidy up after him. But he didn't like her coming into his room too often, so it tended to get cluttered. After Sylvie had arrived a couple of days ago, he'd shoved a bunch of junk under his bed. But now he was too full of nervous energy, and he needed something to do.

Plus, he liked the idea of making more room for Sylvie. As if clearing away the detritus from his regular life would give her that much more reason to feel comfortable here.

Which was stupid because he wouldn't be here much longer anyway. He'd be leaving for the safe house before long, and he had no idea when he'd be back here.

But cleaning had made some instinctual sense in his head, so he'd decided to go with it.

He stood up from the floor. "Do you know how much longer it'll be 'til they're here?"

"Your answer is as good as mine. I would've thought Sylvie would let you know."

He hadn't heard back from her all day, even though he'd written. Maybe that was another source of his nervousness. He wanted to know what was going on.

He'd managed to talk briefly with Raymond, who wasn't happy at all about the safe house idea. And he'd been outright pissed when he'd heard about the bodyguard detail. Ray had insisted Dominic call off Bennett Security before he'd even consider anything like the safe house.

Dominic didn't understand his brother's reticence. Maybe the kid was afraid to accept that their lives weren't normal, wouldn't be anything close to normal until they could both get away from the Syndicate.

Raymond was going to need more convincing. Dominic was still counting on Lana to help him there.

But at least they had some time before the move. He wanted to spend as much of that with Sylvie as possible.

By the time Sylvie and Tanner arrived, Dominic's room was spotless. He'd showered and shaved. He met Sylvie at the door and swept her into his arms, capturing her mouth in a passionate kiss. He was putting on a show for the cameras because he knew Sandford was watching, but he didn't have to fake his enthusiasm.

When Dominic broke off the kiss, Sylvie said, "Wow. Hello to you, too."

"Just wanted to make sure you knew how much I missed you."

Sylvie pulled him down again, locking their lips. Dominic knew she was playing along, but he liked to think her show of affection was mostly sincere. Their chemistry certainly felt like the real thing. His breathing was shallow, and his focus was soft. No one had ever fit so perfectly into his arms.

Maureen cleared her throat. "All right, I think that's plenty. We've all got the idea. Either you two head upstairs for privacy or turn down the thermostat. I'm having a hot flash over here."

Tanner snorted, shaking his head as he wandered toward the kitchen.

They acted normal for a while, chatting like this was just a regular visit, in case the Syndicate had binoculars trained on Dominic's windows right now. He didn't want to do anything that might set off their suspicions.

But there was a different kind of tension in the air this afternoon. All four of them knew they had an important objective today.

Dominic took solace in the fact that they were all finally working together toward a common goal. Every time he touched Sylvie or kissed her hair, he felt the relief of knowing they were being completely honest with one another. That he wasn't hiding anything at all.

Maybe this was what it felt like to really be himself. Smiling and laughing easily, feeling at home in his skin. Not worrying about what anyone thought of him, despite the danger waiting just beyond their door. He wished it hadn't taken such extreme circumstances to make him stop playing the role of "Dominic Crane" and just be *Nic.*

All he knew was that he wanted to feel this way all the time.

They'd choreographed the whole evening. Sylvie had already dropped off her overnight bag in Dominic's room. When she and Maureen started making dinner, with Tanner helping out, Dominic went upstairs with the flash drive Sylvie had given him. It contained the modified code she'd created.

She'd promised all he had to do was plug it in to her laptop, just like the one Sandford had given him before. To the

Russian hackers, it would be indistinguishable from the programs they'd created to infiltrate Bennett Security. Of course, this one had the secret malware Sylvie had devised.

Dominic didn't understand how it all worked, but he could manage this part of it. He took Sylvie's laptop out of her bag and set it on the dresser. Even pretending to violate her trust bothered him. It reminded him of how close he'd come to doing the real thing.

He plugged the drive into the USB port on the side of Sylvie's machine. She had told him the screen would come to life, and a small window would appear with code.

So far, so good.

He'd asked Sylvie if she should handle the install herself in case anything went wrong. But she was worried the slightest misstep could alert the Syndicate that something was amiss.

As he waited for the code to stop scrolling, the only sound he could hear was his own breathing.

When the little window on the screen disappeared, he removed the drive and shut the lid on the computer. The last thing he had to do was use his phone—the regular one the Syndicate knew about—to notify Sandford.

Dominic: It's done.

He stared at the screen, waiting for a response. But none came. He had to assume everything was fine. Sandford would let him know what to do next.

He went back downstairs to meet Sylvie in the kitchen.

"Did it go okay?" she whispered, her eyes wide.

"It was exactly what you said. Plugged it in, the window did its scrolly thing, then I pulled it out. That was it."

She nodded. "Okay, that's good. I guess now all we can do is wait."

"When will we know it's working?"

"When I get back to the office and access the data that

should be coming back from the Russian hackers."

"You can't check on the laptop upstairs?"

Sylvie smiled at him patiently. "I can't do that because then they'd see it. They have access to everything on that machine, but it's just a decoy. A copy of my real laptop. The malware I wrote is going to send the Syndicate data directly back to Bennett Security."

He stood behind her and kissed the side of her neck until Maureen and Tanner started to complain.

Then Dominic's phone chimed with an incoming text. He checked the message.

Aaron Sandford: We need to talk. Urgently. Get somewhere you won't be overheard and call me.

Dominic cursed. "It's him. Sandford needs something and says it's urgent. What if it's the program? What if something's wrong?"

Sylvie's face gave away her anxiety. It was the same thing he felt.

The four of them went upstairs to the game room. Maureen, Sylvie, and Tanner sat out of sight on one side of the room. Dominic lowered himself onto the couch and dialed Sandford's number.

The lawyer switched the call to video. His face appeared, eyes glittering with animosity.

Dominic forced himself to act calm. "What do you want now?" he whispered, as if he feared being overheard. "I did what you asked."

"I know. It's a step in the right direction, but unfortunately, that's no longer good enough. Charles wants to see you in person. You need to deliver your endorsement to the captains, and besides that, Charles is tired of having to guess about what you're really doing."

Dominic's stomach lurched. "You want me to leave my

house? Did you forget the ankle monitor?"

"So get rid of it. You've been giving far too much credence to those rules. It's really making Charles have doubts about you. He heard you were going soft, and your tendency to hide in that house is only confirming those rumors."

Dominic could feel Sylvie and Maureen reacting on the other side of the room, but he didn't dare raise his eyes from the screen.

"But consider this an opportunity," the lawyer said. "You'll finally get out of that house, just like you wanted. Don't worry, Charles will keep you hidden. He's very anxious to keep you close."

Dominic tried to think fast. "All right, I'll make it happen. Just tell me when and where to meet Charles, and I'll be there. But I'll need at least a week. I have to wrap some things up here, pack, make excuses to Sylvie and Maureen…"

"That's not possible. We're sending a car for you tomorrow."

"*Tomorrow?*"

"Someone will call you in the afternoon when the car is nearby. They'll tell you where to meet up with them. All you have to do is ditch the ankle monitor and walk away. If the police figure out you're running, it's not a problem. Our car will get to you faster." Sandford smirked. "Until then."

The lawyer's face disappeared.

He hadn't even given Dominic a chance to argue, to ask questions. Nothing. Because there was absolutely nothing he could do.

Charles was demanding he come in and put himself at the mercy of the Syndicate.

Dominic didn't just turn off his screen. He powered down his phone completely. "He's gone."

Sylvie raced across the room. "Why are they doing this? Do you think they know about our plan to target their hackers?"

Dominic shook his head. "I don't think so. I think they've been planning this all along. I gave them what they wanted, so now they have no more use for me. Maybe Charles really does want me to put in a word with his captains. But after that..."

They were going to kill him. Dominic was sure of it.

He hardly felt anything, just numb. Like the shock hadn't worked its way through his entire brain yet.

"You're not going with those people, are you?" Maureen asked.

He huffed a laugh. "Not if I want to live through the week."

Sylvie covered her gasp with her hand.

Charles had trapped him. Left him no way out but to run.

Lana had told him they might be able to move up the schedule if circumstances changed. But could she find a way to get him out of here by tomorrow?

He reached for his phone. Then he remembered he had to use the burner. "I need to contact Lana and see if the Feds can get me and Maureen out of here tomorrow."

"They have to," Sylvie said. "There's no way they'll just leave you at the Syndicate's mercy. You're a witness."

Tanner walked toward them, his hands tucked casually into his shorts pockets like always. "Or we could just skip the bureaucracy and deal with Bennett Security instead. We'll get you out of here tonight. No messing around. We'll get you into one of Max's safe houses until we can figure out a more permanent arrangement."

"You think Max would do that?" Dominic said. "You'd be helping me violate bail. That's a crime."

Tanner shrugged. "Pretty sure he would."

Sylvie sat on the couch and took Dominic's hand. "Even if Max wouldn't help you, he would do it for me. I'm not going to let anything happen to you."

He wasn't sure he believed her. But it meant a lot that she'd said it.

Chapter Twenty-Seven

"We're going to fix this. It's going to be okay." Sylvie was trying to reassure herself as much as Dominic.

He didn't answer, just sat on his bed, staring into the half-packed suitcase at his feet.

She and Tanner had already made secure phone calls to Max and the rest of the Bennett Security bodyguard team. Of course, Max had agreed to set up Dominic, Maureen, and Raymond in one of his safe houses.

Tanner had made some very good points to their boss. They couldn't count on the bureaucracy suddenly becoming efficient. This had to happen fast. If Dominic raised the alarm right now, the entire police department would hear about it, and somebody might leak it to the L.A. police, too. The more people who knew he was going into hiding, the more likely the news would get back to the Syndicate.

None of them knew what the DA's office would have to say about the arrangement. Max hadn't told Lana because he didn't want her to know Dominic was going to break his bail conditions. *We'll have to ask for forgiveness instead of permission,* her boss had said.

If the Feds or the DA didn't like the plan, they could point fingers *after* Sylvie and her friends got Dominic to safety.

His burner phone rang on the dresser. He jumped up and grabbed it. Sylvie stood beside him.

"It's Raymond. Thank god." He answered.

"Nic? I got your message. What's going on?"

"Ray, I've got you on speaker. Sylvie is here with me." Dominic smiled at her shyly. "The one I mentioned?"

"Hey, it's nice to meet you," she said.

"Oh, Sylvie. Hi." Raymond's voice was as calming as his brother's. "Is that why you wanted to talk, Nic? To introduce her?"

Dominic's eyes closed. "I wish that was all. Turns out we need to make that move I was talking about sooner, rather than later."

"How much sooner? I already told you, I don't want people hanging around here, watching me. That creeps me out."

"I know. And I called off the bodyguards when you asked. But now, I'm not just talking about precautions. This is serious. We have to leave tomorrow morning. Before dawn."

Raymond cursed. "I can't just pick up and leave. I have class in the morning. I have a test."

"If there was any other way, I'd do it. But they're coming for me tomorrow. And that means they might come for you."

There was a pause. "There's something you're not telling me. I want to know what's really going on. Why is this all happening *now*?"

Dominic exhaled, glancing at Sylvie. She nodded her permission. If Raymond needed this information to get onboard, she had no problem sharing it.

As she listened, Dominic told his brother everything—the cyberattack on her computer, the orders from their uncle to install the malware, and the plan to infiltrate the Syndicate's hackers.

Raymond kept making choked sounds of dismay. "This is just nuts. All of it." But Sylvie could already tell he was giving in.

"Please," Dominic said. "Sylvie's friends are going to get me out of here, but I can't go without you. We'll come pick you up on the way. Be ready to go by four."

"Four in the morning? That's when you'll be here?"

"Or a little after. Just watch from your window. Wait for my call. Then come downstairs. Don't come out for anyone else."

"Damn, Nic. I don't want to do this."

"But we don't have any other choice."

"I get that. So, I guess we'll just do what we have to."

Dominic had lowered the phone when Ray said, "Wait. Nic, I love you. Okay? I'm sorry...about all this."

"Hey, you have nothing to be sorry for. I love you, too. I'll see you soon."

"Yeah."

Sylvie thought of Ethan back home. The Syndicate knew who she was, even if they didn't know she'd modified their code and used it against them. They knew she was here right now and that she and Dominic were sleeping together.

Sandford had threatened her. Did that mean they might go after her cousin, too? Maybe she should tell Ethan to stay at Luis's for a few days.

For the first time, Sylvie had fully come out from behind her computer screens. She didn't have her anonymity to protect her. She'd never had to worry before about her loved ones being hurt because of her work. But it was something Max had been through. She didn't know how he could stand it.

She was afraid of what might be coming. But she also knew Dominic was worth it.

He set the phone back on the dresser.

Sylvie glanced at the time. It was nearing eleven o'clock

now. Only a handful of hours left. "We should get some sleep."

"I'm not ready."

"Just pack enough for a few days. I'm sure someone can come get the rest later."

"I'm not worried about clothes. I'm not ready to leave *you*. I don't know when I'll see you again." He sat on the edge of the bed. Dominic circled his arms around her waist, pulling her closer until she stood between his knees. "Or when I'll be able to touch you."

"Probably not for a while. You'll be surrounded by Bennett Security bodyguards."

"Then we'd better make tonight count."

They undressed each other, one piece of clothing at a time. Sylvie ran her hands over his smooth chest, the defined ridges of his abs. But Dominic seemed just as enthralled with her body as she was with his. He picked her up and laid her on the mattress, touching and kissing and licking her everywhere. Under her breasts, just above her hipbones, the inner hinge of her elbow. Like every part of her was worth cherishing.

He turned her over and ran his finger across her back. "I haven't spent nearly enough time studying your tattoos."

The ink spanned the top half of her back, spilling across her shoulders and down her arms to her elbows. She wasn't sure how many more she wanted to get. When she looked in the mirror, she still saw an unfinished project, slowly being filled in toward the edges. Someday, she figured she'd be done, but she also didn't know what that would feel like.

"You said this was your newest one, right?" He pointed at the heron on her left shoulder. "When did you get it?"

"A few weeks ago."

"Before the first time we met? Or was it after?"

"I think...after." Definitely after.

He put his lips against her ear and whispered, "See how its neck is outstretched? That's not a heron. It's a crane."

"Is *not.*"

"Maybe you didn't like me then, but your subconscious did."

"How conceited are you?" She tried to turn over, but he wouldn't let her. Instead, Dominic spread his body over hers until he was completely covering her. His warm weight pressed her into the mattress, and his erection lay snug against her rear. She had her head turned to the side, just able to see his face in her peripheral vision as he kissed her neck. The feeling of him was extravagant, over the top. She didn't ever want to move from this spot, yet she also wanted even more of him. All of him she could get.

"I need you."

"I need you, too."

"I mean, I need you *inside* me." He'd told her before he'd been tested. "We're both clean, and I'm on the pill. You don't have to use a condom."

He kissed the heron tattoo. Okay, the *crane* tattoo. "You're sure?"

"Very."

He reached down to grip one of her thighs, spreading her wider, then did the same on the other side. His fingers stroked between her legs. She tilted her pelvis to give him better access, though his body still held her down.

He lifted off her a bit and slid his hand beneath her stomach to raise her higher. She felt his tip against her entrance, and he pushed his way in. The sounds she made were needy and desperate.

"Nic, *yes.*"

His hips drew back and flicked forward again as he buried his shaft to the hilt. His body was everywhere, sheltering hers, pinning her into place. His cock rubbed against the inside of her channel as he withdrew. Every sensation was exquisite, the pleasure acute. She felt herself stretching anew as he filled her over and over.

"Sylvie. No one's ever felt as good as this."

She moaned in response.

"I'm going to turn you over. I want to see your face." He pulled out to roll her over, then plunged inside of her again. She loved how easily his cock glided in and out of her, their bodies so wet and eager. Their breathing grew ragged. She dug her fingers into his hair. They were both sweating. She pulled him down and licked his neck, tasting salt.

"Can you grab the lube?" he asked. The bottle was sitting right beside them on the nightstand.

"I don't think we need it."

"For my fingers. I want to make you feel even better."

"I don't see how that's possible."

He grinned wolfishly. "Humor me."

She grabbed the bottle and popped it open, though it was hard to focus on even this simple task with his dick sliding into her like that. He propped up on one elbow, holding out his other hand. Sylvie tipped the bottle and lube poured onto his fingertips.

Dominic brought his hand down to where their bodies were joined. He pressed his slicked fingers to her clit. Sylvie gasped.

While his fingers worked at her most sensitive spot, Dominic pushed his tongue into her mouth. His hips drove his cock between her legs. There was just so much—almost too much—all of him overwhelming her senses.

She felt the change in her body. It was small at first. The pleasure was already so intense. But then the tension that had been coiling inside her suddenly ratcheted up by a thousand, and she was coming apart, shuddering. The power of it shocked her. Her body was convulsing completely out of her control. How could anyone bear so much pleasure at once?

She cried out, and if Dominic's mouth hadn't been fixed to hers the whole house would've heard.

He kept pumping into her, and wave after wave of sensation kept crashing through her. She felt him start to shake too, his cock throbbing and somehow drawing even more indulgent pleasure out of her body. He growled against her mouth as he came.

Dominic collapsed on top of her, both of them panting. She was trapped beneath his weight, his cock still pulsing every few seconds inside of her. Every last bit of energy had left her body. She couldn't imagine how she'd stand up again. Her joints all felt detached.

Their breathing slowed, and Dominic drew up onto his elbows to look down her.

"Hi."

"I came." She could hardly believe the words.

"I know."

"It was…"

He nodded. "Yeah. It was." He kissed her lips gently. Sylvie wrapped her legs around his waist, not wanting him to leave her yet. She didn't want any of this to end.

His cheek nuzzled against her. "I want to keep seeing you." His eyes met hers, his gaze hesitant. As if he could have a doubt about what she'd say.

"I'd like that. And not just because you gave me my first orgasm. Though it helps."

"Yeah, I even impressed myself." His grin flashed, then faded. "I just wish I knew when that would happen. Or even…where I'll be."

She tucked his hair behind his ear. "I'll chase you down if I have to."

"Then I'll be waiting."

Chapter Twenty-Eight

They dozed in each other's arms. But after a couple of hours, Sylvie's alarm went off. They jumped in the shower and stayed under the spray as the minutes counted down, kissing and touching until the water ran cold. They didn't try for any more orgasms, and Dominic wasn't even sure if he'd be able to get there himself. He was too exhausted and worried about would happen today. And his throat was tight with the agony of already missing her, even though she was still in his arms.

When they'd been making love, he hadn't even been trying to make her come. Not necessarily. He'd just wanted to show her how much he appreciated her, how much he cared. Dominic didn't have a lot to offer anyone, so he'd wanted to give her everything he had, meager though it was.

His life was heading into a black hole, a place he couldn't see the end of. He didn't even know if he'd *ever* make his way out again. He'd agreed to turn on the Syndicate, on the Crane family name… Who would he be when he woke up tomorrow in some safe house, with the West Oaks DA and the US Attorney calling and making demands?

How much was his testimony worth? How much were his very life and identity worth?

The thought of still having Sylvie was a comfort, as was the knowledge that Maureen and Raymond would be safe with him, too. But none of them would be out of danger for a while, perhaps an indefinite amount of time.

Would Sylvie have to go into hiding as well? They hadn't even talked about that. He figured she could handle herself, especially as an employee of Bennett Security. Max would see that she was safe.

They got out and toweled off. Sylvie dressed quickly and went downstairs to confer with Tanner. Dominic's limbs moved slower than they should as he dropped random clothes and items into his suitcase. How did he know what he would need in this new life? He didn't even know who the hell he would be.

A soft knock interrupted his thoughts. "Dominic?"

"Come in."

Maureen opened the door and stepped inside. "I made some food to take with us. I wasn't sure what they'd have."

"Thanks. I didn't think of that." He figured Max wasn't going to let them starve. It was surreal to think of something so basic as food right now. But at least that was one thing that wouldn't change. They needed to keep breathing and eating and sleeping. He knew how to do those things.

Except for the fact that he barely knew how to feed himself without Maureen's help.

I'm thirty-three years old, he thought, *and what the hell do I have to show for it?* Except for an ankle monitor and bail conditions he was about to violate. Just one more thing he was leaving broken.

"I'm going to miss this place," Maureen said. "I've enjoyed my time here with you."

He lifted his head. "You have? Why?"

"Well, it's certainly never been dull. It's like my own

personal soap opera. Romantic trysts, dramatic entrances. By the SWAT team or otherwise."

"Glad you haven't lost your sense of humor."

She took a few more steps into the room, hands clasped together. "And I've enjoyed getting to know you. You don't let many people do that. So, it was a privilege."

He pushed air out of his nose, shaking his head at the absurdity of that statement. "Knowing me is dangerous. It's no privilege."

"I disagree. I'm proud of what you're doing. It takes courage to do what's right. I don't think it matters how long it takes to get there. As long as we find the right path in the end."

He hoped so. But he realized he wasn't going to miss this house at all. He'd miss mealtimes with Maureen, their conversations. He'd miss some of his old memories of summers with his brothers. And he would always remember the time he'd spent with Sylvie here. But the rest of it? The rest of it could stay behind, along with the parts of himself he was giving up.

He knew this was the right choice. But he wasn't courageous in the way Maureen thought. He was just stuck without any other options. Yet maybe, for now, that was enough.

He and Maureen had packed a suitcase each. They met Sylvie and Tanner downstairs, careful to keep out of the view of the front door cameras. Sylvie was going to disable the alarm system at the very last moment, right before they left. They didn't want to tip off the Syndicate a moment sooner than they had to.

None of them were speaking. It was so quiet Dominic could hear the faint roar of the ocean crashing into the cliff below his house.

Sylvie received a text. She nodded at them.

Then she went over to the security panel by the front door and input a set of commands. The screen went dark. "The cameras are disabled. If the Syndicate is watching, I assume they'll guess pretty quick what we're up to."

Tanner went to the front door. He wore a shoulder holster Dominic had never seen before, an odd match with his usual flip-flops and shorts. "Let's go." Tanner opened the door and ushered the rest of them outside. "I'll get the bags."

There were two black SUVs, one parked in front of the other at the curb.

Tanner pointed Dominic to the rear SUV. But he put a hand on Maureen's shoulder and directed her to the one in front. "You and Sylvie are taking this car to the safe house here in West Oaks. Dominic is going to Los Angeles."

Maureen reached for Dominic, her expression full of panic. "No, I thought we were staying together."

Sylvie's gaze darted from one man to the next, her uncertainty clear on her face.

A bodyguard stepped out of each SUV, opening the doors into the backseats. "Mr. Crane," one of them said, "we need to go."

"Hold on. This isn't what we planned." Dominic retreated, backing away toward the house.

Tanner walked over to him. "Dominic, you have to go with us to get Raymond because it sounds like he won't come with us otherwise. But Sylvie and Maureen don't need that much exposure. This is the safest choice for both of them."

Dominic didn't like it. But he knew the man was right.

Sylvie marched over, pushing against Tanner's muscled arm. "This is bullshit. You spring this at the last minute and expect me to go along? No. I'm going with Dominic."

"You're not a bodyguard."

"But I have training. So unless you want to get Max on the phone to fire me right fucking now, quit telling me what to do."

Dominic made a decision. "Maureen, you need to go with

them. They're going to take care of you, and you don't need
to be driving all the way into L.A."

She pulled him into a hug. Her eyes were shining. He'd
never once before seen Maureen cry.

"All right, I will. But you take care of yourself. Since I
won't be there to do it for you."

"I'll see you soon."

"You'd better." Maureen got into the first SUV. Tanner
loaded her suitcase, snapped shut the trunk, and then banged
on the roof. The driver pulled away.

"The rest of you, let's get out here. We've wasted enough
time."

"You should've told me about your stupid plan in the first
place, so I could reject it," Sylvie said. "Nic, did you take off
the ankle monitor?"

"Uh, not yet." He'd nearly forgotten about it. He took out
the pair of pliers he'd stowed in his pocket and pried the strap
apart, both terrified and relieved to finally have the thing off.
He left it right there on the sidewalk. An alarm would be
going off at the police station now, alerting them about the
tampering.

Dominic stepped across the invisible barrier in his front
yard and into the street.

Sylvie slid into the backseat of the SUV next to him.
Tanner took shotgun. The car doors slammed.

"You should've gone with Maureen," Dominic murmured.

"Don't give me any reasons to stop liking you. I was
starting to get attached." Sylvie clasped his hand, and he quit
arguing.

He took solace in her presence, even though he knew he
was putting her in danger. But he'd been doing that all along,
hadn't he?

The driver put the car in gear, and Dominic heard the
door locks snap into place. He didn't look back at the house as
they drove away.

Chapter Twenty-Nine

They raced down the freeway. Normally, the trip from West Oaks to Los Angeles was over an hour, but at this time of night traffic flowed smoothly. Sylvie knew Tanner was keeping a close eye on the vehicles around them, watching for any signs they were being tailed.

She leaned forward in her seat. "Everything look good out there?"

Tanner nodded. "So far."

She checked her phone. The Bennett Security office was full of people right now because of this operation. She'd asked Priyanka to keep her apprised of any data coming in from the Russian hackers. But Priyanka's last update, from just a few minutes ago, said she hadn't seen anything yet.

Sylvie cursed under her breath. There should've been something by now. It was daytime in Russia. The black-hat hackers would be active.

"You all right?" Dominic's shoulder leaned into hers.

She exhaled, forcing a smile. "Of course. Everything's going to be fine."

About twenty minutes into the drive, they got word that

Maureen had arrived at the West Oaks safe house. "You should call Raymond and let him know we're on our way."

Dominic took out his burner phone. He'd left the other back at the house. He punched a button and lifted the phone to his ear. Sylvie heard it ringing.

But Raymond didn't answer.

A crease appeared between Dominic's eyebrows.

"I'm sure he's just getting ready," Sylvie said. "None of us had much time."

Dominic nodded, though his frown remained.

"You should try to sleep. I can wake you when we get to your brother's dorm.

He smirked. "How about you rest, and I'll wake *you* when we arrive."

They both knew that nobody was going to be sleeping on this car ride. So she snuggled against him instead, enjoying these last few minutes of being together.

"When we get to the safe house with Raymond, you won't be able to stay," Dominic whispered. "Will you?"

"Maybe for an hour or two, but that's probably it. When we get there, Tanner and the other bodyguards will be in charge. It won't be so easy for me to boss them around."

"Too bad. I enjoyed that."

The safe house was about ten miles from Raymond's West Los Angeles campus, according to the Google maps search she'd run earlier. The distance wouldn't take too long to cover at this time of night. During peak L.A. traffic, it could've taken an hour just to make that small piece of the trip.

From there, the Bennett Security bodyguards would take over, and Tanner or Rex—the man driving them right now— would take Sylvie back to headquarters. She had no idea when she'd be able to see Dominic again, or even speak to him. Sylvie hoped the security measures wouldn't be that drastic. But it all depended on what the Syndicate decided to do next.

"Where will you go afterward?" he asked.

"I'll be somewhere safe. Don't worry about that."

She had the feeling Max and Tanner would insist she not go home for a while just in case Charles Traynor decided to send someone after her. She wasn't looking forward to it. Max had an apartment on the third floor of their headquarters building, and he'd recently moved out of it to get a new place with Lana. Max would probably tell Sylvie to hole up there. At least she'd be close to work.

She didn't want to discuss the topic with Dominic, though. He needed to focus on himself right now, not on her.

They pulled up outside Raymond's dorm just after four. The building was a large rectangular brick structure. A few students wandered the sidewalks, obviously on the way home from parties.

Tanner unbuckled his seatbelt. "Have you reached Raymond yet?"

Dominic was trying his brother again. "He's not answering. This isn't right."

"Tanner, what about our surveillance on Raymond?" Sylvie asked.

"We pulled them, just like the kid wanted." Tanner sent an accusatory glance back at her. "Starting to wonder about that."

So was she, though she didn't want to say it aloud.

Dominic unbuckled his restraint and reached for the door.

Sylvie grabbed his arm. "Wait, you can't go. That's not the plan. Raymond's supposed to meet us out here."

"But if he doesn't come out, then we need to go in." Dominic got out of the car.

She met Tanner's eyes in the rearview mirror.

"I figured you both would get pissed if I activated the child locks. I'll go with him."

"Then so will I. Rex can wait here for us."

"Sure," Tanner said breezily. "Why don't we stop by a frat

party, chug a few beers while we're at it? Fuck." He tugged on a windbreaker, clearly meant to hide the gun in his shoulder holster.

They hurried after Dominic, who had already charged up to the building's entrance. The door was locked, but a couple of girls had just gotten out of an Uber and were tottering toward the door, their keys in hand. Their eyes widened when they saw Dominic. Sylvie didn't know if they were afraid of him or stunned by his attractiveness. But it didn't really matter.

She stepped forward. "We were just heading in. Can I help you with that?"

The girls gave Sylvie their keys. She unlocked the door and handed them back. She had half a mind to follow them to make sure they got back to their room safely, but Dominic was already running down the hall.

He stopped at a door. "This is it. Raymond's in room 104." His knuckles rapped on the wood.

"Does he have a roommate?" Tanner asked.

"It's a single." Dominic knocked again, louder. Then he tried the door, but it was locked. Sylvie could feel his panic. He was running his hands through his hair, cursing. "This can't be happening. Where is he?"

A couple of people opened other doors, peering out.

"Anyone know Raymond Crane?" Tanner asked. "He could be in trouble. We're trying to help."

Raymond's neighbors said they knew him, but they had no idea where he was. Then a shirtless guy stepped out of the room across the hall and said, "I saw him earlier, leaving with a bag. He said he was taking a few days to go see his family."

Dominic practically pounced on the man. "When was this?"

"Um, midnight maybe?"

After they had the phone call with Raymond. But why would he have left so early? That was hours ago.

Tanner thanked them, and the students went back into their rooms. "Wherever Raymond is, he's not here. We need to go. We could be blown."

Dominic was pacing frantically across the hall. "I'm not going without him. There's been a mistake. He wouldn't have just left."

He raised his phone to his ear again, probably trying Raymond's number. He turned around and paced away from them, muttering to himself.

A terrible thought had just occurred to Sylvie. Priyanka hadn't detected any data coming in from the Russian hackers' system. Did that mean they already knew what she and Dominic had tried to do?

Had they gone after Raymond?

But then why would Raymond have left on his own?

Tanner pulled Sylvie aside. "This situation could get very bad very fast. We need to get him out of here. If those Syndicate people show up, we could be putting every kid in this building in danger."

"Okay, but then what? We have to do something."

"Yeah, we'll call the police on the way. But we're not doing anything else until after Dominic's in the safe house. This is more than we can handle right now. The best we can do is get him secured so this doesn't explode in our faces. Then we'll see to his brother."

Dominic turned around. He'd dropped his phone to his side, looking deathly pale.

"Did you reach him?" Sylvie asked.

Dominic shook his head, his mouth a thin line.

Tanner walked over and put a hand on the other man's shoulder. But Dominic shook him off. "I am not getting back in that car. I'm not leaving without my brother." He took off down the hall, but he wasn't going back toward the entrance they'd come in.

She chased after him. "Where are you going? Tanner is right. We need to get out of here."

"You don't understand."

"Nic, wait." She tried to grab his hand. He yanked himself out of her grip, whirling around.

"What are you going to do, have Tanner grab me and carry me back to the SUV? He's welcome to try. I am not leaving here until I know what happened to Raymond. He's the one person I was always supposed to protect, and I... He..." Dominic's hands were shaking.

"We'll figure out where Raymond is, and we'll help him. But you can't do that if the Syndicate grabs you, too."

"I don't care what they do to me!" Dominic's eyes locked with hers. "There's no point in hurting my brother, except to get to me. It's *me* they really want."

The realization washed over her. Terror followed.

He was going to trade himself for Raymond.

"Don't do this, Nic. Please."

"I'm sorry, Sylvie. You'll have to shoot me if you want to stop me."

Dominic had reached the rear exit door at the very end of the hall. "Don't follow me," he said over his shoulder. "Unless you want to give me a weapon, Tanner? Like a dumbass I left all of my guns at home, like you told me to."

"Am I arming the fugitive? No thanks. I'm not doing the paperwork on that one."

"I didn't think so. Don't come after me, Sylvie. *Please.*"

Dominic pushed the door and went outside. Where, for all they knew, the Syndicate could already be waiting.

"Shit," she yelled.

Tanner's large palm rested on her arm. "Let him go. If he doesn't want to come in, he's right. I'm not going to make him. It's not going to be pretty when the district attorney finds out we helped him skip his bail. We're going to have a shit ton to answer for. But if he's running, it's his choice. We'll just have to let the police handle it."

"No. I'm not letting him." Sylvie ran after him.

"Damn it all." Tanner kept up behind her, talking into his phone to their driver, Rex. "Yeah, the other side. Bring the car around. No, I don't fucking know what's going on. Call the police to report a possible kidnapping. Be careful and be ready. Yeah. That's what I'm afraid of, too."

Please let them be okay, Sylvie thought. Both Raymond and Dominic.

Tanner dashed ahead of her, barring her path with his arm. "You know, believe it or not, being a bodyguard is usually pretty damn boring. So at least this assignment has been interesting."

He pulled out his backup weapon, handing it to her. She checked the magazine. Fully loaded with .38 rounds.

"I'll go first," Tanner said. "Stay behind me, and if I tell you to run Sylvie, you'd better fucking run."

Chapter Thirty

*D*ominic cut across a grassy lawn. He was supposed to lose his bodyguard detail, and he'd taken care of that. But he didn't know where the hell he was going. He'd only been to see Raymond at his dorm once before, and that hadn't been in the middle of the night.

When he'd called Raymond in the hallway, he'd finally gotten an answer. Except it hadn't been his brother on the line.

I'll give myself up, Dominic had whispered into the phone. *Just don't hurt Raymond.*

On the phone, Sandford had told him to get to the street that cut through the campus.

Dominic stopped a student and asked for directions. The guy was so drunk he barely made sense, but he pointed, and Dominic went that way, skirting between two buildings.

Finally, he saw cars parked along a curb. Streetlights made all the concrete look pale yellow.

Sandford had said they wouldn't hurt Raymond if Dominic turned himself in. But what if the lawyer had been lying? What if something terrible had already happened to his brother? His heart was beating so hard he didn't know how he could keep functioning.

"Dominic!"

He turned. Sylvie and Tanner were running after him. Shit. "I told you not to follow me. Both of you need to get out of here. *Now*."

He didn't have time to warn them about what was coming. A black sedan with tinted windows roared up the narrow street. The window of the backseat was open, and Aaron Sandford pointed a gun barrel out of it.

Tanner cursed, drawing his weapon. Sylvie held a gun too, and she aimed it at the car.

"Tell your friends to drop their guns, or you and Raymond both are going to die."

Dominic looked over. "Tanner, just let me go. Please do what he says."

The bodyguard and Sylvie both laid their guns on the concrete.

Sandford leaned forward through the open window. "Dominic, you too. Get rid of your weapons, or you'll never see Raymond again."

"I don't have any weapons."

"Are you shitting me? Get over here, and we'll find out if you're lying." He looked towards Tanner and Sylvie. "Anybody tries anything funny, then you all know what's going to happen. Pretty boy's brains will get plastered all over the sidewalk."

Dominic approached the vehicle, keeping his arms raised.

Then Sylvie screamed, and Dominic pivoted to see a huge man in a black leather jacket lurch from the shadows.

Tanner's arm lashed out, knocking the gun from the new guy's hand. They grappled with one other. Sylvie reached for one of the weapons on the ground, but a gunshot rang out, splintering the tree trunk beside her. Sandford had fired. Dominic yelled, starting toward her. He heard Sandford telling him to stop, but Dominic didn't care. He had to get to her.

Yet another Syndicate enforcer appeared. They were coming from around the side of the building, like they'd split up to flank Dominic from multiple sides. The newcomer brought a blackjack down on the back of Tanner's head, and Sylvie's friend collapsed onto the concrete.

The leather jacket guy grabbed Sylvie by the arm and dragged her toward Sandford's car.

"No," Dominic said. "Leave her alone." He kept hoping Tanner's other friend, Rex, would drive up and help somehow. But the Bennett Security car was nowhere in sight. *Because you wanted to lose him, idiot, and now they've got Sylvie, too.* This had all gotten so fucked up so fast.

The man holding the blackjack drew a gun and pointed it at Dominic. "Both of you in the car. Now."

"That wasn't the deal. It's me for Raymond. Leave Sylvie out of this."

Nobody even bothered to respond to him. The car doors opened. They shoved Dominic and Sylvie both inside. The tires peeled as they drove away.

Alexi, the massive Neanderthal who'd visited Dominic's house with Sandford, was driving. Dominic was squeezed in next to another Syndicate enforcer, with a gun barrel pushing into his abdomen. The man had worked for him—Patrick. That was his name. Though if Patrick had shown the slightest bit of loyalty to Dominic, Sandford would never have brought him tonight.

Sandford had Sylvie on his lap. It made Dominic's skin crawl to see the lawyer's hands on her arms, pinning them to her sides.

But just a few seconds later, the car swerved into a turnout and stopped. Another vehicle, this one a gray Lexus, waited at the curb with its engine running. Sandford's door opened, and someone grabbed hold of Sylvie, transferring her into the other car.

"Where are you taking her?" Dominic demanded.

Sandford smiled. "She's coming with me. You shouldn't have brought her, but I'm glad you did. It'll save us another trip."

The lawyer moved to the other car, and the door closed. Patrick scooted over, still aiming the gun at Dominic's stomach.

This was so bad. He could barely keep himself from screaming. But he had to. Raymond and Sylvie were both counting on him now. He had to calm down and think.

"Where are we going?"

It was Alexi in the driver's seat who answered.

"To your uncle's house." The man had a strong Slavic accent.

"Is Sylvie going there, too?"

"Think so. Yes."

"Why's she in a different car?"

"More room."

More room for what? If Sandford hurt her, Dominic would end that fucker's life. He'd choke him out and enjoy watching the light leave his eyes.

But right now, he was powerless. Sylvie had stuck by his side, and because of that, she was at the mercy of the kinds of men Dominic had feared becoming.

He eyed Patrick's gun, but the man just glared back.

Dominic wondered about the Russian hackers who now worked for the Syndicate, and about Alexi. Was he Russian? Were these his uncle's new friends?

Maybe Uncle Charles had done more than Dominic realized to take over the Syndicate. He might've needed new allies who provided him with foot soldiers and money.

But these new connections had to be dangerous, too. There was a reason Dominic's own father had never relied on outsiders to run their business. Because the more powerful your friends, the more likely they'd eventually decide to take over your business and run it in your place. The kinds of people who were ruthless enough to help Charles conquer the Syndicate's warring factions wouldn't hesitate to stab anyone in the back.

They raced onto Wilshire Boulevard, leaving Raymond's campus behind.

Dominic's uncle lived in Bel Air, which wasn't far. He figured it wouldn't be long before he saw his uncle in person and learned exactly how far the man intended to go.

He tapped his fingers against the door, praying to the universe that Sylvie was okay.

Chapter Thirty-One

"Sylvie, I'm Aaron Sandford. What a pleasure to finally meet you in person."

Sylvie was trying to inch away from the man, but he was squeezed in next to her. Men with guns sat in the other seats, staring at her, while the driver gunned the engine.

How had everything gone to shit so quickly? One minute, they'd been headed for the safe house. The next, Raymond was missing, Sylvie and Dominic had been kidnapped, and Tanner was lying on the concrete with a gash on his head. Rex would find him soon, but she hoped he wasn't badly injured. The man had a hard head, but he wasn't invincible. None of them were.

Could she throw herself out of the car? She was afraid to reach for the handle with those guns aimed at her. Besides, Tanner might've failed to engage the child safety locks, but she bet the Syndicate wouldn't be so generous.

"It's rude not to answer when you're spoken to," the lawyer snapped.

"I know who you are. Where are you taking Dominic?"

"Aren't you more worried about yourself? Or are you just

too blinded by love? It's sweet. You've certainly been going to a lot of effort for him. I promise you, he's not worth it."

"What about Raymond? Where is he?"

Sandford gripped her chin and forced her to look at him. "Let's not get distracted. Aren't you wondering how we caught up to Dominic so quickly? It's because he's been working with us all along. How else do you think we knew from the beginning about the little program you wrote and installed on that computer last night? The one that was supposed to trap our hackers?"

Icy dread shot through her. There was no way Dominic had told. It was impossible. "Dominic would never do that."

He pinched her chin hard between his fingers and let go. "You're right, he's always been too soft when it comes to women. But it was still a mistake to ever trust him. It's his fault you're sitting here. His fault and your own for thinking you could outsmart us."

His voice was so smug. He wanted her to know there was more he wasn't telling.

How had the Syndicate found out about the malware? Had she screwed up with the code? Were their hackers just that good, and she'd underestimated them?

Or had someone else betrayed them?

Aside from Bennett Security, the only people who'd known were Maureen...and Raymond. Sylvie couldn't believe Dominic's brother would give that information up voluntarily. What had they done to the kid to make him talk? Her heart ached with worry. She didn't know Raymond at all, but Dominic loved him, and that meant Raymond was important to her, too.

The car turned off the boulevard into a neighborhood. Massive houses stood behind shade trees and hedges. She didn't know exactly where they were, but it had to be near Beverly Hills.

"I don't see why Dominic is so attached to you, though," Sandford said. "You don't seem that special."

"Is that supposed to offend me?"

She felt his shoulder shrugging. She tried to put space between them, but there was simply nowhere to go. She laid her head against the cold car window.

"But maybe your best qualities are more evident once you're undressed?" Sandford's hand slid onto her thigh.

She slapped it away. "Touch me again, and you'll lose whatever body part you use to do it."

The gunman in the front seat flinched, his gun barrel inching closer. But Sandford just laughed.

They pulled into a driveway. It wound through trees, skirting a palatial Spanish-style mansion.

The car stopped, and the driver got out to open Sylvie's door. Sandford pushed her outside. They seemed to be at the rear of the property. Tall hedges and more trees surrounded them, as if they were in a dense forest instead of a fancy West L.A. neighborhood.

Sandford took her arm and led her through a wrought iron gate. They passed a swimming pool glowing with blue lights. Guards were everywhere, many of them carrying submachine guns. There was no chance of running. Yet her mind still searched for some means of escape. If she could just get a hold of one of the weapons, maybe... But if she even tried, she'd probably get gunned down in three seconds flat.

They reached a carriage house. Sandford pushed her through the door.

Dominic sat in a straight-backed chair with three more guards nearby. Neither she nor Dominic were restrained in any way, like these people didn't have the slightest concern about them getting free.

Dominic looked up when she came in. "Sylvie!" A livid bruise marred his cheek.

She started toward him, but Sandford kept hold of her, pulling her closer.

"Behave yourselves, both of you. Wouldn't want anything else to happen to Dominic's face."

"I'll do whatever you want. Please just let Sylvie go. Don't hurt her."

"Your father would be sick to hear you pleading like that." Sandford's fingers tightened on her elbow. "You got her involved in this. No one can come after us and get away with it. Not even a Crane. You thought you could rat out your family, and there wouldn't be consequences? You think we won't force you to watch what happens to each and every person you love?"

Even with all the guns aimed at him right now, Sylvie could tell Dominic was fighting to keep himself seated. He had hatred in his eyes as he glared at his former lawyer.

"There must be something you want," Dominic said through gritted teeth. "If Charles needs me to endorse him, I'll say whatever he wants me to."

"None of the captains want to hear the opinions of a traitor."

"But Raymond is innocent. And he's a Crane, too. I know some of the captains are still loyal to my father and to Warren. So do what you want to me, but let Raymond go. Let him take Sylvie, and neither one of them will ever bother Charles or the Syndicate again."

Sandford started to laugh. "You really haven't realized yet how fucking dumb you are? How you could've walked away with your new friends and bought yourself some time? Of course, we would've gotten to you eventually. But at least you could've fucked your girlfriend for a while longer in blissful ignorance instead of delivering yourself up on a silver platter."

"What are you talking about?"

No, Sylvie thought. *Please say it isn't true.*

The door opened behind them. The guards in the room all stood straighter, and Sandford tensed beside her. An older man with sleek black hair strode into the room. He wore khakis and a gingham button-down shirt, like somebody's rich dad relaxing on the weekend. The man nodded at several people as he entered, then his eyes fixed on Dominic.

"Uncle Charles."

"Nephew. This isn't the family reunion I was hoping for. But I suppose it's the only one we'll get."

Another man stepped into the room, this one far younger. He was tall and lean, with similar features to his older brother's, though they were sharper. Not quite as beautiful. Raymond wore a look of sad determination on his face.

Charles reached out to put his arm around Raymond's shoulders. "We weren't expecting you so soon, Dominic. But it's good you'll get to see this. Your baby brother is finally taking his place in the family business."

Chapter Thirty-Two

*R*aymond, Dominic thought. *What have you done?*

His brother's eyes didn't meet his.

Dominic's hands were sweating. He rubbed them against his jeans. His cheek ached where Alexi had hit him. He'd gone for the man's gun when they were getting out of the car, so he'd deserved it. But hell, that fist to his face had really hurt.

Not as much as this, though. Seeing Raymond here with their uncle's tentacle around him. Charles Traynor was far shorter than the Crane men, and he didn't have their looks. But he had the cold dead eyes of a shark. Charles gazed fondly at his younger nephew.

"Raymond here arrived last night. My original plan had been to draw you out by telling you we had him. I know you have a soft spot for your brother, so I was sure you'd come running. But Raymond didn't think so. He thought you'd see through the ruse. So we were just going to let you stew for a while, until we could track you down. But you see, Ray? Your brother did come for you the minute he found out you were missing. I should've put a bet on it. You would owe me a drink right now."

Dominic was glad to see Raymond unharmed. But his

rational mind didn't want to acknowledge the truth, even though it was standing literally in front of him. He stared at his brother, both needing and dreading to see the confirmation in Raymond's eyes.

"You didn't. Please tell me you didn't."

Finally, his brother looked back at him. And there was nothing. No trace of the boy Dominic had thought he knew.

"You were going to betray our family. From the minute you were arrested, we all knew you would cave. Warren never should've put you in charge. If he'd trusted Charles back then, none of this would ever have happened."

"He's right," Charles said. "You just weren't cut out for this sort of thing, Dominic. Your weaknesses were always going to condemn you, and Warren should have seen that. But it was your choice to take affirmative steps against us. I tried to warn you. If you'd just done as I said, you could've come back into the fold. It's too late for that now."

Dominic could barely speak. How long had his brother been lying to him? How long had he been working with their uncle, plotting this takeover? Was it really since the arrest months ago?

That was what Raymond had suggested—that he'd never believed Dominic was strong enough to withstand the government's pressure. And he'd been right. But the one accomplishment Dominic had thought he'd made in his time as leader was keeping Raymond *out* of it. That was the single truly decent thing he'd ever done.

And he'd failed at that, too.

Raymond was part of the Syndicate now.

Charles was going to have the younger man ruling their family business right by his side. For how long, it was hard to say. But it wouldn't last. Charles would already be looking for the first opportunity to rid himself of Raymond Crane the moment the kid was no longer useful.

Maybe even as soon as Dominic himself was out of the way.

"I'm sorry it had to be this way, Nic. I tried to give you a chance. You should've just let me go."

Dominic cringed at the nickname. "If you expect me to beg for my life, I won't. But Raymond, are you sure you truly know what you're doing? Haven't you noticed our uncle has some new friends hanging around? He's got Russian hackers working for him. You know our dad would never have invited outsiders into his circle. Who are they, Russian mafia? You really think you can control them, Charles?"

His uncle put his hands in his pockets. "You're right, I do have some new allies. They've proved very useful. We have a joint venture, and it was your father's shortsightedness that limited him rather than protected him. It kept the business from growing."

"But how long until they decide to take you for everything you've got?"

"That's where loyalty comes in. I wouldn't expect you to know much about that. But my friends also know what I'm willing to do for them. And they show their gratitude back to me. For example, later today they're going to send a car for you. I expected it might be difficult for Raymond to see his older brother suffer. So my friends are going to take care of your punishment, and they will make sure it fits the severity of your betrayal."

The room was starting to spin. "What about Sylvie? What's going to happen to her?"

"Don't worry, you'll stay together. I'll let them decide how they want to...use her. Maybe for her hacking skills, or something else."

Dominic closed his eyes, swallowing down the bile that had risen into his mouth. "Raymond, I am begging you. If you ever loved me at all, don't let them do this to her. It's all my fault, so I'm the one who should be punished. I know you're a decent man. Help her. Please."

"You're just making yourself look pathetic," Charles said. "You might as well just accept that—"

"*All right.*" Raymond pushed his hands into his hair. Sweat had broken out along his brow. "I'll keep Sylvie with me."

Their uncle's expression turned menacing. "That's not your decision."

"Am I your partner or not? I say she's mine. Nobody else is touching her."

Dominic couldn't breathe as he looked between his uncle and his brother.

Charles's mouth slid back into a toothy smile. "All right, fair enough. If you want her, then she's yours. I'll talk to our friends and let them know." He gestured at Sandford, who reluctantly pushed Sylvie toward Raymond. She wouldn't walk forward, so Raymond reached out and grabbed her by the wrist. Her lips puckered like she'd spit at him, but thank god she didn't.

He won't hurt her, Dominic told himself. He'd been wrong about his brother in some ways, but not about this. At least, he hoped so.

Maybe the best Dominic could do right now was choose between something bad and something even worse. The story of his fucking life.

"Our friends will be here in a few hours. Let's all get some rest before then, shall we? It's been quite an exciting night."

Charles left. Raymond followed next, dragging Sylvie along with him toward the main house. Her anguished gaze didn't leave Dominic's.

"Get up," Sandford commanded. Alexi emphasized the point by extending the arm holding the gun.

Dominic stood. They put him in a room with bars on the windows and a bucket in one corner for the toilet. Sandford followed him inside. Alexi hulked in the doorway, the machine gun held across his body.

"Not so defiant now, are you?" Sandford aimed a punch at Dominic's nose, but Dominic shifted easily out of the way.

"You'll have to do better than that."

Scowling, Sandford beckoned his fingers at Alexi. The Neanderthal stepped aside, and two more guards entered the room. They each grabbed hold of one of Dominic's arms, and Alexi aimed the gun at his legs.

"Nobody said you had to be able to walk when we deliver you. So you'd better stay still unless you want Alexi to take out your knee caps."

The lawyer's fist pulled back again, and this time he didn't miss.

Chapter Thirty-Three

*R*aymond passed Sylvie over to a guard, who deposited her in a bedroom upstairs in the mansion. She banged on the door for a while, until the guard outside yelled at her to shut up or he'd come in there.

She backed away, scanning the room for anything that might help her. A weapon, a phone they might've overlooked. Of course, there was nothing because the Syndicate wasn't that stupid. Unlike her. She'd been such an idiot, thinking she was several steps ahead of them, when they'd been playing her and Dominic the whole time.

Charles had made no secret of the fact that the Russians were going to murder Dominic. Her heart wouldn't accept it. She wanted to scream and kick at the walls, as if that could somehow save him. But she was helpless. Dominic was going to die, and there was nothing she could do. She dug her fingers into her hair, pulling at the strands.

They'd told Raymond their entire plan. The kid was a good actor, she gave him that. It seemed like Raymond and Dominic had that in common. Dominic had changed his personality depending on what other people expected, and Raymond had learned to do the same.

What did he plan to do with her, exactly? Dominic clearly thought she was better off in Raymond's hands than with the Syndicate's Russian mobster friends. She was inclined to agree. But that was a small consolation when she was trapped in this room with no way out and nothing to defend herself.

The furniture was screwed into the walls, and the light fixtures were all mounted into the drywall. Not even a lamp she could bring down on Raymond's head if he got too close.

There was a bathroom, but it held little except a spare toothbrush.

She found a duffel bag in the otherwise empty closet. The bag had men's clothing inside, which she guessed belonged to Dominic's brother. There was a pair of running shoes, but they didn't have much weight to them.

Finally, after what felt like ages, exhaustion started to overcome her. There was no window, but it had to be past sunrise by now. She sat in a corner of the walk-in closet and let her head fall against the wall.

She woke with a gasp when the door to the bedroom opened. She peered out of the closet.

Raymond had just stepped inside.

"Were you sleeping in there on the floor? Don't you think you'd be more comfortable in the bed?"

It didn't sound like he was making any sick innuendos, but she couldn't be sure. Raymond was hard to read.

"I'm guessing *you* weren't sleeping," she said. "It's no wonder, since you're giving up your brother to be tortured and murdered. You should feel some kind of shame after the sacrifices he's made for you. He loves you."

"And I loved him. That's why I took responsibility for your welfare."

"Well, don't expect me to thank you."

He shrugged. "Get yourself cleaned up. You smell."

"Fuck you. I'm not taking off my clothes."

"I wasn't asking. I was telling." He marched into the closet, grabbed her by the arm, and hauled her up. He was thinner than Dominic, a decade younger, but he was strong. He shoved her into the bathroom. "The sooner you learn to take orders, the easier this will be."

She braced herself against the wall across from the toilet. "Try to come near me, and I'll kick your balls so hard you'll be spitting them out."

Raymond stood in the doorway to the bathroom. He reached into his pocket. She sucked in a breath, thinking he would produce a gun.

But instead, he held a stack of note paper.

The first one said, *I'm not going to hurt you. But they're listening.*

He raised a finger to his lips. All she could do was stare. As she watched, he put the piece of paper into his mouth and chewed.

The next note said, *Scream.*

Raymond nodded at the paper, raising his eyebrows. She opened her mouth and yelled. He banged his fist into the wall, and she yelped in surprise.

He poured a glass of water and drank to wash down the paper, grimacing. It looked awful.

The next note said, *Do everything I say if you want to get out of here.*

What about Dominic? she mouthed silently.

Raymond nodded. She took that to mean Dominic would get out, too. But she didn't understand what was going on. She held out her hands and shook her head, trying to convey her confusion.

Her eyes widened at the words on the next piece of paper.

I'm working with the FBI.

That note he ripped into small pieces before shoving it into his mouth, chasing it with another swig of tap water.

She had a million questions, but she couldn't ask them. Then she had an idea. She switched on the water in the shower, then beckoned Raymond closer. He shut the door to the bathroom.

"Can we talk now?" she whispered into his ear.

He hesitated. "We have to be careful. There's a bug in the light over the bed, and it picks up a lot. It might help if you scream every once in a while."

She cringed. She tried not to think of how close she'd come to ending up in the hands of the real Syndicate members.

Raymond told her a brief outline of what happened. After Dominic's arrest, Uncle Charles had approached him, asking him to join forces to unite the Syndicate.

"All my life, I've seen what this business has done to our family. To my brothers. Nic saved me by keeping me out of it, so I had to do something to return the favor. I went to the FBI. Offered to infiltrate the Syndicate in exchange for my brother's safety and immunity. But they expected me to deliver the Syndicate before they lifted a finger to help Dominic."

"But they wanted him to testify. Why did they need your testimony, too?"

"Because they're greedy? Dominic's testimony could get them what they needed in case I failed. Which I still might. The two of you being here has fucked all my plans."

With each new bit of information Raymond gave her, she only had more questions. But this wasn't the time. "What are we going to do?"

"Can you fire a gun?"

"Yes."

"I'll get you a weapon as soon as I'm able. I can tell you mean a lot to my brother, so I'll do my best not to let anything happen to you. But if we're going to pull this off, I need your help."

"What about the Russians who're coming to get Dominic? We can't let them take him."

"I thought Dominic would be at the safe house right now,

but then he went and tried to trade himself for me. I guess I should've known he would do something stupid like that. I just figured... I didn't think he'd be willing to go that far."

She hadn't either. Maybe Dominic himself hadn't known until he did it. But doing something courageous often seemed impossible until the moment that you stepped up.

Raymond had done it, though. He'd been working under-cover for months now. She couldn't believe the guy was only around twenty years old. But Raymond had the kind of back-bone that might have made him an effective leader of the Syndicate. Thank goodness Dominic had saved him from going down that path. It had given Raymond the chance to see another way and take it.

"I'm improvising at this point," Raymond whispered. "The FBI can kiss my ass if they don't like it. It's going to be messy. But with some luck, we have a decent chance of making it out of here alive."

Some chance was better than none. "Tell me what to do."

Chapter Thirty-Four

*D*ominic lay on the concrete. His lip and nose were swollen, and blood matted his hair. His stomach ached where Sandford had kicked him. The coward would never have dared if those three enforcers hadn't been pinning Dominic down.

He touched the deep scrape on his cheek. It was still oozing blood. Sandford's ring had done it.

No more pretty boy, the lawyer had mocked.

Like Dominic cared about his fucking face. He wanted to know where Sylvie was and what the hell Raymond was doing to her.

He dozed and woke up when a key scratched in the lock. Dominic had no idea how long he'd slept. His stomach gnawed at itself with hunger, so he assumed several hours had passed.

When the door opened, he saw daylight. He'd been lying in the dark. The brightness made him squint.

"Who's there?"

"It's me." Raymond switched on a light. He was holding a gun.

Dominic sat up. "Here to finish me off? Is that your idea

of mercy?" Maybe it was. A quick gunshot wound to the head would be far preferable to whatever the Russians had planned for him later.

Raymond said something to a person in the hall and closed the door. They were alone. That probably meant this was his last chance to beg.

"I'm sorry for failing you." Dominic's voice sounded strange, probably because his nostrils had swollen shut. "I never wanted you to be a part of this. But please take care of Sylvie. I get that you're angry at me, but don't take it out on her."

"Shut up. You have no idea how sick I am of hearing you talk."

Dominic flinched at the harshness in his brother's voice. Had Raymond ever spoken to him that way? He sounded like Charles.

"The least you could do is hold yourself together and take what's coming like a man. Don't embarrass our family any more than you already have."

"That's how you really see me?"

An embarrassment. Weak. Dominic had thought he couldn't sink any lower, but every word his brother uttered was another stone pushing him down into the depths.

Raymond knelt beside him. "Be quiet," he whispered in a completely different tone altogether. "You have to trust me, Nic. Stay close, and I'll help you." For a split second, he held Dominic's hand and squeezed it.

"What?"

But his brother had already stood up again and opened the door.

Patrick, the guard Dominic had seen yesterday, came into the room and lifted him up to standing. More guards flanked them as they walked him into the main room of the pool house.

"Dominic, I hope you slept well." His uncle smiled like he

was enjoying this. "I would've invited you in for breakfast, but I'm afraid our chef's not here."

Dominic licked at his bloody lip. "Can we get this done without any more bantering?"

Raymond elbowed him in the side. "I told you to stay quiet." The harsh tone was back, but the words reminded him of what Raymond had whispered. *I'm going to help you.* Dominic didn't see how, but he decided to go with it. He didn't have any options left.

To either side of Charles, crowding the room, stood the other Syndicate captains. Men Dominic had known most of his life, who'd worked for him, who'd treated him like their own son. Most of them just eyed him with stony expressions, but one man spat at his feet when he came near.

To them, he was already dead.

Charles raised his arms, and everyone else quieted. "The Crane brothers are back among us. Two of them, at least. I know I'm not the only one who's gratified to see it, even in a different form than we all were hoping. I wanted to bring both of my nephews into the fold again, where they belonged. But life doesn't always deal out the hand we'd like to get. I'm confident you'll all welcome Raymond as he takes his place at my side, and not hold any of his older brothers' failings against him."

There were nods and murmurs of agreement. No doubt Raymond's presence was helping them set aside any lingering doubts. A Crane was once again at the head of the Syndicate, even if Raymond wasn't truly in charge.

But Dominic guessed his betrayal had united the factions behind Charles more than any endorsement ever could.

Again, Dominic thought of Raymond's whispers in that room. Had he imagined it? Maybe he'd been hallucinating, his mind grasping for anything to hold onto.

"Sadly, we have less pleasant business to handle today. A righting of wrongs. Unpleasant, but necessary. Gentleman, if you'll come with me? I believe our friends are arriving as we speak."

Charles and the captains filed out through the pool house door.

Patrick pulled Dominic to follow them.

Yellow glare bounced off the swimming pool. Dominic raised his hand, shielding his eyes from the sun. He stumbled, and Patrick yanked his arm to keep him going. Raymond stayed close to Dominic's other side.

The back door of the main house opened, and Alexi brought Sylvie out to join them. Aaron Sandford trailed after them, his smug smile firmly in place. At least she looked unharmed. Her mouth opened in shock when she saw Dominic, probably reacting to the state of his face.

Raymond elbowed Dominic again, like he was warning him to keep his mouth shut.

But what the hell was Sylvie doing out here? Raymond was supposed to be protecting her. He'd said he wasn't going to give her to the Russians. Dominic wanted to scream. Raymond's whispers earlier were the only thing keeping him quiet.

Everyone related to the Syndicate had gathered on the far side of the pool. Now, a new group of people walked through the gate, coming from the direction of the driveway.

A man in his early forties led the way, dressed in business casual like Charles. Then a phalanx of beefy thugs in boxy suits.

They stopped on the other side of the pool, facing the Syndicate.

"Charles, how are you?" the leader of the other gang said. Dominic didn't recognize the guy. He wore a watch that bore a resemblance to a Rolex, but even with blood in his eyes Dominic could tell it was probably fake. The man's clothes were off the rack. This guy was middle management at best.

Whoever this group was, the Russian mob or whatever,

they hadn't bothered to send anyone too important. That just confirmed that Uncle Charles was way out of his league. Dominic would have been, too. The Cranes had always known the Syndicate's place in the scheme of things. That was how they'd survived so long.

"Thank you for meeting on such short notice, Victor," Charles said. "I appreciate the courtesy."

Victor's smile was tight. "Our pleasure." His eyes flicked over to Dominic, probably because he was the only guy who looked like he'd recently received a beating. "Is that our friend?"

"That's right. He's eager to get to know you."

"As are we. And the girl?"

Charles waved a hand at Raymond. "Change of plans, I'm afraid. Of course, you're welcome to question her, given the information we shared with you."

Victor was nodding like he understood just what Charles meant. "Questions. We do have questions. Ms. Trousseau, is it?"

"Yes," Sylvie said in a small voice.

Dominic's entire body seized to see these people focused on her. Raymond's hand circled Dominic's elbow, like he was trying to send some sort of message through his skin.

"I understand you wrote a nasty little bit of code and sent it to some associates of mine."

"Yes," she said again.

Goosebumps broke out painfully over Dominic's back.

"And whose orders were you working under?" Victor asked.

Charles seemed uninterested in this exchange, tapping his loafer against the stone patio—until Sylvie's next answer.

"Charles Traynor. He hired me to do it."

Dominic could hardly believe what she'd just said. "What —" Raymond's hand tightened around his arm, and Dominic clamped his mouth closed.

Uncle Charles couldn't believe it, either. "She's lying," he sputtered. "That's absurd."

Okay, so this was some sort of plan Sylvie and Raymond had cooked up. That was the only explanation. But what was his brother thinking, screwing around with the Russian mafia? How was this supposed to help them?

A dozen different men on either side of the pool had their hands on their weapons. No one had aimed one yet.

Victor's brow wrinkled. "This is a real conundrum, Charles. Because here's what I know. We're the ones who told *you*, just last night, that somebody tried to hack us. And you acted so shocked that anyone would have the *audacity*."

"Yes. Yes, of course. And then I learned it was Dominic. It was *him*. He put her up to it. That's what I told you as soon as I found out."

Victor walked along the edge of the pool, gesturing as he spoke. "But how did we know about it in the first place? Because a source from within *your* Syndicate told us the truth about five minutes before we called you. Told us all kinds of things. That you intended to play us for fools? Learn everything you could about our operation and then fuck us over? You had one chance to come clean when we called you last night, but you played as innocent as a girl at communion."

"But I would never—"

Victor's focus shifted to Raymond. "Why don't we ask your second in command?"

"It's all true." Raymond's voice rang out against the hard surfaces of the pool area. "I heard Charles give the order. Sylvie was supposed to hack your system, and Dominic would take the fall for it. But I never agreed to any of it. That's why I came clean with you. I knew this would blow back on us."

The Syndicate captains were starting to narrow their eyes at Charles. They didn't know who to believe. A Traynor, or a Crane?

"What the fuck are you doing, Raymond?"

Charles grabbed a gun from the nearest enforcer and pointed it at Dominic's brother. Their uncle was several yards away, but still, Dominic sucked in a panicked breath.

"You called me last night to tell me about Dominic's plot to betray *us*," Charles said, "right after I spoke to Victor. I didn't know about the hack until they informed me. *But you* did. Fucking tell them."

Dark metal appeared all over the patio. The Russians pointed their weapons across the pool. The Syndicate did the same, aiming across at the Russians.

Dominic and Sylvie were pretty much the only people in view not holding a gun. *Fuck.* On what planet had this seemed like a good plan?

"You're the one bringing this shit down on our family business, Charles," Raymond said. "I didn't want any part of it. I just want to take my brother and the girl and walk away."

Dominic locked eyes with Sylvie. She seemed just as bewildered as he was. His muscles tensed. If people started shooting, he was going to make a run for her.

He spotted Sandford, who was slowly inching away like he could predict the same future that Dominic could. The lawyer didn't have a gun either.

Victor held up a hand. "Everyone, relax. The timeline of last night's little game of telephone is getting convoluted, isn't it? It's he said/he said. But we're going to work this out. For one, because we've got you outmatched. I have twice as many guys behind me as you do, Charles. Any of yours does something foolish? We'll lay waste to the lot of you, since you've so conveniently gathered for us to play target practice."

Nobody replied. Nobody moved.

Victor sighed, like he was overworked and underpaid. Middle management. "Now Raymond, we already agreed to let you go. You're adding more conditions? That wasn't the deal."

"I didn't know Dominic or Sylvie would be here. I—"

"No!" Uncle Charles screamed. "I'm not letting you roll on me, you little fucking punk."

He opened fire.

And so did everyone else.

The pool area exploded with gunshots. Raymond tried to drag Dominic to the ground. But Dominic was already scrambling toward Sylvie. She dove behind a concrete planter.

People were shouting and falling left and right. Blood spattered the patio.

Dominic made it behind the planter and grabbed for Raymond, who was right behind him, panting like he'd sprinted a mile. Dominic looked around for Sandford, but the lawyer had vanished.

Raymond dashed out beyond the planter and back again, grabbing a gun from a fallen Syndicate member. Pieces of concrete exploded from the planter as bullets plowed into it. Dominic couldn't even tell who was shooting at them. People had scattered everywhere.

Then Dominic noticed his brother's leg was bleeding. "Jesus, are you hit?"

"It's nothing. I'm fine." Raymond handed the gun to Sylvie. "Where's Charles?"

Sylvie checked the magazine and slapped it back into place. "He's facedown in the pool. Tends to happen when you start shooting and a bunch of Russians with machine guns are already aiming at you."

He couldn't even tell how many Syndicate members were still alive. But Dominic didn't expect any favors or mercy from Victor and his men. He just wanted to get the people he cared about as far away as possible.

"We need to get out of here," he said.

"You two go ahead of me," Sylvie shouted over the noise. "I don't know where the exit is." She jumped up and squeezed the trigger, laying down cover.

Dominic took a split second to admire her. Damn, this woman was incredible.

Raymond went first, crouching low as he headed for the side of the house. The lower part of his pant leg was drenched with blood, which made Dominic's gut wrench. That wasn't some scratch. But the kid had shaken it off.

Dominic saw a body a couple of feet away. Alexi. The man lay on the ground in a puddle of red. Dominic crawled forward to pluck a handgun the guy had dropped. He pushed Sylvie ahead of him, then took over the job of firing behind them to provide cover.

They reached a side yard, where ferns and palm trees hemmed them in. Here, it was relatively quiet. Over by the pool at the back of the house, the gun battle continued. The lots in this neighborhood were huge, but the neighbors had to be hearing all this noise.

"Think someone's going to call the police?" Dominic hadn't enjoyed his recent experiences with the SWAT team, but it was the lesser of evils at the moment.

Raymond took out his phone. "How about the FBI?"

"The *what?*"

His brother smiled. "Sylvie knows. She can explain if she wants. I'm just trying not to piss myself at this point."

"I doubt that." Dominic eyed the blood on his brother's pants, worrying over how bad the wound might be. Did he need to stop and bandage it? But Raymond had kept going, edging along the side of the house.

Sylvie went next, with Dominic bringing up the rear. There was another gate up ahead. It appeared to lead into the front yard, which covered at least an acre on its own. But he'd seen dense trees when they were driving in, so there would be plenty of places for them to hide.

Raymond swung open the gate and hobbled forward. Then he skidded to a stop. Sylvie bumped into him. Dominic stopped several paces short.

Aaron Sandford stood in front of them, aiming a machine gun.

"Drop the gun, Sylvie. Slowly."

She lowered her weapon to the ground. While Sandford's eyes were on her, Dominic tucked the gun he'd taken from Alexi into the back waistband of his jeans.

"The Crane brothers. First it was Warren, then I had to deal with Dominic. And then it's Raymond who shows up. Every time I think I'm done with you, one of you pops back up again. Do you know how annoying that is? Having to clean up your messes?"

As he spoke, Sandford moved the gun around like it was some toy. Aiming at Sylvie. Then Raymond.

"And the whole time, I knew you'd run your father's business into the ground. But did anyone want to hear what I had to say? No. Nobody listens to the lawyer."

"What are you going to do, Sandford?" Dominic asked. "Without us, you're out of a job."

"You think I want this job? I fucking hate you, Dominic. God, it feels good to say that. I hated Warren, too. I danced the day he went to prison. None of you ever respected me. I warned Charles not to trust Raymond—never trust a Crane brother—and now look what's happened? I told him. I knew."

Dominic took a step forward, keeping his hands raised, palms out. "You're right. Charles should've listened to you."

"So now, what do I do with you? If anybody from the Syndicate is still alive, they might like to watch you get roasted on a spit."

In the back yard, guns continued to pop like fireworks.

Dominic edged forward another step. "Or you could turn us over to Victor and his friends. They might give you something for us."

Dominic kept slowly advancing, arms out. Sandford was backing up, the gun muzzle still pointed at them.

"Why the hell would they do that? They'd shoot you just

to be rid of you. I'm sure they're regretting their partnership with Charles and just want to wash it all away."

Dominic was even with Sylvie now. Just one more step. That was all he needed.

Raymond had moved to the side, looking from Dominic to the lawyer. As if he could sense what was about to happen.

"What I really want," Sandford said, "is to watch you bleed out on the ground. I think that would be sufficient payment for all the years of suffering you boys have put me through."

"If that's how it has to be, then I get it. But let Sylvie walk away. That's all I ask."

"You know, I'm really tired of hearing you say that. I'm tired of all of you. So the answer is no. You like her so much, then you can die together." He extended the arm holding the machine gun.

Dominic stepped in front of Sylvie.

She grabbed the gun from his waistband, raised it past his shoulder, and fired. Sound exploded in Dominic's ear. The shot hit Sandford in the upper chest. His finger pressed the trigger on the machine gun, and bullets strafed the house. Raymond, Sylvie, and Dominic dove to the grass, but the bullets hadn't come anywhere near them.

The lawyer slumped onto the ground.

Minutes later, the place was swarming with FBI agents and police. But Dominic could barely hear, much less respond to their questions. He could only look at Raymond and Sylvie, his ear ringing, and think of how close he'd come to losing them.

But this wasn't over. He could still lose them yet.

Chapter Thirty-Five

*S*ylvie had never been questioned by the FBI before.

They took her to a local police station, where the agents asked if she wanted a lawyer. Shooting Aaron Sandford had to be a clear case of self-defense, but her hacking activities were gray area, at best. And then there was the part where she'd helped Dominic evade bail. So, she said yes.

The agents called someone, who consulted with her. Sylvie answered a few of their questions before the interviewers seemed to lose interest. They said they might bring her in for further information later on.

After they were finished, the agents told her she could leave. She insisted on speaking to Dominic but was still surprised when they actually allowed it.

He was sitting in an interview room, looking like hell. Bandages crisscrossed his face. "Sylvie." He stood up from his chair, and she ran into his arms. He pulled her against his chest.

"I'm so sorry." His voice was hoarse.

"I know. Are you okay?"

He paused, like he was trying to think. "No."

Paramedics had treated him and Raymond at the scene

for their injuries. Everything had been so chaotic. Ambulances, SWAT, FBI, and police—it all blurred into shouts and lights and sirens in her mind.

"Do you need a doctor?"

"No, that's…" Dominic seemed listless, his eyes unfocused. Was he on pain meds?

Raymond limped in wearing a fresh pair of pants. According to the medic at the scene, the bullet had gone through his calf muscle, missing the bone or anything vital. He'd been lucky. But his skin was about five shades paler than normal.

"Nic. Jeez, they wouldn't let me out of there 'til now." The brothers embraced. Raymond asked the same questions—was he okay, was he hurting—but Dominic's answers were equally disjointed. They all sat down.

"What are they going to do with you?" Sylvie asked Dominic.

"Keep me here, then they're going to transfer me back to West Oaks. No more bail. I don't know why they haven't stuck me in a holding cell yet."

"One of the FBI guys is a friend," Raymond explained. "He told me he'd wait on that as long as possible, so we could talk. Given the circumstances."

Dominic touched his injured ear. The paramedic had said hearing loss was probably temporary, but Sylvie didn't know if it was bothering him.

"At least I'll get a new lawyer," Dominic said. "When are you two leaving?"

"I just spoke to Max. He's sending cars for us." Sylvie had borrowed a phone to call Bennett Security. She'd lost her device in the chaos of the last twenty-four hours. Max had confirmed that Tanner was safe at the hospital. He had a concussion, and the doctors were keeping him there for further monitoring.

"And you're going to Max's safe house?" Dominic asked her.

"Raymond is. I'm just going back to headquarters, but I'll be fine there. I'm still trying to understand how all this happened, though." She turned to Dominic's brother. "Were you *trying* to get the Syndicate and those Russian mobsters to kill each other?"

"Not exactly. Not at first." Raymond wiped a hand over his eyes. "I told you that Charles contacted me after Dominic got arrested, asking me to help him unite the warring factions of the Syndicate. That's when I went to the FBI. But I didn't want to seem too enthusiastic. I had to be careful, build up my uncle's trust. And I didn't want to leave school yet, either. There was a lot I had to get ready for. But the deeper I got, the clearer it was to me that bringing down the Syndicate was the only way to save Nic."

Dominic walked away from them, hands on his hips, cursing under his breath. Raymond sat down at the small table, resting his elbows on its surface.

"From the beginning, Charles was dropping hints about how Nic would be better out of the way completely. I kept hoping I'd get enough evidence that I could nail him, but in order to do that, I had to officially join. But that would just make Charles want to get rid of Nic even more, because he wouldn't need Nic's endorsement. So I was kind of stuck. Charles made friends with the Russians and took power on his own. He kept pressuring me to join and solidify his claim, but he wanted to keep Nic in his back pocket, too."

"But then we called you," Sylvie said. "About going to the Bennett Security safe house."

"Exactly. You told me Charles wanted Dominic to come in. I panicked. I figured there were two possible outcomes. One, Uncle Charles was going to get rid of Nic, just like he'd threatened to do. The other possibility? That the Russians would figure out about your whole hacking plan, and they'd send people to torture you to death. I knew I had to do something, and it wasn't going to be bringing the FBI into the loop, because there was no way they'd act fast enough. I had a few hours to work with. That was it."

"Then what did you do?"

"Because of hanging around Charles, I'd already met some of the guys who work for the Russians. Like Victor. I called up Victor and said I had information for him. I told him Charles was planning to hack their computer experts. That Charles intended to betray them. And I already knew they'd be able to find the evidence—that program you'd uploaded. I didn't want to tell them about your plan, Sylvie, but I had to give them something to make them trust me. That was all I could come up with."

"No, I get it. But what did you say to Charles? He said you called him, too."

Raymond nodded. "I had to come into the Syndicate fully, and I couldn't act like the timing was just a coincidence. They would've been suspicious. So I said that Nic had betrayed the Syndicate, and I wanted to stop him. And of course, by then Victor had already said something to Charles about Sylvie's hacking attempt, so I had corroboration to back me up."

"And that made Charles trust you, too."

"Yeah. I packed my stuff, left my dorm, and headed straight for my uncle's house in Bel Air. My entire purpose was to buy you time to get to the safe house. I thought once you and Dominic and his housekeeper were safe, I would focus on finding the evidence I needed to testify against the Syndicate. But I couldn't just abandon all that work and go into hiding until I had something to show for it."

"Why didn't you warn Dominic about what you were planning?" She wasn't upset at Raymond, but it might've saved a lot of the mess they'd gotten into.

"If I told him, that would've *guaranteed* he'd come after me."

Dominic was still staring at the wall, arms crossed. But she was sure he was listening.

"And your deal with Victor?" Sylvie prompted.

"That was my backup plan. I had to make sure Charles had his hands full with a bunch of pissed-off Russians, and that the Russians were too distracted by my uncle's supposed deception to pay attention to you and Nic anymore."

Jeez, the kid had definitely been panicking, because his "plan" sounded more like a bunch of desperate moves without a clear strategy in mind. But he'd done the best he could.

"I hadn't expected you and Nic to end up at my uncle's house. When that happened, it made Charles call his Russian friends for help getting rid of you. But Charles had no idea Victor would read that request as an overt attempt to lure them closer. Victor rolled up with an army of guys, ready for war."

Dominic finally turned around. "So you decided to poke that giant fucking hornet's nest and tell everyone *you* were the source who ratted out Charles? How did that make any kind of sense?"

"I was making it up as I went along. And it worked. We got out of there alive."

"Barely. Your leg is bandaged up. You could've died if that bullet hit a few inches to the side. And Sylvie had to kill Aaron Sandford!"

"We all did what we had to." Sylvie didn't like the idea of taking anyone's life, but she wasn't mourning that asshole.

"But neither of you should've had to do *any* of it."

Raymond stared at his brother a moment, then sighed. "The FBI found important documents during their raid of Charles's house. It's going to make a difference. And at some point, I'll testify to what I know about the Syndicate. I'm not even sure how many Syndicate members are still alive. I know things about the Russian guys, too. I've spoken to people who work for the US Attorney, and they're applying for witness protection for me."

Dominic stepped forward, shock on his face. "WITSEC? Like...permanently?"

"Yes, Nic. The new identity stuff. Everything."

"But you have school. I don't understand."

Raymond sighed again, as if he were the older brother explaining the real world to the younger one. "This was always the plan for me since I started working with the FBI. I knew this was coming."

"You can't give up your life."

"I already have. I haven't had a girlfriend since this started. I barely talk to my friends. They wouldn't have been safe."

"Jesus, Ray. Do you know how fucked up that is? My baby brother had to sacrifice himself to save me?" Dominic's eyes were shining with tears.

"Because you saved *me*. And I would do it all again."

"It would've been better if you'd just let them kill me."

Sylvie's heart twisted. "*Nic.*"

He sank back into his chair, head in his hands. "I don't mean I want to die. Of course I don't. But it's not right that anyone else has to pay for the things I've done."

"You didn't ask to be born into this family any more than I did. I *want* this fresh start. Maybe you should think about it, too. As long as our last name is Crane, we'll never truly be safe from our family's past."

Sylvie couldn't believe how much Raymond had taken upon himself. Dominic just shook his head, not so much disagreeing as despairing at the truth of what his brother had said.

Raymond got up slowly and headed for the door. "I'm going to find some coffee or...something. I need a minute. I'll be right back."

After the door closed, Sylvie asked, "Do you think you

might go with him? Move to a new place? Change your identity?"

She'd known this could happen. Yet she still couldn't begin to get her mind around it. Or what it could mean for her. As if her own needs were even relevant to this conversation.

"I don't know." Dominic would barely even look at her. "I'm so sorry for what you've had to go through because of me."

"I feel the same way Raymond does. I'd do it again. I care about you."

He didn't respond. He'd dealt with too much today. She understood.

"So you might be in jail for a few days?" she asked.

"Or more than a few."

"I could come visit you."

"*Please* don't do that. I'm serious."

Maybe he didn't want her to see him that way. "But is there some way I can reach you?"

He didn't answer.

"I know it's really hard right now. But we probably won't have another chance to talk for a while. You said you wanted to keep seeing each other, and I still want that, too."

Dominic's eyes were hollow. "I did. You're amazing. You're *everything*. But I have nothing to offer you. No home, no money, no future, or security. I don't know who I am now."

"You'll figure those things out." Her voice sounded high. Desperate. Like she was pleading with him not to say the next thing, even though she could tell it was coming.

"Sylvie, I'm not a whole person." He looked down at his hands, fingers spread wide. "I'm just…shreds."

You're beautiful, she wanted to say. *And I'm not talking about what's on the outside.* But she knew that wasn't what he wanted to hear right now. She looked around for a piece of paper. "I'll give you my cell and work number, and you'll call me when you're ready to talk."

"It would be better if you forget about me."

She turned back to face him. "I can't do that. How could I do that?" Sylvie's eyes stung with tears.

He got up and walked toward her. "Getting to know you is one of the best things that's happened to me." Dominic cupped her cheek and kissed her on the corner of her mouth. "You have no idea how much I'm going to miss you."

No. Don't do this.

But what else *was* he supposed to do? She didn't know, either. The bail thing would get resolved. She was sure of it. But then the DA would still expect him to testify, and he'd probably want to stay with Raymond. Sylvie might have to testify about some of these events, too, yet she wouldn't possibly be in as much danger as the Crane brothers. How could she have a future with Dominic when he might be living in some other city, under some new name?

Raymond popped his head in. "Sylvie? Your friends are here."

"I'll be right there." She turned back to Dominic. "Can I hug you goodbye?" Her voice was breaking.

"Of course."

She held him as tightly as she could, trying to memorize his scent, the sound of his breathing, the feeling of him against her. As if those countless pieces of him could add up to something that would fill his absence.

He brought his lips to her ear. "Goodbye, Sylvie."

"Bye."

Raymond stayed in the room to say his own goodbyes to his brother. But Sylvie forced herself to walk away, wiping the tears from her eyes.

Chapter Thirty-Six

Four Months Later

*D*ominic waved when Max Bennett stepped into the pub. His fingers drummed the table as he waited for the man to order a drink at the bar.

It had taken a lot of courage just for him to invite Max here tonight. Now he had to figure out the right things to say.

I can do this, he thought. *I have to.*

Max set down his glass and slid into the other side of the booth. "Dominic. It's been a while."

"Thanks for meeting me." Dominic had to speak up over the noise. It was a rowdy place in Culver City, crowded with twentysomethings in T-shirts and flannel. Not his usual hangout, but Dominic had picked a location where he wasn't likely to see anyone he used to know.

"No problem," Max said.

"This is weird, right?" The two of them, meeting for drinks. Like they were friends.

"A little weird." Max gestured at the beer in front of him.

"I mean, they've only got fruit-flavored beers on tap here. I don't get it."

Dominic barked a laugh. "Yeah. I'm drinking a pineapple IPA. It's better than it sounds."

"Some things are like that." Max shrugged, sipping from his pint glass. "You seem different."

Dominic stared into his beer.

"Not in a bad way. I was surprised to get your call, though. I thought you'd left."

"I left West Oaks. Still in L.A. County. I live in Burbank at the moment."

The man's brow tightened. "Don't you miss the ocean? Why the valley?"

"It's anonymous. And very slightly less expensive."

Max tilted his head, acknowledging the point. "But you're alive, I see. That's good news." He lifted his drink like he was toasting.

"I'm glad you think so." That was the closest Max had ever come to complimenting him.

Only a couple of Syndicate captains had survived the massacre at Charles Traynor's house. The US Attorney had filed charges against them for murder, racketeering, and whatever else. Dominic hadn't paid attention. He just knew the trial was at least a year away with all the complications involved.

Raymond was living in some city where Dominic couldn't reach him, except through special channels. He wasn't allowed to know his brother's address or the new name the US Marshalls had given him. They'd see each other at the trial to testify, but that was a long way off.

The West Oaks DA's Office had dropped Dominic's murder charge, as well as any charges related to him skipping bail. He was a free man now. In some ways.

"Why did you decide to stick around?" Max asked.

"Wasn't ready to give up completely just yet."

There were still people he cared about here. One person, especially. He probably didn't have any chance with her now, but he couldn't completely break those ties, either.

At first, when he'd gotten out of jail after the massacre, Dominic hadn't really cared if the remnants of the Syndicate came after him. He'd almost been daring them to do it by staying in So Cal, living under his real name, and meeting with government agents all the time.

But nobody showed up to deliver vengeance.

As the months went by, Dominic hadn't felt anybody following him. Like he wasn't even important enough to kill anymore, which might've hurt his feelings back when he was pretending to be the ruthless leader of the Silverlake Syndicate.

Dominic had spoken to Warren since, and the eldest Crane brother assured him nobody was going to bother him. Warren said the Syndicate was finished, their territory and market share absorbed by rival groups. Those few people the Feds had rounded up to prosecute hardly amounted to anything, and even they blamed Charles and Raymond more than Dominic himself.

Victor and many of his Russian mafia henchmen had survived the massacre. But the Feds had decided not to bring any sweeping charges against that group. Instead—according to Raymond—the US Attorney wanted to flip more of the low-level guys to bring a racketeering case against the higher ups later on. The massacre at the Traynor house barely ranked on the scale of shit those Russian mob guys were into.

Dominic felt like just one more cog in a big machine, where defendants constantly turned into witnesses to save themselves and pass the blame along. He assumed the US Attorney would eventually get to the top of the criminal food chain, but by then, he and Raymond would be long forgotten.

Max took another sip of his beer. "Do I need to keep an

eye on the exits? In case your old friends are planning an ambush?"

"Anybody who cared enough to kill me is already dead."

"I heard something about that. Might have made the news?"

That was an understatement. "There were a few articles." Some with his face on them.

Max pointed at Dominic's cheek. "I'm guessing that's where you got the scar. Too bad."

"Doesn't bother me." He touched the spot where a thin, white line of scar tissue striped down his cheek. Courtesy of Aaron Sandford's ring.

"I hear some women are into scars."

Dominic appreciated Max's attempt at optimism. "I wouldn't know. I'm steering clear of women these days." And that just made him think of Sylvie. He'd promised himself he'd wait at least ten minutes before asking about her. But now he couldn't think of anything else.

"How's Sylvie doing?"

Max grimaced, setting down his drink. "I doubt you want me to answer that. If she's good, then you'll feel bad. And if she's not good, you'll feel worse."

"Is she good?"

Max shook his head.

Damn. He was right. Dominic did feel worse.

"Is she seeing anyone?" Hope made his breath catch.

"I *really* shouldn't answer that."

His stomach dropped. "Because she is?"

"No, because it's not my business." There was an awkward silence. "Is that why you wanted to meet? You could've asked me about Sylvie on the phone. I would've given the same nonanswers."

"That's not why. Not really." Dominic's finger ran through the condensation on his glass. "I was hoping for advice. I *need* advice."

"From me?"

"You seem like somebody who has his shit together. And mine's all over the place."

"Thanks. It's only a recent development for me, actually."

"Really?"

"Believe it or not, Crane, I had a crappy childhood, too. Different from yours, but still bad in ways it took me a long time to work through."

Dominic decided not to mention that his name wasn't "Crane" anymore. He'd just gotten the court order changing it to "Anderson." Nice and generic. Not a brand-new identity, like his brother in WITSEC. But the new name felt like something he'd needed. A baby step toward moving on.

"Tell me what you've been up to," Max said. "How've you been keeping yourself busy?"

Aside from living in a shithole apartment off money his brothers sent?

"I've been consulting with the FBI and state task forces on organized crime. Sharing everything I know. There's a ton of stuff I can't testify to in court, but that could still help law enforcement strategize."

"That's admirable."

"It's really not. No need to patronize me." He was just paying back a small part of his debt to society.

"Okay, then I won't. So, what's the advice you need?"

"Can I turn this into a more permanent gig, do you think? Former bad guy consulting with the good guys? I'm short on career options. No degree, and my past employment references have limited usefulness."

Max knew all about the private side of security and investigative work. Dominic had figured the man would have some ideas. But he had to do something because he couldn't keep mooching off his brothers. Warren was making license plates or some shit in prison, and Raymond was a college student for god's sake, though he did get some money through the WITSEC program.

The government had seized most everything else, except the house in West Oaks. But they'd sold that property to fund their dad's long-term care in a home for people with dementia, and Dominic donated the extra proceeds to a charity for crime victims. None of them spoke to their mother.

Maureen was a little like a mother to him, and she'd offered to help from her meager savings. But aside from the occasional home-cooked meal, he couldn't accept. Even he wasn't that contemptible.

"There are opportunities like that, sure. But is that really what you want to do? I get that you're starting from scratch, but that also means you could do pretty much anything. Why not pick a job that suits *you*, and not who you used to be?"

"Who else would want anything I could offer? My past is all I have." Sad as that was.

"I could be wrong, but from the things you've told me— and things Sylvie has mentioned—I would've thought you'd be trying for something different."

Suddenly, it didn't seem like they were just talking about career options. "I did want that. I do. But it doesn't seem possible for…someone like me."

"Here's some real advice. It's the best I've got, and it comes from experience. If you want someone else to believe you deserve a second chance, then you've got to forgive yourself first."

Can I do that? How would he even know if it happened? What would it feel like?

"If I figure out how to do that, do you think someone *else* might forgive me, too?"

"I can't tell you that. Probably depends on what you need her to forgive. But if she cares about you, and you earn it, she will."

"Is that something else you've learned from experience?"

The corner of Max's mouth ticked up. "I'm going to ask Lana to marry me. I...don't even know why I just told you that." He exhaled. "I've been stressing about it. See? Not *all* of my shit is together."

"Stressing because you don't think she'll say yes?"

"Not really. It's because I worry I won't be enough. It's not about any single thing I've done to prove myself. It's being enough every day." Max shrugged. "But she's worth it."

Dominic was happy for them. But if a successful guy like Max still doubted himself, Dominic didn't know what hope *he* had.

They finished their beers, chatting about less serious topics. The weather, the Dodgers' current record. When Max left, Dominic saw a note the man had left behind on the back of his bar receipt.

Sylvie's cell, it said, along with a number.

THAT NIGHT, Dominic stared at the contact he'd programmed into his phone. He wanted to write to Sylvie more than anything. But he didn't know if he should.

The last time they'd seen one another, at the police station, he'd been reeling from everything they'd been through. Watching so many people die and knowing that, because of him, Sylvie had blood on her hands.

Yet that day, he'd also felt like he was seeing things clearly for the first time in a while. He'd been a fool to think he and Sylvie could have a future together. He could hardly take care of himself, so how could he have taken care of anyone else?

You have to forgive yourself first, Max had said.

Dominic didn't hate himself. He just hadn't seen how he'd get beyond the limitations of his past.

But he'd been making progress in the last few months. Digging himself out of the hole he'd made. Maureen had been teaching him some basic cooking skills. His apartment only had a hot plate, but he could make pasta and scrambled eggs. He'd liked going to the local government offices in the mornings and grocery shopping at night, which wasn't glamorous but made for a routine.

Nic Anderson had a simple existence, but at least he was doing something to make the world a little better.

After four months of surviving, he didn't feel quite so much like a shell of a person. It was getting easier to sleep through the night. He thought of himself as Nic, and that was how he introduced himself whenever he met people now. He was still Dominic, too—but the sharp edges had worn off the old memories. Thoughts of his brothers, and even his flakey former friends, made him smile. The darker spots in his past just made him sad instead of debilitating him with guilt.

So maybe he *had* forgiven himself, at least part way, and just hadn't acknowledged it yet. And didn't know what to do with it.

But he missed Sylvie. So fucking much.

The feeling wasn't going away. With each day that passed, the agony of missing her only intensified. Her smile and her soft kisses. The way she'd seen the best parts of him and wasn't afraid of the rest. In his mind, he'd replayed every hour they'd spent together in the West Oaks house, every conversation.

Now, his yearning for her was a gaping hole in his chest, his heart ripped clean away.

And he was staring at the phone in his hand, thinking how easy it would be to reach out.

Would she answer?

Dominic: Hi. It's Nic. You said we could talk when I was ready, and—

No. That wasn't right at all. He deleted it.

Dominic: Hi. It's Nic. I really miss you and I was thinking if you miss me too, then—

> Fuck. No. Terrible. Delete.
> He lay on the couch for a while. Then he started typing.

Dominic: Dear Sylvie, I hope you're doing well. I'm better than I was, but still working on myself. I can't think of what to say except I miss you, and that doesn't begin to describe how I feel. I would love to talk with you sometime if you're willing, even just on the phone. I would love to hear your voice.

It's hard staying positive, but it helps to remember the beautiful things. Music and art and books I've enjoyed. People who've made me see the world—and myself—differently. The very top of that list is you.

Love,
Nic

> He hit send.
> Dominic stayed awake as long as he could, checking his phone for a response. But it didn't come.

Chapter Thirty-Seven

Sylvie got home from work and dumped her things in her room. It had been another crappy day, the latest of many in the last few months. Nothing seemed to go right. Her codes were buggy. Her focus was inconsistent. Even her photographic memory had been erratic. Today, she'd completely botched the video analysis Max asked her to do. Priyanka had swooped in and finished it for her.

I need my mojo back, she thought. Though she didn't know where to find it.

She started up the stairs to check in with Ethan and find out what he wanted for dinner.

Then she heard a voice she hadn't encountered in a long time—not in person, anyway. She ran up the rest of the way to her cousin's apartment.

"Faith?"

"Sylvie!"

Faith leaped up from the Ethan's couch, her long blond hair flying. She tackled Sylvie in a hug. "It's so amazing to see you. Look at you." She pulled back and held Sylvie at arm's length. "You're so beautiful."

"I was thinking the same thing about you. What on earth are you doing here?"

Sylvie had written to her former high school best friend over four months ago, just before all that happened at Charles Traynor's house. Since then, she and Faith had been exchanging texts and talking on the phone several times a week.

Faith had told her how sorry she was for cutting off contact between them. She'd gotten stuck in a loveless marriage at nineteen, right after Sylvie left, for reasons that she still hadn't shared. Faith had just hinted at a shotgun wedding and some traumatic events. But she'd always regretted losing her best friend.

Sylvie couldn't deny that the rejection still hurt, even after Faith's explanations and apologies. But she'd wanted Faith back in her life more than she wanted to hold on to some pointless old grudge, especially now that she understood the real story was complicated.

"I left Jon."

"Oh. God. I'm sorry." They settled onto Ethan's couch, holding hands.

"I'm not."

Faith smiled at both the cousins. She'd always had the whitest, straightest teeth Sylvie had ever seen. Like a dentist's commercial, which fit because Faith was a dental hygienist.

"Do you two realize this is the first time I've left Texas? I feel so free. I want to see everything. The beach and the Hollywood sign and Rodeo Drive. I want to go clubbing on Sunset Boulevard."

"Okay, slow down," Ethan said, laughing. "You should pace yourself."

"Tell us what happened."

Faith swept her hair over her shoulder and twisted it around her hands. "My marriage had been a mess for a really long time. But I kept trying to fix it, even though it was a losing battle. Talking to you lately, Sylvie, it gave me the courage to finally choose my own happiness. You and Ethan have done so much with your lives. I can't wait any longer to have the life I want. And there was just no way I could ever have it back home."

"Wow. Okay." Sylvie was trying to be happy for her friend. But she didn't think she should be anyone's role model.

Just leaving everything behind and starting over? It was going to be brutal. She didn't know if Faith was truly prepared.

"You realize how rough this is going to be, right? My life is nowhere near perfect. Actually, it sucks at the moment." Oops. Maybe that was more honesty than Faith needed. Unless it was *exactly* what Faith needed. Maybe it wasn't too late to change her mind.

Ethan glared at her. "But we're proud you're taking this step, aren't we Sylv? Leaving is probably the hardest part." He patted Faith's hand.

Sylvie snorted. "You think so? It should be the hardest part, and I used to think it was. But then more difficult things just keep coming at you. And then something great comes along, something beautiful and amazing, the thing you always wanted, and then the universe snatches it away again and breaks your heart." Her eyes filled with tears. "And you're right back to feeling lost again."

Ethan jumped up from the couch. "Okay, I think Sylvie's had a long day. Let's get some dinner and discuss this later." He grabbed her arm and pulled her toward the stairs. "What is wrong with you?"

"I'm being realistic."

"No, you're putting your problems onto Faith. Maybe listen to her before making this all about you?"

"Ugh, tell her I'm sorry. I'm... I don't even know lately."

"Apologize yourself—later. You need a time out."

She went into her room and fell onto the mattress. Ethan shut the door.

A while later, the hinges squeaked open.

"Can I come in?" Faith asked.

"Yesh." Sylvie's face was mashed against the pillow. She didn't have her glasses on, so Faith was a blur across the room.

"Ethan tells me there's a guy."

Sylvie groaned. "There was. And there is. Sort of." *Nic*, her heart whispered. A flood of tears responded, gathering in her throat.

"That's not mysterious at all."

She swallowed down her emotion and tried to explain. "I met someone through work. I really liked him, and he liked me. But if you think you and I have family issues, it's nothing on him. He had to leave to try to deal with it." That was the grossest oversimplification Sylvie had ever made, but she didn't want to get into the drama surrounding the Syndicate. "Just recently, he wrote me again. He wants to talk. But I don't know if I can."

She got her phone and showed Faith the message Dominic had written her a week ago. It made her cry every time she read it—because she heard his sorrow in his words, and she felt the same thing in her heart. But she still couldn't see a path forward. He hadn't mentioned where he was living or what was really going on in his life.

Faith's expression showed everything she was thinking as she read Dominic's text. "That's the sweetest thing I've ever heard. But I don't see a response in the thread. Haven't you written him back?"

"Not yet. I want to. But it's so complicated."

"Why?"

"It's not just him. It's *me*."

Faith sat on the edge of the bed. "How so?"

She struggled to pull her thoughts together. For the last several months, she'd been trying to figure this out.

And then, suddenly, the words just came.

"Some things have been missing from my life for a long time. But I thought I was satisfied. I have a great job, friends. Then I met Dominic, and I realized it was okay to want more. I thought I could actually have it. He's the reason I wrote back to the card you sent. I wanted to give you a chance, even if I was afraid of getting hurt again."

"Then I owe him. I'm so glad you did."

"But there's still my family back home. My brother and sister have written to me and tried to call over the years, and I never respond. Why haven't I given them the same chance? What am I even so afraid of?"

Since she'd left home, Sylvie had convinced herself she was the one who was brave. That her family was to blame for being scared of anything new or different.

But it had been *her* choice to hold onto her anger and resentment all these years. And to lie to herself, pretending she was over it.

She didn't know about her parents, but her siblings clearly wanted her in their lives. Maybe they were sorry for their mistakes. But she'd never given them the opportunity to prove it.

"You're afraid they'll disappoint you again."

"Am I? That would just confirm what I already thought of them."

She always said people didn't really change. After meeting Dominic, she allowed that sometimes people weren't able to be their true selves. They could make mistakes and have regrets later.

Sylvie hugged her pillow. "But when my family let me walk away when I was nineteen, they were telling *me* I wasn't good enough."

"So you're afraid if they reject you again, it's because of you?"

Tears welled from Sylvie's eyes and slid down her cheeks. Faith scooted closer and circled her arms around Sylvie's neck.

"What if they were right?"

Back then, Sylvie had called to tell her parents she was dropping out of the University of Texas a few days before she'd done it. They'd listened in stony silence and hung up on her. They hadn't tried to argue or beg her to stay in Texas. They'd simply washed their hands. Like she wasn't even worth the breath it would take to tell her they loved her.

Even Dominic's family hadn't done that. The Cranes had tried to shape him into someone else to suit their needs, but he'd always had a place among them.

Sylvie remembered why she'd first been drawn to hacking —the egalitarianism. It didn't matter who you were or where you'd come from. The hacking community would accept you based purely on the quality of your coding and the creativity of your solutions. She'd hidden behind the anonymity of her computer screens ever since. There, she knew she'd belong because no one truly knew her as an individual. They only saw the evidence of what she could do.

"In a way I've been hiding since the moment I left home. I thought I was accepting my true self by running away, but I wasn't, because I almost never showed it. Not completely. I was always holding something back."

Maybe that was why physical pleasure had eluded her for so long. She'd reached a climax with Dominic because he'd come the closest to seeing and accepting her entire self, the good and the bad—because she'd let him. With him, her brain could stop stressing and thinking and just relax.

But having an orgasm hadn't fixed anything about her. She was still struggling with the same issues.

Dominic had wanted to accept her, but she hadn't accepted *herself*.

"Oh my god. I think I get it now. Thank you."

"You're thanking me?" Faith laughed. Sylvie loved her friend's laugh. Bubbly and musical. "I didn't do anything."

"I promise you did." Sylvie sat up against the pillows. "But now I want to hear all about you. You don't have to tell me why you really married Jon, but if you want to? I'm here."

Faith sighed. "That's going to take a while. And a lot of tissues."

"Then tell Ethan to order us some Indian food and open a bottle of wine. We've got all night."

IT WAS ALMOST midnight by the time Faith fell asleep on the couch. Sylvie had offered to share her bedroom, but that could wait until tomorrow. She didn't want to bother Faith now and tell her to relocate.

Ethan had already gone upstairs. The kitchen was littered with takeout containers, so Sylvie cleaned up a bit before heading to bed.

In her room, she unlocked her phone and read Dominic's message for the hundredth time. As usual, her heart twisted with every line. But now, she touched the message box to write back.

Sylvie: Hi.

His response came a moment later.

Dominic: Hi back.

The curser blinked at her.

Sylvie: Tell me something you've never told anyone.

He took only a few seconds to reply.

Dominic: My favorite flavor of instant ramen noodles is Lime Chili Shrimp. Your turn.

Sylvie: My favorite thing about Halloween is candy corn.

Dominic: That's disgusting.

Sylvie: Hey! This is a judgment free zone.

She was smiling, thinking of him holding his phone somewhere in the world, writing his response. Writing to her.

Dominic: How are you?

Sylvie: Feeling judged. Can I ask where you are? Is that allowed?

Dominic: It's no secret. I'm in Burbank.

Her heart raced. He was in the L.A. area. Had he been there all this time? She wanted so badly to see him, even though it was too soon. She'd only just now figured out the whole "self-acceptance" thing. It wasn't going to magically resolve in one night. There was so much she needed to tell him, but she couldn't sort it out yet, much less say it.

But she missed him. She missed Nic so much.

Sylvie: I'm glad you're not far. Can we text again soon?

He sent her a blushing smiley emoji. It didn't seem like the kind of response Dominic Crane would send, but from Nic, it was just right.

∼

THEY TEXTED every night for the next two weeks. He told her about Raymond going into witness protection, about the West Oaks DA dismissing his charges, and his work helping the government understand the methods used by organized criminals.

He said his new name was "Nic Anderson," which was going to take some getting used to, but that she could call him whatever she wanted.

Sylvie told him about Tanner's concussion and the time off he'd taken to recover. About the FBI coming to headquarters to question her and Max, and to seize several hard drives for their investigation into the Syndicate's Russian hackers. She'd spent the last few months revamping Bennett's cyber security protocols to prevent further malicious attacks. Thankfully, neither the Russian mobsters nor their hackers for hire had targeted Bennett Security further.

She didn't tell Dominic she'd been out of touch with her hactivist friends, or that she'd felt disconnected from her work. It had been difficult getting over her failure to trap the Syndicate using her coding ability, even though it hadn't totally been her fault. More time in the gym and the firing range had helped, though she had a long way to go toward getting back her confidence.

She told Dominic about Faith coming to stay with her and Ethan. That led into stories about high school, and then college in both Texas and California. Dominic shared more stories from his school days as well, especially ones featuring his brothers.

One afternoon, she came home to find Ethan, Faith, and Luis all cooking and laughing in her kitchen.

"Guess who's going to be thirty and was totally trying to hide it from us," Ethan said.

Sylvie looked immediately to Luis, and then narrowed her eyes. "Not you."

"Hey!" he protested. "It could've been me."

"Sure, it could." Luis was almost forty, and besides, she'd known him for five years. "Obviously, it's Faith, because her birthday was always about six months after mine."

Faith grumbled at them. "I don't want you to make a big deal of it."

Ethan was slicing mushrooms and tossing them into a skillet. "That's exactly why we have to make a big deal of it. Thirty is a milestone."

Sylvie got a wine glass and poured herself some of the white they'd already opened. The moment anyone had mentioned "party," Sylvie had immediately thought of the one person she most wanted to invite.

"Faith, how would you feel if I invite that guy I told you about? Nic? Would that be too weird?"

All three of them gasped and turned to her.

"You *have* to invite him to my party. That's going to be my present—finally meeting the guy Sylvie's in love with."

She made a face. "I'm not in love with him." Even though her insides were doing a happy dance at someone saying it out loud. Because, wow, she was well on her way.

She was falling for him.

That didn't mean they'd work out. But she wanted to try, and seeing him in person was a necessary step toward actually dating.

That night, she texted him the invite.

Sylvie: We're having a birthday party next Friday at my house. Do you want to come?

Dominic: Is it your birthday?

Sylvie: No, it's Faith's. She wants to meet you.

Dominic: How can I deny the birthday girl? I'll be there. Send me the address.

She sent it, along with a party popper emoji.

Sylvie had trouble getting to sleep that night. She held her phone against her heart, smiling into the dark.

Chapter Thirty-Eight

The day of the party, Nic stood in front of the open suitcase that served as his closet, pawing through his clothes. Should he wear a suit? No, that was too dressy, and he only had flashy "Dominic Crane" suits. But a T-shirt seemed wrong, too.

He decided on items that made him feel most like himself —his usual jeans and a soft gray button-down that he left untucked.

He'd told Maureen about the party, and she'd taken him to a florist shop to pick out a birthday arrangement of flowers. He really wanted to give it to Sylvie, but Maureen had said that would be rude, and that being nice to Sylvie's friend would buy him more points, anyway. Which he knew, of course.

But he felt like a middle schooler going to his first coed dance. He didn't know what the hell he was doing. All the rules he'd learned as a kid about "polite" behavior were taught to him by people who stole and cheated and broke bones for a living. So he couldn't help doubting his instincts.

And he was going to *Sylvie's house*. Even with all they'd been through together, all the moments they'd shared, it had always been in places defined by his old life. Today they were meeting on ground that belonged to Sylvie and her friends.

He wanted to belong there, too.

He drove to West Oaks for the first time in months, memories assailing him the entire way—some uncomfortable, but so many good.

Dominic knocked on Sylvie's front door, shifting the flowers from one hand to the other. He could hear voices inside. The door swung open, and a man with shoulder-length hair and an easy grin stood on the threshold. His eyes made a quick sweep over Dominic from head to toe.

"You must be Nic." He held out his hand. "I'm Luis. It's great to finally meet you."

"You, too." He remembered that Luis was the boyfriend of Sylvie's cousin.

"The party's upstairs at Ethan's place."

Dominic glanced around the first floor as they passed through. The walls were painted in shades of blue and green, hung with framed vinyl album covers. The furniture was plush and undersized to fit into the small space.

Before they reached the staircase, Luis spun around. "You know, you look familiar."

He froze. Had the guy seen pictures of him online in articles about the Syndicate? Dominic cared less about his former associates finding him and more about Sylvie's friends thinking he wasn't good enough for her.

"Have you modeled?"

Dominic shook his head, knowing he must have the same expression as a deer facing an oncoming train.

"Have you thought about it? You have a very distinctive look."

"Um…" *Say something*, he thought. *Why is this so hard?*

Before, he'd never lacked for conversation at a party. But he'd been playing a role for his so-called friends. Now that he was just trying to be himself, he was struggling to find the right words. Shouldn't it have been the other way around? It was like he'd reverted back to some earlier stage of awkwardness. So much for the guy who'd made Sylvie whimper with desire in his entryway the first day he met her.

"Okay, now that I've come across as the stereotypical creepy photographer, we should probably…" Luis pointed at the stairs. "Sorry. I didn't mean to make you uncomfortable."

He found his voice. "Don't worry about it. I've heard that before, about modeling. It's not for me, but thanks." Even setting aside his efforts to separate himself from his old life and name, he didn't want people staring at him. "What kind of photography do you do?"

Luis launched into a discussion about his latest campaign for a popular clothing website. The tension in Dominic's shoulders started to ease. He could do this—relate to people. Make new friends. Right? He wasn't completely hopeless.

He'd better not be, if he wanted to get Sylvie back.

They reached the top of the stairs, and he saw her. Sylvie wore a lacy, sleeveless black dress and her combat boots. Dominic's heart instantly jumped into high gear.

She looked over at him and smiled. "Nic."

"Hey."

Sylvie walked over, her arms flaring like she wanted to hug him. But he was holding the flowers. "Those must be for Faith? That's so thoughtful." She called her friend over.

There weren't many people there, but he seemed to get caught talking to everyone else except Sylvie. Their eyes trailed each other around the room.

He learned that Ethan was a web designer who was into kung fu movies. Faith was in the process of getting divorced, even though she looked too young and innocent to even be married. But people's outsides didn't always match their insides. Dominic knew that well enough.

Luis was talking about his last roommate, an actress who'd brought home "dates" at all hours of the night. "She was running a red-light district out of my apartment. Why can't I find anyone sane to rent my spare room?"

"Maybe the problem is you?" Ethan said. "There's a reason I can't live with you. Aside from the fact that you insist on living near the 405."

"I like things clean, dishes put away, and no illegal activities. That's so demanding?"

Dominic wondered how much Luis was charging for rent. The photographer's apartment sounded much nicer than Dominic's studio, assuming the man didn't run a background check. Or maybe he'd be okay with ex-mobsters, as long as they were tidy.

Finally, the others were all otherwise occupied. Dominic's gaze met Sylvie's across the room. Sylvie set down her drink, rushed over to grab his hand, and pulled him downstairs.

He'd been hoping to see her bedroom, but she stopped in the living area. "Hi," she said, looking down like she was nervous. "Are you having fun?"

"Yeah. Your friends are great." *But I'm here for you.* She had to know that.

"Now you've met all my people. You already knew the Bennett Security contingent, and this is the rest of them. Pretty much."

"You've definitely met mine—all two of them, Raymond and Maureen. There's Warren, but he's not out for another year or two."

Sylvie twisted her hands together. "There's something I've been meaning to say. I loved that text you sent, the first one after we'd been apart? I took so long to write back because I didn't know anything that good to say. But you've made me see the world differently, too. You matter *so much* to me."

Dominic couldn't describe the feeling in his chest. It was like riding a roller coaster as it zoomed into a loop. He pulled her closer. She brushed her thumb down his cheek.

"You have a scar."

"My poor face."

"Yep, you're ugly now." She smiled, and her blue eyes danced. So beautiful. His heart almost couldn't take it.

His hands moved to her hips, enjoying the scratch of the lace against his palms, then traveled to the notches of her waist. Over four months—nearly five now—was a really long time.

God, he wanted her.

He brushed his nose against her temple, just above the frames of her glasses. She smelled like vanilla and roses. He wondered if it was perfume. His eyes closed as he breathed her in. "Since we last saw each other, I've only thought of you. I haven't been with anyone else."

"Neither have I," she whispered. "But I made myself come. Twice. I was thinking about you."

His head rushed with desire. He'd jerked off every day, but not to porn. Only to her.

Dominic brought his lips to her forehead, her cheek, moving toward her mouth. But before their lips could touch, she pulled back slightly.

"I need to take things slow. I don't *want* to. But I need to."

"Okay. That's fine." His dick was protesting that it really wasn't fine. But that would just have to wait. He rested his forehead against hers. "I can go slow. Any particular reason?"

"You said you're working on things about yourself."

"Yeah." He didn't want to admit just how uncertain he still felt about the future.

"So am I. There are things I need to do before I can be with anyone. I'm still holding onto so much anger at my family. I want to let go of that. But I don't know how."

"If anybody can figure it out, it's you." He held her against his chest.

"But I do want to be with you. You have no idea how diffi-cult it is not to drag you into my bedroom right now."

"I can guess." Five. Freaking. Months.

"But I don't want to mess this up. It's not just sex."

"No. Not at all."

"So we'll be patient a little longer."

"Yes?" His voice went high at the end, making it a question.

"Yes." She kissed his jaw. "But I'm imagining all the things I want to do to you later."

He made a small, needy noise that sounded distinctly like a whimper.

Ethan called from upstairs. "Everyone, cake!"

Chapter Thirty-Nine

Sylvie and Tanner strolled along the beachside path. It was seventy degrees, not a cloud in the sky. They passed a beach volleyball game, and people in various states of undress lazed on the sand. Apparently, nobody else wanted to work this Friday afternoon, either.

"Did you know Dominic Crane is back in town? And that Max met with him?"

Sylvie glanced sharply at her friend. "Max? He hasn't said a word to me about it."

"About Dominic being back? Or about the fact that they talked?" Tanner's smug tone conveyed that he already knew the answer.

"I knew Dominic was in the area. I've seen him. He never really left." She hadn't seen Nic since Faith's birthday party several weeks ago. It was the right choice for them both. Sylvie knew they wouldn't be able to resist jumping into bed. She wanted to know they were each in a good place before that happened.

The waiting was tough, though.

"But what did Max say?" she asked.

"He asked me to check up on Crane to make sure his old

Syndicate buddies were leaving him alone. Because Max figured if you were hanging around the guy, we needed to ensure you'd be safe. It really does seem that he's out of his old life, and that the Syndicate—whatever's left of it—has decided to let him go. *And* they haven't been sniffing around you, which is much more important. Thought you might want to know. But if you want to yell at Max about it, say you found out through some hacking voodoo, not from me."

Why was she even surprised? Max would always be protective of the people he cared about, and Sylvie was glad to be one of them.

Briefly, Max had made her wonder if people really *did* change, but it was comforting to know Max was the same as ever. There was enough uncertainty in the world already.

"What a crack investigator. Did you even know 'Crane' isn't his name anymore?"

"Nic Anderson, whatever." Tanner shrugged one of his beefy shoulders. "He'll always be Crane to me."

In some ways, Dominic was still 'Crane' to her, too. If only because of that tattoo on her shoulder, which made her think of him every time she saw it. For her, the name reminded her of his grace and inner beauty, rather than his family.

"So, are you two together?"

"We're not…together. Not exactly. We're figuring it out."

Dominic was renting Luis's spare room in Los Angeles now. It had made her nervous at first, knowing he'd be closer to people who could recognize him. But Dominic had assured her over and over that he wasn't in danger anymore, and Tanner's investigation soothed her concerns further.

Of course, he'd told Luis the truth about his past, and the photographer had loved the story. The whole mafia vibe had given him ideas for an ad campaign for a leather goods client.

And ever since he'd moved in with Luis, Dominic had been busier. It was good. She was happy for him. She'd had plenty of time to think through her feelings about her family, which she'd needed to do.

A couple weeks ago, she had written to her siblings the old-fashioned way, since she didn't know their emails. Nor had she been brave enough to dial the phone.

She figured if she never heard anything, she could chalk it up to the post office losing her letter, rather than her siblings deciding not to respond.

They reached the fish taco stand and put in their orders. "You do seem happier lately, though," Tanner said. "I know you think being in a relationship shouldn't make you different. But I gotta say, that's bullshit. I've seen you depressed, and you can't tell me there's no difference."

"I guess." She hadn't wanted to admit that having certain people in her life dictated her happiness or well-being. But she'd been looking at it the wrong way. Being with the right people just made her more herself.

"What about you?" she asked. "How's your head?" Tanner had been out of commission for a few weeks after the concussion. Months had now passed since he'd returned to work, but she knew it could be difficult to recover from a head injury.

And lately, Tanner had seemed slightly off from his usual laidback self. Distracted, maybe. Sometimes he went still and stared into space for minutes at a time, or frowned when before he would've worn a breezy smile.

Just like he was doing now.

Then the smile returned. As if nothing had changed, and she'd been imagining it. "You know me, I'm just cruising along. No worries."

"Everyone has *some* worries."

He hooked an arm around her shoulders. "Except me. Besides, you've had enough in the last several months to go around."

That was for sure.

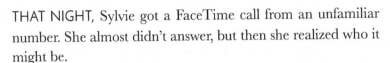

THAT NIGHT, Sylvie got a FaceTime call from an unfamiliar number. She almost didn't answer, but then she realized who it might be.

When the video loaded, she saw her sister Trina staring back at her.

"Sylvie, is that you?" her younger brother asked in the background.

"Of course it's her. Don't you know our sister?" Trina was the oldest of the three of them, and she'd always been their spokesperson. Their younger brother tended to sit quietly and go along. "Sylvie, how on earth are you?"

"I'm..." Where could she even begin? "I'm sorry it took me so long to get in touch."

"You're sorry?" Trina waved her hands. "Okay, I need to say this, 'cause it's been building up a long time. I know we hurt you, Sylvie. We didn't fight back against mom and dad when they cut you out of our lives. But I need to know if you can ever forgive us, because that guilt is damn near killing me."

Trina's voice shook, and their brother wiped his eyes. Sylvie was fighting back tears of her own.

"Of course I forgive you." As she said it, she realized she already had.

They talked for another hour. The minute their call ended, Sylvie called Nic's number. He was the person she most wanted to tell about her conversation with her siblings.

He didn't answer.

She'd never in her life been a jealous person. So why did she keep imagining him at parties with the gorgeous people who frequented Luis's photo shoots?

You're being ridiculous, she told herself. If Dominic had more friends in his life, then that was great. It was what he needed.

She went upstairs to find her cousin. Ethan had his feet

propped up on an ottoman, watching an episode of whatever obscure martial-arts-film director he was into these days. Faith was at a yoga class down the street.

"I just got off the phone with my siblings."

He switched off the TV. "Really? How was it?"

"Better than I would've thought." She told him about their conversation, which had been cathartic in many ways. Sylvie had learned she had five nieces and nephews—*five*—whom she'd never even met. She'd missed so much. And the more they'd talked, the more she'd heard herself opening up about college, her friends, even her favorite memories from home that she hadn't thought of in a long time.

"They'd like to get in touch with you, too," she said. "I couldn't speak for you, but I promised I'd ask."

Ethan looked thoughtful. "I guess it wouldn't hurt to chat. I don't need to make peace with our family to find closure, but it would be nice to catch up. Do you need a hug?"

"Yes. A hug is exactly what I need." *And Dominic*, she thought. She was so ready for that. But was he?

The cousins put their arms around each other, heads bent together. "Are you going to Luis's gallery show tomorrow night? He said you didn't RSVP."

"I almost never go to his events. They're so…L.A."

"Yeah, but this one's going to be special. You have to go."

She sat up, looking at him. "Why?"

"Do you have to ask so many questions? Trust me, you'll want to be there."

She wanted to ask if Dominic would be there, too. Judging by her cousin's sudden weirdness about the subject, she guessed that he would.

"Stop trying to figure it out," Ethan said. "Just enjoy being surprised for once."

"All right. I'll try."

Chapter Forty

"Quit watching the door." Luis grabbed a glass of champagne from a passing tray and shoved it in Nic's hand. "She and Ethan are stuck in traffic. Now come on, I have so many people for you to meet."

They were at an art gallery owned by Luis's friend. Dominic glanced at the black-and-white photos on the walls as they walked through the space, weaving in between guests. These images were now as familiar to him as the ones that used to be in his bedroom back in West Oaks. Pride swelled in his chest, then diminished as he thought again of Sylvie. Why wasn't she here yet?

What if she didn't come at all?

Luis pulled him into a circle of people. "Everyone, this is Nic. He's who we have to thank for tonight."

He put on a smile, shook hands, and tried to remember all the new names.

Dominic was starting to suspect he was an introvert because this was exhausting. He'd never liked big groups much, but he'd always faked his way through without thinking much about it. He was learning all kinds of new things about himself these days.

When nobody was looking, he snuck away to a quiet corner, looking at a photo of the Walt Disney Concert Hall.

He felt a tap on his shoulder and turned around. Sylvie stood there, smiling hesitantly. "Hi, I was hoping you'd be here. We didn't mean to be so late."

She was wearing a pair of simple black pants and a silky top with thin straps that showed off her ink.

"You look incredible."

"You don't look so bad yourself." She pointed at his black suit, which he'd worn with a white shirt and no tie. It was one of his old suits, but there was no way he could afford a new one this nice, so he'd decided to go ahead and wear it. He didn't have to get rid of *everything* about Dominic Crane. The guy had known how to dress.

Across the room, Luis was talking animatedly to a group of people that now included Ethan. Nic liked that about his new roommate. Luis usually took care of the conversations.

He decided to escape before Luis noticed them and introduced him to anyone else. He grabbed Sylvie's hand and walked her through the crowd to a back room, which was less busy.

"I tried to call last night," she said.

"I know, I'm sorry I missed it. I was working late, and I've been busy here all day. I wanted to surprise you." He held out his arms, gesturing at the framed photos around them.

"They're beautiful. But what's the surprise?"

"Luis's friend owns this gallery. She's been wanting to have a show of his work, the artistic stuff he does on the side in between ad campaigns. But Luis never had time to put it together. So I offered to do it. He had a ton of raw shots just dumped on his hard drive. I went through them and came up with the themes for this show."

He led her around the space, showing her each photograph and explaining why he'd picked it. Luis had a great eye for a light, shadow, and composition. Most of these were shots from downtown Los Angeles. Luis had managed to find beauty amid the gritty buildings and concrete, as well as the dark edges to the fancier architecture.

"This is amazing. Why didn't you tell me you were working on this?"

"Because I was afraid Luis and his friend wouldn't like it. But the woman who owns the gallery—" He looked around and spotted her, a silver-haired woman in her sixties. "She loved what I came up with. And she offered me a job. You're looking at her new photography curator."

Sylvie gasped. "Nic. Oh my god. Congratulations." She hugged him around the neck.

His arms closed around her. "It doesn't pay that much, but I love it. It feels like…me." He was still consulting with law enforcement, too, but just volunteering his time.

"I'm so happy for you."

He'd been amazed how many hours he could spend poring over photos and thinking about how they could all come together into one exhibition. He'd never been so engaged in something that he could call "work" before.

And he was proud he could show this to Sylvie. Her opinion mattered more to him than anyone else's. Her approval lit a warm glow in his center.

"But what was it you wanted to talk about last night? When you called?"

"Oh. I spoke to my sister and brother back in Texas. Something I should've done a long time ago, but I didn't get up the nerve to do it until recently. It was a really great conversation. But we can talk about that later. This is your moment. It's a very big deal."

He wanted it to be her moment, too. Without her, none of this would've been possible.

"Can I tell you something I've never told anyone else?"

She lifted her eyebrows, waiting.

"I'm in love with you."

Sylvie drew in a breath, her hand going to her mouth. He really hoped that was a good reaction.

"I've been in love with you for a while," he said, "but I wanted to show you I could be someone worth loving back."

"You always were. I've loved you for a while, too. I'm *so* in love with you."

He'd thought tonight couldn't get much better, but she'd managed to do it.

He curved his fingers around the back of her neck and bent down to kiss her. Almost six months since he'd tasted her mouth.

Just as plush as he'd remembered. God, he'd missed her.

"There's a back exit," he said in between kisses. "Want to get out of here?"

"Don't you need to stay?"

"I've been here for hours. I've met nearly everyone." And if he hadn't, he could meet them next time. He wanted to get this woman home and show her just how much he loved her. Preferably two or three times. "The only person I want to be with right now is you."

THEY STUMBLED into Luis's apartment, still kissing. He'd left a good tip on his Uber app to make it up to their driver, since they'd been all over each other in the guy's back seat.

"Luis is going to West Oaks with Ethan tonight," he said. "We have the place to ourselves."

"He just moved up the list to my second favorite person ever. Right after you."

Dominic picked her up and headed straight for his bedroom. Then there was a lot of frantic removing of clothes, kicking away of shoes. He nearly ripped the button from his pants getting them off. Sylvie was fumbling with her bra, so he found the little zipper at the side of her pants, sliding off the outer layer and her panties at once. He pulled her against him, running his hands over her skin. His cock was thick and needy between them. He rubbed himself against her.

"This first time needs to be fast and dirty." She sounded breathless. "I'm not patient enough for anything else."

"Fuck, I'm glad you said that."

"Six months…"

"Is a really damn long time."

He lifted her onto his dresser and shoved her knees apart. His tongue wasn't teasing or sweet. He was starving for her. His fingers pushed inside of her as he flicked his tongue over her clit, then sucked the sensitive flesh between his lips. Every trick he knew was coming out to play to get her where he needed her.

He was a little worried she'd get overstimulated, but that didn't seem to be an issue, at least not right now. His middle finger curved inside of her, aiming for her G-spot. He felt her start to convulse.

"*Nic.*"

When she stopped shaking and moaning, he tongued her opening one last time, drinking in her wetness. She tasted so fucking good.

She dropped her feet to the floor, then turned around and stuck her ass out, her arms braced against the dresser. "I need you to fuck me now. Hard."

He couldn't manage a coherent verbal response. But he didn't really need one, anyway. The tip of his cock found her entrance. He buried himself inside.

She was soaking. When he drew back, his dick was covered in her slickness. His hands gripped her by the hips and pulled her back against him while he thrust forward, colliding their bodies together. In the mirror, he could see the ecstasy on Sylvie's face. Nic lost himself in the feeling of her.

He roared when he came, the orgasm so fast and intense that he'd couldn't have stopped it if he'd tried.

Thank goodness she hadn't expected him to last a while because that would've been embarrassing.

Dominic kissed her shoulders, then pulled out and looked down, watching his cum drip down her inner thighs. A spark of possessiveness flared in his stomach. He pulled her upright, holding her against him. Sylvie was his, and he'd never been so grateful for anything.

They both collapsed onto the bed. The room was quiet for a while as they lay there, just looking at each other while Dominic traced his fingertips over her arms.

Their second round of lovemaking was slower, sweeter, full of tender kisses and I-love-yous.

The third time was up against the wall of the shower, water spraying on Dominic's back, after he'd made her climax with his fingers.

Then they were both completely spent. They wrapped up in a blanket and ate leftover takeout from the fridge on the living room couch. He had no clue what time it was, nor did he care.

"Tell me about the conversation with your siblings. Did it go well?"

"We all cried a little. We apologized and asked for forgiveness and talked about what was important in our lives. I told them about you."

That made him smile.

"They want me to come visit."

"Wow. That would be a big step. First time back there in over ten years?"

"Yeah." Her blue eyes lifted to his. "Would you come with me?"

"Me? Really? Yeah, of course I will. If you think... I don't know if they'll like me. I'm weird around people now. I don't know what to say."

"Number one, who gives a shit if they like you? You'd be

there for me. And second, just be yourself. That's how *I* like you." She kissed him on the nose.

"But what if they ask about *my* family?"

Hi, Sylvie's mom and dad. I'm in love with your daughter. My background? Let's see. Dad's a former mobster, just like me. My uncle tried to have me tortured and killed, and my brother's in federal prison. Oh, and my other brother is in witness protection after setting up two gangs to murder each other. Pass the potato salad?

"I can't tell them the truth, right?"

She burst out laughing. "No freaking way are we telling them the truth about your family. But that's okay. They don't need to know everything. Just that I love you."

"That's good enough for me."

Epilogue

Sylvie had forgotten just how hot Central Texas could get in the middle of summer.

She'd only wanted to see her immediate family on this trip, but of course, her mother insisted on inviting all their relatives and half her knitting circle to a picnic to stare at Sylvie and her strange boyfriend from Los Angeles.

They waited in line for the buffet table while Jason Aldean played over somebody's speaker system. Sylvie introduced Dominic to all the local delicacies. "That's my aunt Rita's Frito pie. She adds green onions. And cornbread casserole, that's going to be good. But skip that mess—Janice's turkey tetrazzini. Bleh. Oh! Hold on." She added a scoop of seven-layer dip to his plate. "Can't miss that. For the tortilla chips."

He grinned at her and grabbed a fork.

By the time Sylvie had finished with her own plate, several of her cousins had cornered Nic by the kiddie pool. The women were slack-jawed, gazing at him as if hypnotized. Sylvie could sympathize with the feeling.

"What's a photography curator?" one cousin was asking, eyes narrowed under his camo hat. "Sounds made up."

"It's an L.A. thing, don't worry about it," Sylvie said, taking her boyfriend's elbow and steering him away.

Before she'd agreed to visit, she'd waited until her sister Trina invited Ethan as well. But Sylvie's cousin had politely declined, offering instead to host anyone at their place in West Oaks. Trina was already planning a beach trip with her kids.

Nobody had asked about Faith, which was for the best. It wasn't Sylvie's place to say anything about Faith's decision to leave Jon. And thankfully, neither Jon nor Faith's family were here today.

"You're being very patient," she whispered to Dominic. In her head, sometimes he was "Nic," and sometimes "Dominic." With her, he happily answered to both.

"It's not so bad. This food's good. And I like the music."

"Of course you like the music. Jason Aldean rocks. I have so many amazing country artists to introduce you to."

She'd almost brought her violin—a gift from Dominic that he'd saved from his house in West Oaks. He'd insisted she didn't have to play for him, that it was a gift for her. But of course, she loved seeing him smile as he listened.

"I just wish I could've skipped the cousins who think Los Angeles is Satan's playground," she said.

"My uncle had you kidnapped and tried to turn you over to Russian mobsters. I can handle a few impolite comments from your extended family."

True. But she was tiring of her mom's friends remarking how "interesting" her clothing choices were. She certainly wasn't the only cousin with tattoos, though. And plenty of people had welcomed her back warmly, as if she'd never left.

Her parents were still awkward, but they were trying. Her mom had hugged her, and cried, and professed to have no memory of how they were ever separated. Sylvie figured it was the best she could hope for, at least for now. She wanted to have a more candid conversation with them, but it was one step at a time. She could love her family and disagree with them.

And Nic was here beside her to laugh at all her snarky comments. He cuddled with her when tears threatened, too. He was sweet like that.

She'd been remembering all the things she loved about home, and she was sharing those with him as well. The limestone of the hills, the smell of mesquite on the air, and the wind blowing through the trees.

Thank god Trina had offered to let them stay in her guestroom. That meant Nic could be spared the ancient couch at her parents' house, and she could avoid her childhood twin bed.

Trina's two boys were seven and nine, and Sylvie had enjoyed seeing Nic roughhouse with them. It was a side of him she'd never witnessed before. She loved seeing him laugh so easily, and he was patient with them, too. It made her wonder about their future in a way that made her chest swell.

She and Dominic, having a family of their own. A family they'd love unconditionally, with open hearts, without fear.

She wasn't ready for that yet, and neither was he. But it was nice to think about.

Sadly, Trina's guestroom mattress was squeaky, so they couldn't get too frisky at night. But Sylvie was planning to borrow one of her brothers' pickups to reenact the countless country songs about truck beds in the moonlight.

Nic set down his plate on a nearby tree stump. "I love every part of you. Even the parts you don't love."

She hooked an arm around his neck. "It's a good thing you're so attractive. It makes up for how mean you are."

"Can't help it. I'm a bad boy." He dipped down to kiss her. Sylvie could feel people staring, and she didn't care.

"*Such* a bad boy."

"But you like that."

"I *love* that. And I love you."

She spent the rest of the picnic teaching him to two-step as the sun went down.

~

Don't miss the next Bennett Security book,
HOLD TIGHT, Faith and Tanner's story!

Tanner was supposed to be her first-date wingman. Faith never planned to fall for him. But the former Navy SEAL is battling demons of his own. As their chemistry and the danger both heat up, the path forward will force them to take the ultimate risk—saving each other.

Acknowledgments

Many thanks to my editor and my criminal law consultants. Any mistakes—and creative license—when it comes to legal proceedings in this book are entirely my own.

I'm so grateful to my beta readers and advance reviewers! Your support means the world to me.

Also by Hannah Shield

THE BENNETT SECURITY SERIES

HANDS OFF (Aurora & Devon)

To keep her safe, he has to keep his hands off…but she has other ideas. A steamy, action-packed romantic suspense.

~

HEAD FIRST (Lana & Max)

He's protecting his former flame… But can he resist falling for her? A second-chance steamy romance with courtroom drama and heart-pounding danger.

~

HOLD TIGHT (Faith & Tanner)

He was supposed to be her wingman. She was never supposed to fall for him. A steamy, friends-to-lovers military romance.

~

HUNG UP (Noah & Danica)

Coming August 2022

Her brother's worst enemy is the only man who can protect her. A second-chance romantic suspense between a former Navy SEAL and a billionaire's daughter.

~

And more books coming soon!

About the Author

Hannah Shield once worked as an attorney. Now, she loves thrilling readers on the page—in every possible way.

She writes steamy romantic suspense with feisty heroines, brooding heroes, and heart-pounding action. Bennett Security is her debut series. Visit her website at www.hannahshield.com.

Made in the USA
Middletown, DE
13 January 2024

47797233R00188